Georgiana L. Bloomfield

Reminiscences of Court and Diplomatic Life

Vol. 2

Georgiana L. Bloomfield

Reminiscences of Court and Diplomatic Life
Vol. 2

ISBN/EAN: 9783337094836

Printed in Europe, USA, Canada, Australia, Japan

Cover: Foto ©Raphael Reischuk / pixelio.de

More available books at **www.hansebooks.com**

COURT AND DIPLOMATIC LIFE

VOL. II.

Nicholas I.
Emperor of Russia

REMINISCENCES

OF

COURT AND DIPLOMATIC LIFE

BY

GEORGIANA BARONESS BLOOMFIELD

WITH THREE PORTRAITS
AND SIX ILLUSTRATIONS AFTER ORIGINAL SKETCHES BY THE AUTHOR

IN TWO VOLUMES

VOL. II.

FOURTH EDITION

LONDON

KEGAN PAUL, TRENCH, & CO., 1 PATERNOSTER SQUARE

1883

(*The rights of translation and of reproduction are reserved*)

CONTENTS

OF

THE SECOND VOLUME.

CHAPTER XII.

CHAPTER XIII.

CHAPTER XIV.

CHAPTER XV.

CHAPTER XVI.

CHAPTER XVII.

CHAPTER XVIII.

REMINISCENCES.

CHAPTER XII.

Extracts from Letters written to my Husband after I left Russia.

Breslau, June 6, 1851.—This is such a fine picturesque old town. I cannot tell you what a difference there is in the appearance of every-thing, as soon as one crosses the Russian fron-tier. Such a far greater air of comfort and civilisation. The cathedral here is Roman Catho-lic, but there is a fine large Protestant Church, and they contain beautiful tombs. There is a large painted glass window in the Protestant Church, which was given by the king, but I did not admire it. The Hôtel de Ville is extremely picturesque, and there are fine public walks, which were crowded with people.

British Embassy, Paris, June 27, 1851.— I went to the Assembly with the Normanbys yesterday. M. Thiers was to have spoken, but unfortunately M. de St. Beuve made such a long speech on his free trade motion, that M. Thiers put off answering him till to-day, when he spoke for an hour. He has the most wonderful command of language, and such a memory for figures that in the most complicated financial debates he hardly ever refers to notes. His voice is audible, but uncommonly harsh.

I saw the President Louis Napoleon and his suite returning from the Parade yesterday. There was rather a Socialist demonstration as he was going there in the morning, and he was met with cries of 'Vive la République, démocratique et sociale,' so he thought it prudent to return a different road. Everything seems quiet for the moment, but no one anticipates a continuance of the lull; on the contrary, the general opinion seems to be that it precedes a storm. The revision of the Constitution is to come on in the Assembly soon, and it is to be hoped the President will get an extension of power, or rather that his re-election will be legalised, but no one knows whether this very important point will be carried or not. I saw Lamoricière yesterday at the Assembly, Changarnier, Molé, and both Baroche and Fould spoke. We are invited to dine with the President to-morrow. The heat just now is tremendous, but the air much lighter than it is in hot weather in Russia.

17 *Eaton Place, July* 8, 1851.—I had a most interesting conversation with Prince Albert the other day, and he expressed himself strongly about the line the Emperor took respecting the Great Exhibition here. I said how delighted and thankful we had been to hear that everything went off so well, and that in my last interview with the Empress at Warsaw I could not help dwelling upon the complete success of the whole undertaking. The Prince smiled and said, ' Yes ; but what they cannot understand in Russia or forgive is its being, as it were, a *national fête.* Brunnow said the other day we have no nation, we only recognise the Emperor ; now though unfortunately this may be the case, in these days it is a very dangerous doctrine to promulgate. I understand the Emperor was very angry at the Prince of Prussia coming here, and said all he could to alarm the King, who wrote

to me to state he knew there was danger, and asked whether I would be responsible for the Prince's safety. I answered that if the King knew there was danger, in God's name not to let the Prince come, as I could not be answerable for anything; but that as far as my own convictions went, I considered the only danger was in people's own minds, and I classed that danger with the malicious reports the enemies of the undertaking had industriously spread about fifty millions of sparrows spoiling the goods, the roof of the building not being waterproof, and the whole enterprise being an arrogant, wicked work, which would infallibly bring down God's wrath upon us all.

'All these things I say I classed together, and the King was then ashamed, and allowed his brother to come, but you know just at the last the Diplomatic Corps failed us, and were very ungracious. The Empress of Russia also wrote a letter, in which she only dwelt upon the great fatigue and excitement of the Exhibition, and said she wondered how we had been able to bear it.'

The Queen was most kind, and said she hoped we should like Berlin, which she considered a most desirable change on my account. She said how very fond she is of all the Prussian Royal family, especially the Princess of Prussia, to whom she had particularly recommended us. I saw Bunsen at the concert at Buckingham Palace last night. He was very cordial and civil, and said he was delighted to hear we are going to Berlin, and that the other day he had had the satisfaction of presenting a letter to the Queen from the King of Prussia, expressing his very great satisfaction at your appointment. The party last night was not large, but after Russia it amused me to see how many members of the Corps Diplomatique were invited, when comparatively few of the society were—very different from St. Petersburg!

Berlin, July 17, 1851.—Lord Bloomfield presented his letters of credence to King Frederic William IV., at Belle Vue Palace. His Majesty was particularly gracious, spoke most affectionately of the Queen, and most properly about England, and he wore no order on that occasion except the garter. Baron Manteuffel, the Minister President and Minister for Foreign Affairs, was present, so politics were not discussed. Baron Manteuffel was a small man, nervous and embarrassed in society, but shrewd and intelligent. I returned to Berlin on August 2.

We made a very pleasant though rather fatiguing expedition to Mecklenburg Strelitz, where my husband was accredited, as well as at Mecklenburg

Schwerin and Anhalt Dessau.   The first thing that
occurred after our arrival was that I learnt, to my
great surprise and dismay, that there was to be a
great court reception the following day in honour
of the King of Prussia and the Grand Duke of
Mecklenburg Schwerin, and that I should therefore be expected to appear in full court dress, for
which I was not in the least prepared.   The shops
were already shut, nevertheless I sallied forth to
try and purchase material for making up a train,
and owing to the good nature of the lady at whose
house we were lodged (there being no room for
us in the Schloss), I succeeded in finding that and
a tailor, who, with my clever French maid, made
up a handsome court dress.

The next day at 12 o'clock we were invited
to a breakfast, when I was presented to the
King and the Grand Dukes and Grand Duchesses.
They were all extremely gracious, and expressed
great satisfaction at my having accompanied Lord
Bloomfield on his first visit.   After standing
about for a long while we rushed home to
dress in full court attire, and then returned to the
Palace, where we had to stand for about two
hours and a half during the reception, and then
marched straight to the banqueting-hall, where
there was a magnificent dinner for 200 people !

Nothing could be handsomer than the plate, liveries, and arrangements. The dinner lasted till seven o'clock, when we were allowed an hour's rest, and then had to go to a ball and dance, which we had neither of us done for some years. The Grand Duke, who was an agreeable and most courteous old gentleman, was the brother of Louisa, the beautiful and unfortunate Queen of Prussia, who was so insulted by Napoleon after the battle of Jena. The Hereditary Grand Duchess was the daughter of the Duke of Cambridge, and inherited all the charm of manner of our Royal family, often reminding me of the dear Duchess of Gloucester, my mother's best and kindest friend.

Lord Palmerston having given my husband six months' leave to take me to Italy, we left London on November 11, and spent a few days with the Normanbys, my brother-in-law being then Ambassador at Paris. We were invited to a party at the Elysée, and presented to the President, Louis Napoleon. There was nothing striking in his general appearance ; he was short, with rather a heavy expression of countenance, and his manners were quiet and dignified. He was extremely civil to us, expressing regret at the shortness of our visit to Paris, where he said he hoped to see us again. He spoke with kindness of the reception the late Lord Bloomfield gave him at Woolwich. Louis Napoleon fancied he was predestined to be the saviour of France. Alas! how little he then foresaw the humiliation and ruin his policy would bring upon that unfortunate country. One day Lord Normanby was at the Elysée, when he saw the Emperor conversing with San Giacomo. They beckoned to Lord Normanby to approach, and then Louis Napoleon said he was reminding San Giacomo of a curious interview they had when young men with a somnambulist. The President added she predicted three things :—That I should be some time in prison, then reign over an empire, and lastly that I should die a violent death. He added, 'deux de ces choses sont arrivées, l'autre arrivera.'

We twice visited the Assemblée Nationale, and were amazed at the shamefully disorderly conduct of the representatives. They paid no sort of deference to the attempts of the President to maintain order, and the howling, shouting, and noise of all kinds was deafening ; one really could not have conceived that a like confusion could prevail in the mode of carrying on the business of a great country. The Mountain were like ravenous wolves, and unfortunately they were a very strong party, amounting to nearly 300. Their support of the President maintained his advisers in office, and the Conservative party were furious. Paris was quiet, but it was like the lull before a storm, no one felt secure or seemed to know what was pending, and there was a general feeling of mistrust in the Government, which was fully justified very shortly after by the famous *coup d'état*.

We left Paris on November 21, stayed one day at Lyons, and then embarked on board a miserable dirty steamer for Valence ; unfortunately it did not leave Lyons till the afternoon, so instead of reaching Valence as we had hoped, we had to spend a wretched night at Ste. Valérie. The weather was excessively cold, the hills about Lyons covered with snow ; and the following morning before daybreak we had to embark, but were again doomed to disappointment, for we had hardly started before such a dense fog came on, that we were forced to anchor for six mortal hours. Fortunately our carriage was on board, so I was able to sit in comfort ; but there was no food to be had, and the captain consoled us by saying that sometimes the fogs lasted forty-eight hours, at that season on the Rhone. Luckily the fog cleared sufficiently to allow of our reaching Valence, where, having had enough of the boat, we landed and proceeded to Avignon by land, where I was much interested in seeing the cathedral and the ancient Palace of the Popes. The next day we proceeded by rail to Marseilles, and were fortunate in witnessing the most glorious sunrise I ever saw. The railroad passed through rather a desolate country, bounded to the east by mountains, behind which the sun rose majestically, lighting up the whole landscape with such gorgeous golden tints. The sky was perfectly clear, with just one or two little bright clouds ; and then, to use the expressive language of Scripture, the sun 'came forth like a bridegroom out of his closet, rejoicing as a giant to run his course ;' neither before nor since have I ever seen so striking an effect.

There was a tunnel five kilometres long before we reached Marseilles, which seemed interminable ; but when we emerged from it the first view of the town, with the blue Mediterranean beyond, and the orange groves and vineyards delighted me. The road from Marseilles to Nice was bad, the inns and the food detestable. When we got to Fréjus the best apartment was taken and my husband, who had a dread of damp beds, insisted upon it that the mattresses were not aired ; after vainly attempting to tranquillise his fears the chambermaid at last got impatient, and vociferated : ' Mais votre excellence, quand j'assure votre excellence que deux commis voyageurs sont sortis pour faire place à votre excellence!' I thought to myself, 'where ignorance is bliss, 'tis folly to be wise;' and after that I implored my husband not to inquire too narrowly as to who had preceded us in the rooms we occupied. Fréjus is a pretty little place, where there is a small Roman amphitheatre, and it is also interesting as being the spot where Napoleon I. landed when he escaped from Elba.

We spent three delightful weeks at Nice, which was then a pretty quiet country town, surrounded by beautiful gardens. The weather was brilliant and the society very agreeable. I there made the acquaintance of Monsieur Paul de la Roche, and visited his atelier, where I saw three of his famous pictures, the Two Princes in the Tower, a Stabat Mater, and a small but most beautiful Descent from the Cross, painted for Lord Ellesmere. Paul de la Roche was then a middle-aged man, with a remarkably intelligent expression, dry and rather caustic manners, satirical, but full of animation and quickness in conversation. He was living at Nice for the benefit of his two sons, Horace and René, who were both delicate, and to whom he was very much devoted, and he also found the quiet of the place conducive to his art. We met him at a pleasant dinner given by Countess

Delphine Potocka, who though no longer young, had still great traces of beauty and a lovely voice, which she managed with consummate skill. When poor Chopin was dying he asked her to sing to him, and I have been told that the effect of her singing at that solemn moment, when the room was filled by his friends all in an agony of grief, was most touching.

On leaving Nice, which we did with regret on December 22, we proceeded along the beautiful Corniche to Genoa. The luxuriant growth of olives, palms, myrtle, and cactus all along the road delighted me, and I was much struck by the first view of Genoa the superb, from Arezzano. It may well be called the city of palaces, but on entering the town we were much struck by the exceeding narrowness of the streets, as well as by the picturesque dresses of the inhabitants. We visited the Balbi, Brignole, Durazzo, Doria, and Pallavicini Palaces, and were delighted with the treasures of art they contained. We also drove to the Villa Pallavicini, about six miles from Genoa, where it is said the garden and grottoes cost three millions of francs. Water, conveyed a distance of five miles, supplies a cascade and small lake, or rather pond, and the grotto, which is considered the chief wonder of the garden, is formed of rocks and stalactites brought from Spezia and other parts of the coast. The day was bright, but bitterly cold, and though the place was worth seeing as a specimen of Italian taste, I regretted the time we spent in going there. The costume of the peasants struck me as very picturesque : they wore a scarf of coloured cotton over their head and shoulders, gracefully draped, and producing a very artistic effect. On January 30 we left Genoa, and spent a delightful afternoon at Sestri, which is one of the most beautiful spots on the Riviera. The sunset was glorious, and the eye stretched far away across the Gulf of Genoa to the snow-capped Alps behind the Corniche.

After visiting Spezia, Lucca, Pisa, and Siena, we reached Rome. I shall not attempt to describe our stay at Rome, but merely record that we had hardly settled ourselves comfortably in a nice lodging, with the hope of spending at least two months there, when one day, to our surprise and dismay on fetching our letters at the post-office, one arrived for my husband with the terrible letters O.H.M.S. He immediately said, 'Oh, that is to order me back to my post!' and sure enough it was an official letter from Lord Granville, who had just succeeded Lord Palmerston as Minister for Foreign Affairs in England, desiring

Lord Bloomfield to return to Berlin at once. This was a terrible blow and disappointment to us both. I had been ordered to Italy for my health, and durst not undertake the long cold journey north, so after considerable hesitation it was decided that I should remain in Italy with one of my nephews till the spring. This unfortunate *contretemps* of course spoilt all my pleasure in Italy, but 'contre la force il n'y a pas de résistance,' and we had to submit and bear our disappointment as best we could.

On February 2 we attended Candlemas in the Sistine chapel, where the Pope officiated in person surrounded by the cardinals. After blessing the large wax tapers, the Pope distributed them to whoever approached him; and after the cardinals, bishops, and clergy had received theirs, the Corps Diplomatique approached, and after kissing the Pope's toe each received a taper. I was struck by seeing that not a single *un-official* person approached his Holiness except a few English, who had lately joined the Roman Catholic Church ; among others, Lord Campden, Lord Fielding, and Aubrey de Vere. The Pope was seated under a canopy to the left of the altar, with a white mitre on his head, and attired in a crimson cope. During the procession he was carried on a chair raised on men's shoulders. He gave his blessing as he passed, and all the Roman Catholics prostrated themselves before him. During high mass the Pope was seated before the altar on a low sort of throne, whilst mass was said by one of the cardinals assisted by the bishop. The music disappointed me, and I thought it much less fine than the church music I had often heard at St. Petersburg. The ceremony lasted about a couple of hours, and though the *coup d'œil* was fine it did not impress me at all, or excite the smallest feeling of devotion.

One day before Lord Bloomfield left Rome Count Rayneval, then French Ambassador at Rome, and an old friend of my husband's, invited him to go to a *chasse* he had at Ostia. They were to start very early in the morning, but the weather was so extremely wet my husband gave up the expedition. That evening we dined at the Embassy, and he asked Count Rayneval whether he had had a good day's sport. He answered, to our great amusement, ' Non, mon cher, pas trop. J'ai tué un corbeau et une grive,' having travelled forty miles there and as many back to accomplish this remarkable feat. On February 3 my dear husband left me.

Tuesday, February 17.—I went to the Usedoms'

balcony on the Corso to witness the end of the Carnival.   People were pelting each other to any extent with bouquets, bonbons, flour and lime. The races began about five o'clock, and were run by about six poor horses without riders. As soon as it was dusk the moccoletti or candles were lighted, and then came the great excitement of the day, every one trying to extinguish his neighbour's light.   The view up the Corso was very gay and pretty, but the general effect was spoiled, because the mob, to show the discontent which prevailed generally, had no candles.   When Charles Albert entered Milan the Pope permitted the populace to testify their joy by carrying moccoletti, but they have never carried them since.

Early in March I left Rome for Naples, where I had the pleasure of making Sir William Temple's acquaintance, who was then Minister there.   I had some very interesting conversation with him about the state of the country, which though quiet was then much oppressed.   The King was completely in the hands of the Jesuits, and was a despotic sovereign.   The number of people imprisoned for political offences was great, and they were treated with brutal severity, chained two and two night and day, and the state of the prisons was said to be deplorable.   I heard that about forty prisoners who had been confined at Ischia were removed in the dead of the night to another prison in the interior of the country, where they were confined in a dungeon and treated with great cruelty. The surveillance of the police was insufferable, but led sometimes to very funny stories. Once ten or twelve young men dined together, and having drank freely they expressed their opinions more openly than prudence permitted, so the next morning each went to make his report to the police, and there were as many reports as there had been guests!

Florence, April, 1852. (*Extract of a Letter to the Hon. Mrs. Trotter.*)—I have just arrived from Naples; unfortunately the weather was as bad as any I ever felt at Brighton in March, viz., bitter N.E. winds and hot sun. The mountains were covered with snow, which is rare at Naples even in mid-winter, so I saw the place to great disadvantage, but certainly the bay with Vesuvius towering up above it, is most lovely, and Sorrento and Castelamare must be enchanting in the spring. I think it is a mistake coming to Italy when the leaves are off the vines, and I have been seriously disappointed in the mildness of the air, especially in the spring, which is as backward as it is in England. When I left Rome a week ago the hedges were still quite brown. I travelled a lovely road, *viâ* Terni, Perugia, and Arezzo. I went at Rome to hear a famous French preacher, the Abbé de la Vigne, who was giving a course of Lent lectures. He was eloquent, and his lectures were very edifying, and, as he did not touch upon our doctrinal differences, I listened to him with great pleasure and I hope profit. I think I have never felt the differences which rend the Church of Christ more painfully than I have done since I came to Italy ; for there is certainly much that is great and good in the Roman Catholic Church, much we might do well to imitate. A devotion to the cause of religion, a self-denial, and conscientiousness about what is believed to be right which often shames me ; and though the superstition is painful, I cannot help thinking that sometimes we fall into contrary extremes equally grievous. As far as I am able to judge, I certainly think that the Church of England is the *juste milieu* ; and the more I see of other forms and other churches, the more I cling to the simple, scriptural, and beautiful Liturgy of our own Book of Common Prayer, and hope that in time it may be more generally adopted throughout Europe than it is now. An attempt is being made in Piedmont now to unite with the Vaudois, and the first Protestant Church is being erected at Turin, which possibly may be the beginning of a better and purer worship throughout Italy. One thing seems quite certain, viz., that the Papacy has received a shake from which it will not recover, and though many still nominally belong to the Church of Rome, I believe thousands would leave that communion if they dared. The power of the priests is gone, and there is a great spirit of inquiry abroad which I believe is the precursor of a great change.

As to describing Rome, that is quite out of the question. There is such a strange mixture there of past and present, palace and hovel, luxury and filth, one feels quite bewildered; and at the same time such deep interest is attached to almost every stone in the place, there is abundant food for the mind. After the Holy Land, I think there is no place so full of interest as Rome; and it is impossible to see so many spots connected with the early days of Christianity and the martyrs without deep emotion, mingled with regret that so much which calls forth our best and holiest feelings should be mingled with such gross superstition, not to say idolatry. I cannot tell you, for instance, the sort of turn it gave me on first entering the Coliseum to see it filled with little altars dedicated to different saints, and two small crosses let into the old walls, with an inscription on them offering a hundred and forty days' plenary indulgence to whoever should kiss them ! Then the feelings of intense wonder and admiration St. Peter's calls forth are considerably damped when one reflects that the riches of art it contains were bought with the price of indulgences ; and it is melancholy to see people prostrating themselves before the bronze statue of St. Peter (said to be that of Jupiter Tonans), whose toe is completely worn away with being kissed. Of course, every church has its relics, and yesterday at St. John Lateran, we were shown the table where our Saviour took the last supper, the well where he spoke with the woman of Samaria, and a block of granite, said to be our Lord's height. I own these things do not touch me, but there are some places in Rome which certainly call forth one's deepest feelings of veneration. For instance, there is no mistaking the Coliseum, Titus' Arch, with the bas-reliefs of the golden candlesticks, the table and trumpets of the Temple at Jerusalem. Then the main features of the surrounding country are doubtless very much the same as they were when St. Paul entered Rome by the Appian Way : with so much that is real, one need not care about what is doubtful or false.

From all I can learn, things here are going on as badly as possible, and there is but one voice as to the misgovernment of this wretched country and the oppression of the priesthood. If it was not for the French army things could not go on for a day, and a zealous Roman Catholic told us a few days ago that he believed if the troops were withdrawn there would be a massacre of the priests—they are so hated. I know for a positive fact that a Roman *dare* not have a Bible in his house, domiciliary visits are constantly taking place, and people are exiled and imprisoned without trial; in short, if you have read Mr. Glad-. stone's account of the state of things at Naples, you may have some idea of what they are at Rome at this moment. As for the poverty and dirt of Rome it exceeds all belief, and when Cardinal Wiseman talks of the purlieus of Westminster, I only wish he would turn his attention to those of the Vatican. During the Revolution a vast number of Bibles were sold, but they were bought up and burnt, and neither at Rome nor in Tuscany would a Roman Catholic dare enter a Protestant Church. Our place of worship at Rome is a large room, which holds seven or eight hundred people, without the walls, but it is always full, and I trust God will hear and answer the prayers that are there offered up for all those that 'err and are deceived,' and enable all who profess and call themselves Christians to 'hold the faith in unity of spirit, in the bond of peace, and in righteousness of life.'

The colouring here is only too lovely, and affords no end of subjects to an artist. The galleries, too, are so rich in *chefs-d'œuvre*, many of which are familiar to me from copies or engravings, and often remind me of our beloved mother, who so enjoyed seeing the beauties of art and nature, but who is now, I trust, in a far more blessed place, with the 'spirits of just men made perfect.'

From Florence I went to Bologna and Venice. There I witnessed a *fête* given in honour of the Archduchess Sophie of Austria. The town was hung with tapestries, banners, and velvet draperies, which added much to its picturesque appearance, and there was a large procession of gondolas, chiefly filled by the lower classes, as very few of the Venetian nobility were present. Not a single cheer was heard, and certainly Her Imperial Highness's reception was anything but hearty. On leaving Venice I proceeded to Berlin, which I reached happily in the beginning of May.

CHAPTER XIII.

Interview with the Empress of Russia—Letters from Lord Bloomfield at the commencement of the Crimean War—Painful state
of political feeling at Berlin—The Kreuz Zeitung party—
Dismissal of General Bonin—Dinner at Potsdam—The Princess
of Prussia—Death of my father, Lord Ravensworth—Visit to
Switzerland—Confirmation of Princess Louise—Letters of the
King—Princess Louise's marriage—Prince Frederic William s
engagement to the Princess Royal.

Berlin, June 1852.—We had not the pleasure
of seeing the Emperor Nicholas during his visit
to Berlin.   The Empress sent for us and received
us with great kindness and cordiality, but gave
us clearly to understand that she saw us as old
acquaintances and not as members of the Corps
Diplomatique, which, as a rule, received but little
attention at the Court of Russia, and the Empress
made a sort of apology for not having seen us
before, by saying she understood my husband
only had asked for an audience, intimating she
should not have received him officially.   We found
the Empress much altered since we took leave of
her the previous year.   She was much fallen
away, and seemed weak, though she said she had

derived benefit from change of air. We never saw Her Imperial Majesty after the Crimean War, and she died on October 20, 1860.

Extracts of Letters from my Husband, written during my absence from Berlin. 1852.

Webster came by express on his way to Constantinople, and brought another cartload of despatches. One to Sir Hamilton Seymour, containing a strong but *amiable* remonstrance, approves of all Lord Stratford has done, and a declaration that we cannot approve of the proposed Convention.

Things look so far bad, and I fear negotiations will drag slowly on. Lord Clarendon writes an excellent *exposé* of the affair, conciliatory but firm, and if the Czar understands our language he will take it in good part, but I fear Menschikoff's disappointment! Prussia is all right; I hope better too of Austria, and if so, it will be hard if the affair does not end satisfactorily.

The Russian boat has arrived, and poor Seymour is frantic . . . I should think that he could not remain at St. Petersburg with any comfort to himself, or even be able to hold, what is called, confidential intercourse with Count Nesselrode and his Imperial master. As to the question of peace or war, I think the Porte will accept the modified Note demanded, which will settle the matter *until next time*! If not accepted, the Russians will enter and keep the Principalities, thus taking another and a good slice of Turkey in Europe. Oh, how thankful I am to the Queen for having removed us from Russia!

Seymour had seen the Emperor, who declares that he will not be satisfied with anything less than a certain recall of Note presented by Menschikoff to the Porte. This is certainly better than the Convention that was required, and, at all events, it opens the way for negotiations. Gortschakoff is to command the army ; and I presume they will march into the Principalities and occupy them as a beginning.

I thought you would be amused at Lord Lyndhurst's opinion of Count Nesselrode's circular. The expressions were very appropriate, and he spoke of the composition as a lawyer no doubt. I think he went rather far, but the tone of every composition which has issued from the Russian Foreign Office within the last few months has the same character. The reasoning is based on false premises, and consequently is easily pulled to pieces. They think their honour engaged in carrying out their schemes, but they have nothing to go on but the traditional policy which characterises their conduct with regard to Turkey.

I have just seen the Manifesto published on the 30th at St. Petersburg, on the rejection by the Porte of the last *generous* (?) offer of the Emperor. It talks of little else than the bounden duty of Russia to protect the orthodox religion ! but though it announces the intended occupation of the Principalities, it declares that Russia does not make *war*. Now, what else is this act ? The stronger, according to Russia, has the right to force the weak to do whatever is required ; there is no other argument ; she will try and tire us out, I suppose !

The Emperor has written to his Belgian brother with a view to his communicating with England on the crisis. This sounds well, and as if the Czar felt he was in the wrong box, and wanted the help of a third hand. But we have now taken our line, and I trust that we shall know our duty and do it. The country, it is evident from the general expression of public opinion, will give the Government all the support that is wanting to make them energetic. There is no use in looking forward to what may not happen, but if the present storm does blow over, we must not easily forget the lesson which we have received, and prepare for coming events, which cannot be very far distant.

I had a long talk this morning with Baron Manteuffel; I read to him portions of the despatch to Seymour, asking for explanations, and left it with him as I was asked to do. He was very satisfactory, but from all I learn I doubt Austria going with us. She is so full of internal weakness and difficulties that I doubt her doing anything against Russia if it came to the point.

The messenger from St. Petersburg came this evening; the accounts are very unsatisfactory, and the further one looks behind the scenes in Russia the greater is one's disgust.

The Emperor *will* enter the Principalities or obtain his Note: but this is not war, and as our ships would not go up the Dardanelles if he entered the Principalities, this complication will be avoided. What I apprehend is that the Turks will refuse the Russian conditions, and that then an interminable negotiation will be opened. The Baltic fleet is being fitted out.

Berlin, June 18, 1853.—The Russian aspersions on the character of our Ambassador at Constantinople are too shabby, and because

Russia fails in carrying out her object of destroying the independence of a country which, by her treaties with other Powers, she is bound to support, she must now cast the blame of her ill success on the English Ambassador, whereas the real cause of the failure was the nature of the instructions under which Prince Menschikoff was acting, and which instructions were quite different from those made known to us!

We had counted on assurances by the Russian Government, and acted a noble and becoming part in believing the Emperor Nicholas incapable of acting otherwise than he had told us it was his intention to do, but we have been taught a lesson which we should not easily forget.

The English Government has no fault to find with Lord Stratford; and his colleagues of France, Austria, and Prussia knew as little as he did himself of the secret and false information upon which the Russian Government based their unjustifiable attacks. England ought to be proud of having in her service so conscientious, so honourable, so straightforward a representative, and instead of meriting blame he deserves the nation's thanks for his conduct. Russia may have one opinion, but Europe has another. of the late negotiation. Further, it stands to reason that Russia expected a defeat, or why should she have prepared 160,000 men to back her negotiation ?

There never was a man more unjustly maligned than Lord Stratford, or one better supported by his own country ! Seymour (Sir Hamilton) told Count Nesselrode that Lord Stratford is quite approved of at home, and if, therefore, he wants to find fault with anybody he should address his complaints to the Government and not to its agent.

At 2 I started the Bishop of Ripon[1] (Dr. Longley, afterwards Archbishop of Canterbury), with Manteuffel and Mr. Bellson (then chaplain at Berlin), to Potsdam. The party have returned greatly delighted, and the Bishop appears to have had an interesting conversation with the King, and a nice drive at Sans Souci. I am so sorry you are not here to talk to him, he is so simple in his ways, and yet very earnest, and has such a nice manner with young people.

Berlin, Sunday, June 19.—This morning the little chapel was crowded to excess. The Bishop preached a most excellent sermon from St. Matt. xxi. 12 : 'My house shall be a house of prayer.' He has a plain, impressive delivery, and his whole

---

[1] The Bishop came to Berlin to hold a Confirmation.

demeanour is exactly what one likes to see. This afternoon he read us the service at 3 o'clock.

I yesterday made the acquaintance of your new French colleague, the Marquise de Moustier, *née* de Mérode. Neither she nor her husband know anything about their profession, but I daresay will soon learn. She was asking me about the Court, and I told her all I could to prepare her; she finished by saying she had never been at a Court in her life, and did not know how she should behave herself! Moustier is a pleasant, unpretending gentleman; very desirous to cultivate the English Legation, which I shall duly reciprocate!

Berlin, July 7, 1853.—I have had a letter to-day from Lord Clarendon, which looks as if public opinion would force the Government to change their pacific policy. The debate to-morrow evening will probably bring the matter out. Austria and Prussia are morally with us, and both Governments are furious with the Russian Manifesto of the [14 o.s.] 26 June, and the entrance into the Principalities has confirmed them in the hopelessness of obtaining any concession. In fact the Czar has treated us all like children, and it is time he should be taught a lesson. If he don't give in he will get more than he bargains for! Budberg has been trying to bully Manteuffel and Moustier, but he finds himself and his policy a good deal isolated. However, the 'Kreuz Zeitung' is Russian to the backbone, so much so that I think it injures its cause. The more one sees of the Russian correspondence—and there is a New Circular come out, which you will probably read in ' Galignani '— the greater appear the fallacies of her arguments. Russia has not, as far as I can discover, been able to establish a single point in her favour, or in support of her position, except that she is strong, and that she is determined at any price to maintain her fallacious doctrines. The treaties she quotes give her no right to the extended protection she claims over the Greek Church. If Austria would act as she ought to do, and as I really believe she would like to do, and we could count upon her co-operation, I am satisfied we must gain all we require. All I now hope is that we may be able to establish something for *hereafter* !

Berlin, July 11, 1853.—The messenger has arrived, but no new light is thrown on the Eastern question. The debate being postponed looks as if the Government does not wish to be forced into war, or to the expression of opinion in Parliament which would render negotiations more difficult. You ask what is to happen if our fleet enters the Dardanelles ? That movement would mean that we had reason to believe that the Russians were preparing an *extensive* attack on the Turkish dominions; which cannot be at present, for Russia declares she does not intend to make war, and has no plan of conquest.

The natural conclusion, therefore, is that our fleet will not enter. If they did, it would be to prevent an attack on Constantinople, or to retard the movements of the Russians in the Black Sea, and perhaps do them as much damage as we could. Our doing this, or advancing, *would be war*, and we should no doubt be able to do them an immense injury and seriously retard their progress though I very much doubt *our* being able ulti mately to prevent their marching south ; but if a general war followed, it is impossible to foresee what complications might arise, and the question would then be who would be on our side, and who against us. If Austria and Prussia were with us, there could be no doubt that with the divisions on her south and western frontiers, and with the movement that would take place in the Caucasus, and the blockade of the two outlets for her trade, Russia would be brought to book, but I fear neither the one nor the other Power will take the offensive. Peace may then be preserved, and *Russia will carry her point*, though she will have lost immensely in moral influence by her conduct. If a general war were to follow, *in a few years we should probably lose sight of the original cause of the quarrel, and finish by fighting amongst ourselves.* Up to this moment we have right so clearly on our side that I feel satisfied we must gain all we want, and I am far from feeling the least uneasiness as to the future. The small Powers are all against Russia, and see in her present pretensions the complete setting of all rights at defiance, and that her law is that of the stronger against the weaker. I trust that all will feel the same, but it is only amongst Russia's immediate neighbours that this will be the case.

There are reported dissensions in the Cabinet in London. The country is united, which is the main thing, and though all are opposed to war, all are for the maintenance of England's honour!

Berlin, July 12, 1853.—The telegraph brings the news that Lord Clanricarde's motion has come on, that he has moved an address to the Queen, and that there are serious rumours of Lord Aberdeen's leaving the Ministry. If so, the war party is rising, and after that second circular of Nesselrode's, I am not surprised at it; for a more ill-judged document, if peace was the object of Russia, could not have been put forth. At the same time I wish some means could be devised to prevent so fearful a calamity.

The Prussians have been writing a good despatch to Constantinople and to St. Petersburg, and Buol, I hear, has spoken out more firmly, so that I hope for better things—but really each day brings forward some new complication, and one's hopes and fears are perpetually rising and falling!

Berlin, July 19, 1853.—I saw Manteuffel this morning, and had a long conversation with him, which I did not think satisfactory. He is evidently put out by the ' Kreuz Zeitung,' and has not carried his point as I should wish him to have done. That party have decidedly got the upper hand, and though if he would but speak out, I think he might beat them, he does not venture to do so. The King wishes to keep him as he is, and to leave the others their paper! The consequence is there can be strength nowhere; but this suits His Majesty, who thus fancies he governs all. I hear the Russians have already got 50,000 men in the Principalities, and are marching more and more to the south. How is it all to end?

On my return from Kreuznach I met the
Prince of Prussia, accompanied by his aide-de-
camp, on board one of the Rhine steamers, but as
I had not had an opportunity then of being officially presented, and was travelling alone, I was
placed in rather an awkward position whilst sitting
close to His Royal Highness all the way from Coblentz to Cologne ; but soon after my return to
Berlin I was presented to His Royal Highness
by the Princess of Prussia, and both condoled
with me on the great national loss we sustained
by the death of the Duke of Wellington, which
took place on September 14, but expressed their
thankfulness that this great man had not outlived
his faculties, and had been spared a long lingering
illness.

Berlin, March 1854.—The state of affairs at
Berlin at this date rendered our position there extremely painful and disagreeable.   Political feeling
ran so very high the town was divided into two
camps, and those who were well with Russia, which
included the Queen of Prussia and the whole of
the ' Kreuz Zeitung ' party, almost cut us and our
French colleagues.   The Princess of Prussia, who
was very English in her sympathies and political
opinions, was looked upon with great suspicion,

her motives were misrepresented, and her desire to strengthen the alliance between England and Prussia, which was so very desirable both in a political and religious point of view, exposed her to the enmity of the 'Kreuz Zeitung' party, so that her residence at Berlin was very trying to her Royal Highness.   It was at this time that we gave a ball to the Hereditary Grand Duchess of Mecklenburg Strelitz, which the King and Queen attended, it being the etiquette in Prussia that the Court should be present at any *fête* given in honour of the members of a Royal family. There were actually bets in the town as to whether the Court would come to our ball or not, and the 'Kreuz Zeitung' party were furious at their doing so, and chose to consider it a political demonstration.

The night of our ball the King asked the Queen at dinner at what hour she intended going to the Bloomfields.   Her answer was that 'indeed she was not sure she should go at all ;' to this the King simply said, 'Du musst' ('you must'). Their Majesties accordingly arrived about 10 o'clock. Lord Bloomfield and I went down to the hall door to receive them, and the Queen took my husband's arm, but the only remark she made was 'Votre escalier est bien roide, Milord.'   She scarcely took any notice of me all that evening, though, of course, I had to attend Her Majesty, and she positively insisted upon the King leaving before supper, which his Majesty wished to stay for, but the Queen stood in her cloak at the top of the staircase, and sent three messages to the King, who at last and very reluctantly was obliged to give way. The Queen tried as a counterbalance to persuade the King to attend a concert our Russian colleagues the Budbergs gave the old Grand Duchess of Mecklenburg Strelitz two days after our ball, but this the King positively refused, saying, ' J'irai chez Lord Bloomfield, et j'irai aussi chez le Baron de Budberg, mais à condition qu'il fasse arriver une Grande-Duchesse de Russie.' I endeavoured as much as possible to keep clear of all political differences and intrigues. I felt that my position was one of conciliation, and that it was my business to try and smooth the difficulties in my husband's path as much as possible, but our position was so difficult and painful that nothing but a strong sense of the duty we owed our Queen and our country would have induced us to remain at Berlin, and we almost envied Sir Hamilton and Lady Seymour when they passed through Berlin on their way home at the breaking out of the Crimean War.

Berlin, March 30, 1854.—The King was completely in the hands of the 'Kreuz Zeitung' party, and acted in accordance with their views, not only without the consent of his ministers, but actually without their knowledge, so that Baron Manteuffel's position was most anomalous, and he only retained it because in the first place he liked being in office, and secondly, because he believed matters would get worse were he to resign. The country had confidence in him, and he was pledged not to go with Russia, though he was unable to go against her. Public feeling at Berlin ran very high against the King, and I believe that if he had attempted to ally himself with Russia against the Western powers there would have been a revolution. The King refused to see any of the moderate men, and the Emperor of Russia was looked upon by the 'Kreuz Zeitung' party as the representative of order and religion *versus* anarchy and revolution.

The Prince of Prussia's views at this time were so completely at variance with those of the King, that they met but seldom, and then studiously avoided political discussion.

Austria sent General Hesse on a special mission, but General Gerlach, the head of the 'Kreuz Zeitung' party, was appointed to treat with him.

When Hesse heard of his nomination he exclaimed he would just as soon treat with Paskewitch !

Berlin, May 11, 1854.—General Bonin's, the Minister of War, sudden dismissal caused a great sensation. He had transacted business as usual with the King when, just as he was leaving the room, His Majesty called him back and told him that although he had the greatest esteem and regard for him, and had always found him a most useful and faithful servant, he now disapproved of his opinions, and therefore wished him to leave the War Office. Poor General Bonin, who was completely taken by surprise, entreated the King to tell him how he had offended ; the King having the previous day signed the ratification of the Convention with Austria, the General could not understand why he should be dismissed so summarily. The King answered by embracing him, and told him General Dohna would give him the desired information, and dinner being then announced General Bonin had to appear at it as if nothing had happened. The next day General Count Dohna came and said he had received the King's orders to offer him (Bonin) a division, and that the reason of his dismissal from the War Office was because about six weeks previously he had made a speech in the Chambers, wherein he guaranteed that the loan of 30,000,000 thalers should not be employed against the Western Powers. General Bonin begged General Dohna to inform the King that his message had been delivered, but declined any further discussion as to his political opinions. He went at once to Baron Manteuffel, the Minister President, and told him what had occurred. He said he could hardly believe the thing possible, but that same evening, to every one's astonishment, Baron Manteuffel countersigned his friend and colleague's dismissal from office. The Prince of Prussia thereupon applied for leave of absence, which the King immediately granted, the King telling him he was delighted to think he had succeeded in breaking up his party. The King was entirely surrounded after this by our bitterest adversaries, and our position at Berlin was so uncomfortable my husband thought it best to abstain from giving his usual official dinner in celebration of the Queen's birthday, as he felt it would be perfect mockery to ask those whom he regarded as our enemies to drink the Queen's health; and yet had he only invited our friends in the opposition party it would have been invidious, and done more harm than good. The members of the English Legation were, however, invited to dine at Potsdam on May 24 as usual, the King having made a rule of celebrating Queen Victoria's birthday by inviting all the members of the British Legation ever since his visit to England in 1842, when he stood sponsor to the Prince of Wales.

Nothing could have been more cordial than the *King's* manner to us, and both the King and Queen congratulated us upon the happy anniversary we were invited to celebrate. In the middle of dinner the King stood up, and addressing my husband, who sat opposite to him, said in English : ' My dear Lord, I beg to propose your Queen's health, and may God bless her . . . . with all my heart,' emptying his glass. The dinner lasted as short a time as possible, and the Queen was evidently impatient to get it over ; and she more than once tried to hurry the King, till at last he got quite provoked. After dinner the King took Lord Bloomfield out on the terrace, and was just getting into conversation with him, when the Queen inquired what train we could return to Berlin by : being informed there was one at five o'clock, she said we must go at once, and she went up herself to the King and told him he must dismiss us, evidently wishing to prevent further conversation, or the King seeing any one who might have what the Queen considered a bad influence. In the few words which passed between the King and Lord Bloomfield, the former referred to M. de Bunsen's dismissal, and said he had written a letter of fifteen pages to explain it to Queen Victoria, adding it was impossible for him to retain as his representative in England a man whose policy differed from his own, and who refused to obey his orders. During dinner I sat next the King, the Queen sat on his other side, next her the Crown Prince of Meiningen, and next him Lady Augustus Loftus, the wife of the Secretary of Legation. The Queen kept telling the Crown Prince to ask all sorts of questions about the war, the size of our army, the operations of the Fleet, &c. ; and at last he summed up by saying, ' Mais après tout que pouvez vous faire ? L'Angleterre est si petite et la Russie est si grande comment pouvez vous l'attaquer ? ' Lady Augustus answered very properly that ' that was not the moment to discuss the relative power of the two nations, but that England had not proved herself insignificant in history, and therefore it would be better to wait and see the result of the war.' The King was determined to maintain his neutral position, but the feeling of the country became more and more demonstrative, and one day at Kroll's

Coffee House in the Thier Garten, the audience asked for the Austrian National Hymn, which was played, after which a number of people marched down the Linden to the Prince of Prussia's palace, where they stopped and gave three cheers, after which they dispersed quietly, but then the little wooden shed where the band played was taken down by the police, and orders were given that the music was to cease, as it gave rise to mischievous political demonstrations !

When first we went to Berlin, the Church of England service was held in a small room in the Hôtel du Nord. It was a very unsuitable place, and often when we were going to church, as we had to pass through the passages of the hotel, we found them encumbered with slops and dirty linen ! This was so very unpleasant, I one day represented the state of things to the King, who immediately most kindly placed a large room at Mon Bijou Palace at our disposal, which was fitted up as a chapel by subscription, and opened for divine worship on Whit-Sunday 1854.

Lord Bloomfield had a curious interview at this time with the captain of an English vessel called the ' Anne M'Callister,' who was indignant at the manner in which he had been treated in Russia.

He was sent to Warsaw by diligence, with only a rouble to pay his travelling expenses, so he only had six meals on the journey, and had it not been for the kindness of the Vice-Consul at Warsaw, he must have begged his way on from there. This man said eight engineers were detained at Cronstadt whom the Russians had done all in their power to keep, but they would not enter the Russian service.

Berlin, June 13, 1854.—The Prince and Princess of Prussia were invited by the King to return to attend a funeral service, which was held in memory of the late king, their father, and a sort of reconciliation took place. Eighty-four addresses were presented to their Royal Highnesses on the anniversary of their silver marriage, and they received many costly presents ; the Princess was so much affected during the presentation of the addresses that she shed tears. It was considered advisable that I should not have my usual audience of the Princess at this time ; it would have been known immediately, and probably have given rise to many false and mischievous reports. I was told some years later by a friend that my house was tabooed in Berlin, and ladies were warned to avoid the society of such a dangerous intriguante. Prussia was governed at that time by a small but most mischievous Camarilla; the country had no voice, every expression of public opinion was instantly hushed and condemned as being revolutionary and disloyal, and whilst making a tour in the provinces the king actually refused to pass through a town which had returned a liberal member, so little were constitutional principles understood or practised. Very little was known as to the result of the King's interview with the Emperor Francis Joseph of Austria at Pitschin, but it was supposed to have done more good than harm. The Prince of Prussia went to Königsberg to meet his brother, the Princess returned to Coblentz.

Extract of Letters from my Husband.

All is uncertain at St. Petersburg. The Russians proclaim a willingness to treat, and a desire to do so on all points proposed for consideration, but on the question of the protection of the Christian subjects of the Porte, they say that, *malgré eux*, they cannot yield. So I suppose all this row will end in nothing but loss of time and a feeling of satisfaction to a certain great personage (the King of Prussia), that he has done all he could to maintain peace. I hear the Emperor of

Russia's expressions have quite touched the Court here, and that his generous consideration of the proposals from here have made them quite happy. But there is no question of his yielding an iota upon the all important points. However, that won't make this government prepare for anything beyond protracted negotiations.

Some further details of the shelling of Bomarsund have arrived, and Captain Hall and two small steamers appear to have done a great deal of damage to the steam batteries and forts, and to have completely silenced them. However, we shall never know the extent of damage done, for probably they will have a Te Deum at St. Petersburg, and make out that we were forced to retreat. It appears to have been a well-managed business. A mate named Lucas did a gallant thing ; a shell from the fort fell on the deck ; he took it up and threw it into the sea. The Emperor of Russia would have given him the St. George for such an heroic act. Sir Charles Napier has gone with his squadron to Cronstadt, and was close to it when the last accounts arrived.

Berlin, November 26, 1854.—This morning I had a visit from an English engineer from Odessa, who has been employed by the Russians on the Danube and Black Sea. He is now on his way home to offer his services to the Admiralty.

Ten of the 'Tiger's' crew are here. Two of the lieutenants have been with me. They speak well of the treatment they received from private individuals and from officers of the Russian army, but not so of the Government. They are under the impression that the war is very unpopular, and is causing great discontent in Russia, and that in the provinces through which they travelled the population is already drained away. The troops destined for the Crimea are quite out of heart, and believe that they are only going there to be slaughtered, and that Sebastopol is doomed and must be taken.

Berlin, December 6, 1854.—The extreme party here is in a fearful state of consternation at our treaty with Austria. They do not know what to be after. One of our colleagues said the other day, 'Si la Prusse adhère elle est déshonorée, si elle refuse elle est perdue.' Budberg is frantic, and Gortschakoff considers he has been misled. He knew nothing of our negotiation, and the signature came upon our enemies like a clap of thunder.

Berlin, December 9, 1854.—You will find Berlin in a charming state of excitement about the treaty with Austria. The Prussians are furious because they have been completely deceived, and just at the moment that the King

was proclaiming the happy *entente* with Austria,
she was signing an alliance with the Western
Powers.   Nothing remains for Prussia but armed
neutrality, which will ruin her, and be a most
unpopular measure, or to go with us in a half-and-
half sort of way, or to join Russia, and bring
about a revolution, and that would require more
courage than to go with the Western Powers.
If Prussia were with us the war would be the
sooner ended, but as she never would go heartily
with us I incline to think the best thing is to
leave her alone.

Letter to my Sister, The Honourable Mrs. Trotter.

Berlin, February 23, 1855.—Many thanks for
your last letter, though, alas! it was anything but
cheery, and I fear there is but too much truth in
what you say of our army; but I think you and
the 'Times' are too prone to blame individuals
instead of a system which is undoubtedly faulty,
and requires reforms and changes.   I wish, with
you, we had not begun by talking so big, it is our
national fault; at the same time, the trust Englishmen have in their own superiority leads them to
do marvellous things, and really when one sees,
as at Inkerman, 8,000 Englishmen withstand, and

conquer 60,000 Russians, one cannot wonder at their being rather vain. We have two nephews in the Crimea, and they declare the reports in the ' Times ' are exaggerated, and that though the sufferings of our gallant little army have been very great, it is not true that the French have been exempt from them, and I fear great privations and sufferings are inseparable from a winter campaign. Our losses in the Peninsular War were very heavy, and the Russians admit having lost 116,000 men since they entered the Principalities last year. The other day an Austrian dined with us, who served in Hungary in 1849, and he told us the men were often thirty-six hours without any food whatever, and lay out the whole winter in the snow without any covering except their cloaks. I mention these facts not to defend our system, but simply to show what other nations, and those who pretend to a military organisation very superior to our own, have suffered, and that they have lost quite as many men as we have. Altogether, however, the state of things just now is very deplorable, and makes our position abroad anything but agreeable ; however, we must wait and hope for the best. I trust our Government will be firm and energetic, and not be induced by internal clamour to listen to any proposals for peace inconsistent with our own national honour and what I most firmly and sincerely believe to be the advance of true civilisation and liberty. If Russia is not beaten now, she will be more powerful than ever, not only in the East, but in the West ; and none but those who know, as we do, the fatal effects of her influence in Germany, can estimate the full importance of the present crisis. May God direct and rule the hearts of all who are in authority, so that in the end all may work together for good, and ' peace and justice, religion and piety ' may be established amongst us. I believe nations, like individuals, require chastisement, and I only hope that it will not have been sent to us, as a nation, in vain.

The cold here this winter has been intense, quite Russian ; the thermometer has been as low as twelve degrees below zero, but one feels ashamed of grumbling at anything which happens to oneself now when one thinks of what others are suffering. Distress here is very great, food is very dear, work scarce, and the people are complaining on all sides.

My dear father's death took place on March 7, at Ravensworth Castle, after a very short illness, and was a great blow to me ; the doctors ordered

me to Switzerland, where I spent two pleasant months at Thun and Interlachen with my cousin, Lady Young, and her daughters. On July 25 (St. James's Day) we were reading together on the second floor of the great hotel at Thun, when suddenly the room began to shake and the windows rattle, as if a heavy dray cart was being driven under them. We rushed to the door, which was locked. I wrenched it open and got out of the house; as we ran down the stairs they seemed to rock under us, like the companion ladder of a ship in a heavy swell; and when we got out we found all the inhabitants of the hotel looking pale with terror, standing out on the lawn, and we then realised that there had been a severe shock of an earthquake. The sensation I shall never forget; for the first time in my life I felt the stability of the ground give way under my feet, and as if the mountains and rocks might come down on us. It was very awful, and one felt so utterly power-less. The shock lasted some seconds, and was repeated several times, so that for some nights our rest was much impaired. The village of Wisp, on the Simplon, suffered severely: the waters rose under the houses, and the walls of the great church at Lucerne were rent. Some days afterwards I rode up to see a glacier some miles from Kandersteg : the path was strewn with large pieces of rock which had come down on the day of the earthquake ; and as the mountains rose to my left, and there was a roaring torrent on my right, I could not but feel that I should be in rather a perilous position should another shock occur whilst I was riding up the defile.

An old English lady was staying in the hotel at Thun the day of the earthquake, and we were greatly amused at hearing that she gave her servant strict orders to put her umbrella and galoshes ready next her bed-side every night, in case there should be another shock !

Lord Bloomfield joined me in August, and we returned to England *viâ* Paris. We were at Fontainebleau when the news arrived of the fall of Sebastopol, and the first intimation we had of the victory was hearing the guns, which were fired at Paris in celebration of it. We spent the autumn in Ireland, and returned to Berlin for the winter. The following spring we hired a pretty little villa at Potsdam just under the Pfingstberg, where we spent a very pleasant summer.

Berlin, May 23, 1855.—I had a long and deeply interesting interview with the Prince and Princess of Prussia, Prince Frederick William and

Princess Louise, who were all most kind and cordial.

The Princess of Prussia said she had been most anxious to see me again before she left Berlin, to express better than she should have an opportunity of doing at Potsdam, how unalterable was her affection for the Queen, and she also wished to tell me the comfort she had derived from her beloved daughter's confirmation, which took place the other day. When Princess Louise left the room her mother spoke most feelingly and touchingly of the satisfaction she had experienced at the calm, earnest, and devotional manner in which her child had gone through this solemn event in life; and in the midst of so much that was pain-ful and distressing in the political state of affairs at that moment, the only thing that gave her peace and calmness was her firm trust in God, and entire submission to his will. The dear Princess looked worn and harassed, and each time she came to Berlin her position became more painful and difficult. Her strong sense of what were the real interests of Prussia, her deeply rooted religious principles, and her attachment to England, made her deplore the policy of the Court, which she considered injurious to her beloved country; her noble nature recoiled from the intrigues and unfair means which were employed to influence the King and embitter him against the Western Powers.

We were invited to dine at Potsdam as usual, to celebrate the Queen's birthday, and Lord Bloomfield was the bearer of an autograph letter from Her Majesty Queen Victoria, which arrived at a most auspicious moment. It was with a feeling of real satisfaction that the Princess of Prussia begged the King to grant her a few moments' audience before dinner, and read him the Queen's letter, with which he expressed himself perfectly satisfied. I sat next Prince Frederick William, whom I had scarcely seen since his return from Italy, and his visit to England. He talked a great deal of the interest of his visit to Italy, and especially of his stay at Rome, where both at Christmas and Easter he had witnessed the pompous ceremonies of the Romish Church, which, however, he disapproved, and for which he had no sympathy. The King and Queen took leave of us immediately after dinner, but we returned to Berlin in the same train as the Prince and Princess of Prussia, and the Princess expressed a wish to speak to us for a few minutes in the private waiting-room at the station. She then told us of her conversation with the King, and also kindly read us some passages of Queen Victoria's letter. Nothing could exceed the kindness and cordiality of her manner towards us personally, and when I took leave of her she said it had been such a pleasure and relief to her to express her sentiments and opinions to me, and she added, ' Nous nous voyons de loin, chère Lady Bloomfield, mais vous connaissez tous mes sentimens et vous me comprendrez.' I could not help saying that in our difficult, and often very painful position, it was a great comfort and con- solation to know that we had such a kind and true friend as Her Royal Highness, and that at least there was one person who understood us and our country, to which the Princess imme- diately rejoined, ' Ne dites pas une personne mais dites plutôt deux, car soyez-en bien persuadée mon mari partage tous mes sentimens envers vous et envers l'Angleterre.'

January 18.—We were present at the Court which was held on the occasion of the betrothal of Princess Louise to the Prince Regent of Baden. The Princess, who was extremely graceful and pretty, looked like a fresh rose-bud as she stood next her betrothed. She blushed very much when first she entered the room where all the ladies of the Corps Diplomatique were assembled to present their congratulations, and her pretty eyes filled with tears, but she recovered her composure immediately, and went through the ceremony, which must have been a trying one for so young a creature, with the greatest dignity and self-possession. The Prince Regent of Baden, without being handsome, was nice looking, and had very pleasing manners, and he found a little word to address to every one. The Princess of Prussia was not present, as it is not the custom that parents should appear on these occasions, but Prince Frederick William watched his sister, of whom he seemed not a little proud, with the deepest interest. At the Court receptions a few days previously, both Lord Bloomfield and I were struck with the change in the Queen of Prussia's manner, and Her Majesty was more gracious and cordial than we had ever known her. The King was kind and civil as he always was, but he was beginning to show symptoms of the fatal malady which developed rapidly the following year; his walk was uncertain, which gave rise to the report that he was drunk, instead of which he was a remarkably sober, moral man in all his habits, and had he been a private individual instead of the Sovereign of a great country, I believe he would have been both a happier and a more useful man ;

but he was easily acted upon by whoever happened to be present, and unfortunately during the Crimean War the influence was most mischievous.

At a ball at Court the King, who took a great interest in the Church of England service, asked me whether the Penitential Psalms were always sung in the minor key, and requested me to get him a collection of chants from England, which I accordingly did ; His Majesty then wrote me the following characteristic letter, which alludes to his being refused permission to send a representative to the Congress of Paris.

A Berlin, 27 Janvier 1856.

My Lady,—Vous avez eu l'insigne bonté de copier de votre propre main le Chaunt de Lord Mornington et d'autres mélodies d'Eglise, dont j'avais pris la trop grande hardiesse de vous parler. Je ne saurois trouver des paroles pour Vous remercier de l'active et prévenante indulgence avec laquelle vous avez bien voulu accueillir mon désir de m'instruire. J'espère, Madame, que votre réponse 'mélodieuse' sera d'une influence décisive sur le Chaunt des Psaumes, surtout dans nos vieilles cathédrales à chapitres, de Brandebourg, Mersebourg, et Naumbourg, et dans notre Dôme de Berlin. A cet effet je prendrai le courage, lorsque j'auroi l'honneur de vous revoir (et apparemment entre une valse et une polka), de vous adresser une question, savoir si le Chaunt de Lord Mornington et celui de Dupuis (que l'on chante souvent chez nous), est adapté dans le service anglican à tous les Psaumes sans distinction, ou si certains Psaumes, comme par exemple, ceux de contrition et de repentir, ceux de Babylone où les Psaumes émimment prophétiques ont leur chaunt à part (comme c'est le cas dans l'antique psaltérien de l'Eglise latine), qui exclut les mélodies en question ? C'est là un concert dont on ne me refusera pas la porte et où je désirerois ardemment d'entrer parce que je le pourrois sans crainte et sans scrupule, le sachant dirigé en dernier ressort à Lambeth et par le premier Ministre de la paix de Dieu dans les trois royaumes, qui (soit dit en parenthèse) en valent bien trente sous l'égide protectrice et bénie de votre adorable Reine !

En vous saluant affectueusement je suis, my lady, votre très reconnaissant et tout dévoué serviteur,

FRÉDÉRIC GUILLAUME, R.

I had a long and interesting interview with the Princess of Prussia previous to Her Royal Highness's departure from Berlin. She told me that her position was one of such great difficulty and constant annoyance, that on rising in the morning she always reflected seriously upon all that was likely to occur during the day, and prayed earnestly for strength to accept the period of her stay in Berlin as one of trial. She was satisfied she had done right in bringing Princess Louise to the capital, that she had enjoyed her carnival very much, and had been treated with kindness and affection. Her Royal Highness seemed very hopeless and discouraged at the political state of affairs, and at Prussia not being represented at the Conferences, which were about to take place at Paris, to discuss the differences between Russia and the Allies, though as her policy had been one not only of neutrality, but of isolation, she could not expect to be consulted. I told Her Royal Highness I thought our only chance of converting Prussia was by making Russia 'Westmächtlich;' at the same time there was no doubt of the King's attachment to England and Queen Victoria, but he was so surrounded by those whose object was to hide the truth from him, that he was not aware of the real state of affairs; he lived in a world of his own, and though now and then some startling event occurred, 'contre lequel il se heurtoit,' His Majesty imagined that his policy was wise and dignified, and the most in accordance with the interests of his country. The Princess told me she was perfectly aware of our painful position at Court, and that she herself had been warned of the imprudence of showing us so much friendliness, but she declared that though much obliged for the hint she considered she was at perfect liberty to show favour to whom she pleased, and that she wished to mark her personal regard for Lord Bloomfield and myself. I asked whether Her Royal Highness thought there was anything we could do to improve our relations with the Court, and to tell me plainly whether we had ever displeased the Queen of Prussia in any way, as I was not aware of having done so, and could only attribute her want of common courtesy to the political position we occupied. The Princess assured me that she was satisfied Lord Bloomfield and I had done everything in our power to conciliate, and not only this, but that the English Government had shown the greatest moderation and forbearance towards Prussia in the difficult crisis we were passing through. When the Prin cess took leave of me she gave me a handsome onyx brooch, which she said was the Prussian colours, and she hoped I should often wear it and keep it for her sake.

Prince Frederick William's engagement to the Princess Royal was announced to us by a letter I received from the Queen, just after peace had been concluded with Russia ; the political aspect of affairs began to improve from that time, and our own position at Berlin became much pleasanter and easier. The King announced the marriage at dinner. He got up, to the astonishment of all present, and said he begged to propose a toast, and to drink the health of the bridegroom ; that he durst not mention the name of the bride, as he had been forbidden to do so, but that he left all present to draw the conclusion they liked from the toast. This was related to me by a person who was present, and who added that Prince Frederick William looked so excessively happy and in such spirits it was quite a pleasure to see him.

Princess Louise was married to the Grand Duke of Baden in September in the chapel of the Neue Palais, Potsdam, at half-past six P.M. Dr. Strauss, who performed the service as the senior Court Chaplain, gave a very long commonplace and tiresome sermon. The bride and bridegroom arrived about half-past seven, and the Royal family followed them, and took their places on three sides of the altar. I was just behind Prince Frederick William, and opposite to the Princess of Prussia, who looked very pale and nervous, but whose admirable self-command never forsook her for a moment. The bride looked touchingly young and charming, so pure and virgin-like, and so deeply impressed by the solemnity of the moment every one was struck by her manner. She was a most fascinating creature, and certainly her mother's advice and example were not lost upon her.

Immediately after the marriage the company adjourned to the Weisse Saal, and the Corps Diplomatique and society defiled before the Royal family. Then supper was served, and after that the Fackel, or torch dance, which is an old custom at the Prussian Court, and consists of all the great functionaries carrying flambeaux in an interminable polonaise. I happened to be the Doyenne of the Corps Diplomatique on this occasion, and therefore presented all my colleagues to the bride and the Grand Duke. I told Prince Frederick William that I hoped the next Royal wedding I attended would nearly concern him, and he smiled and said it seemed a long time to wait, but the Princess Royal was so young both the Queen and the Princess of Prussia felt it was better Her Royal Highness should not be married till the following year, and they also hoped that by that time party spirit would run less high. The high nobility of Prussia made Princess Louise's marriage an occasion for a political demonstration, and avoided coming to Berlin to attend the *fêtes*.

CHAPTER XIV.

London, February 24, 1857.—I went to England in February, the Queen sent for me to Buckingham Palace, and I had a long talk with the Princess Royal, who is quite charming and very fascinating. Her manners were so perfectly unaffected and unconstrained, and she was full of fun ! I felt sure she would win all hearts at Berlin.

Mrs. Anderson, the Princess's music mistress, dotes upon her, and told me such a nice trait of her yesterday. She was with her when she burnt her arm, and she says the Princess behaved like a heroine, never uttered a cry, and only said, ' Don't frighten mamma, send for papa first.' It was such a mercy that there was a rug in the room, with which the bystanders extinguished the flames, but the arm was a terrible sight, the muslin sleeve burnt into it. Mrs. Anderson remained with the Princess till the wound was dressed, and returned to the Palace in the evening, when Princess Alice ran to her sister and said, ' Here's Andy, I knew *she* would come to inquire after you.' And then the Princess Royal said, ' Then I can be my own postman.' And she gave Mrs. Anderson a letter she had dictated, and signed with her left hand, saying, ' I knew, Andy, you would be anxious and would like to have my own signature, though it *is* all up and down.'

February 25, 1857.—I went to the House of Lords last night, and heard Lord Derby's speech, which lasted above two hours. His address to the bishops was really magnificent, and most effective. Lord Clarendon rose to answer him, but was feeble; and as I could not hear him, I was leaving when I met Lord Redesdale, who told me Lord Lyndhurst would speak next, and he therefore strongly advised me to remain, and I am so glad I did, for Lord Lyndhurst spoke admirably, with so much precision, that it was quite a thing to remember ; and as he is eighty-five, God knows whether I might ever have another opportunity of hearing him. He leant upon two sticks, but his voice never faltered, and he hardly ever referred to his notes.

The marriage of the Princess Royal to Prince Frederick William took place at St. James's Palace, on January 25, 1858, and we celebrated the happy event by giving a great ball, and illuminating our house with gas, which was unusual at Berlin, and created a great sensation. The result was so successful other people adopted the idea, and on the night of the Princess's entry into Berlin, when the illuminations were repeated, we were horrified on our return from the Palace by seeing the English Legation quite dark, with only a feeble glimmer of gas here and there, instead of the brilliant illumination it had been on the wedding day. Unfortunately the Gas Company had undertaken more than it could supply, the consequence being the utter failure of our beautiful design, which was most humiliating and disappointing.

Lord Bloomfield went to Aix-la-Chapelle to meet the bride and bridegroom; I was unfortunately too unwell to accompany him, but received them on their arrival, and assisted at all the *fêtes* which took place on the auspicious occasion, which gave general satisfaction in Prussia.

I have received the Empress of Germany's

gracious permission to publish the letter Her Royal Highness wrote to me after the marriage.

Coblence le 29 Janvier 1858.

Ma chère Lady Bloomfield,—Je saisis avec plaisir l'occasion qui m'est offerte de vous envoyer au nom de la Reine, de notre chère excellente Reine Victoria, le fragment ci-joint de la parure de la jeune mariée, pour vous dire que *tout* s'est admirablement bien passé sans la moindre ombre au tableau d'une fête de famille, devenue fête nationale par le respect que l'Angleterre porte à la royauté, et par l'attachement profond et reconnaissant qu'elle voue à l'Auguste *Épouse* et *Mère* que Dieu lui a donnée pour *Reine*, et que l'Europe apprécie comme sage Souveraine de la plus noble et puissante des nations !

Je sens que la nouvelle patrie de notre chère Princesse Royale vient au-devant d'elle avec joie et confiance. J'ai toujours été convaincue que ce mariage seroit populaire, mais ce que j'apprends dépasse mon attente et me prouve que l'instinct du peuple le dirige du côté où il sent l'alliance de la vérité et de la force, en attendant celle du bonheur dynastique et du progrès. Soyez l'interprète de mes sentimens auprès de Lord Bloomfield et des Loftus. Je ne puis assez me louer

des soins que Lord Clarendon a eu à tous égards.
J'ai retrouvé ce grand homme d'état en pleine
possession des aimables qualités que le plus lourd
fardeau des affaires et des épreuves ne trouble
jamais.   C'est un grand bonheur pour l'Angleterre.
J'ai eu le plaisir de revoir vos sœurs, ma chère
Lady Bloomfield.

God bless you !

PRINCESSE DE PRUSSE.

This letter was accompanied by a piece of
the orange flower and myrtle wreath worn by
H.R.H. the Princess Royal at her marriage with
Prince Frederick William of Prussia, January 25,
1858.

Princess Charles of Prussia who attended a
ball we gave on the wedding day, told me her
son, Prince Frederick Charles, had written quite
enthusiastically about England, and as he was not
usually ' expansif,' this was the more gratifying.
Unfortunately the poor King's malady (softening
of the brain) had increased so much he was not
able to be present at any of the marriage *fêtes*,
but he and the Queen drove into Berlin from
Sans-Souci to hear the salute which was fired
when the telegraphic news of the marriage
arrived.   The *coup d'œil* from the Palace up the

Linden the day the Princess arrived was beautiful; the weather was very bright though extremely cold, and the procession, as it moved up between the crowd on each side, was as striking and imposing a sight as it was possible to witness. The crowd was quiet and orderly, and there was a spontaneous display of loyalty and good feeling which was very gratifying. At the first reception the Princess Royal made a most favourable impression. Her manner was quiet, dignified, and self-possessed, but she found a kind word to say to everyone. After the presentations, which were very numerous, Her Royal Highness polonaised with twenty-two Princes. She looked remarkably well, and her dress was very becoming. I did not see much of Her Royal Highness, as the feeling of jealousy ran so high it was not considered advisable, and we studiously avoided giving any cause of offence. I spent the summer in England, and was not present during the Queen and Prince Consort's visit to Berlin, which took place in September.

In the summer of 1858 I went alone to Ireland, as Lord Bloomfield was ordered to Kissingen. In August the Queen went to Prussia, and the following extracts are taken from my husband's letters.

Dusseldorf, August 11, 1858.—The day has been fine, and everything has gone off admirably. The Queen is looking better than ever. I only had a word from Her Majesty at Aix-la-Chapelle, we were there only a few minutes. I told Her Majesty that you were, I trust, better, but had unwillingly accepted her gracious permission to remain away, and be saved the long journey; but that it was a great privation to you to be absent on the occasion of Her Majesty's visit to Prussia. The Queen was very kind, and looked particularly so.

The night is splendid, and there have been the most lovely illuminations. The Dusseldorf artistes have taken delight in showing off their powers of decoration by lamps and fireworks. It was all spontaneous, and Prussia is showing her attachment to the mother of the Princess Royal! There were about a dozen Rhine boats flagged and moored on both sides of the bridge, and they fired salutes as we crossed the river. I travelled with Lord Malmesbury, and a funny incident occurred as we drove to dinner. One of the hind wheels of the carriage in which Prince Albert of Prussia and Prince Hohenzollern were, came off, and they were upset. So Lord Malmesbury and I, who were in the carriage with the ladies, got out and offered them our places. This they accepted, and we followed in the next carriage, taking the places of the equerries, who went on the box, to the astonishment of the people who looked on !

Potsdam Palace, August 14, 1858.—I have been living in such a state of bustle since we arrived here, that I have not had a moment to myself, or should have liked to give you a detailed account of everything. But you know what Court life is, and what it can be with the thermometer at 83°. The nights too are fearfully hot, so one does not get an over-abundance of sleep. We had such a hot journey on the 12th. Clear sun and clouds of dust !

We got to Hanover at 12.40, and after washing our hands and cleaning ourselves as best we could, we had a long luncheon of 100 people, the Royal family being together. The King made many tender inquiries about you, and so did the Queen. They had come from Nordeney with the reigning Prince of Saxe-Meiningen, who is to marry the Princess of Hohenlohe Langenburg, who, together with her mother, had also come from the sea-side to greet the Royal *cortège*. At Hanover we stayed more than three hours, and departed a good hour after the time fixed, so the

Princess Royal lost much time waiting for us. We tried to keep ourselves cool by taking off all the clothes in our power, and certainly had not the appearance of being part of the Royal society! The Princess met us at the Wildpark station, and got into the Queen's carriage. Potsdam station was illuminated, and we were met by the Royal family, some of the Ministers, Field-Marshals, Generals, &c. &c.

We had some supper, and retired about midnight, but oh! how hot it was. I am grandly lodged—Lord Malmesbury is next door; Bidwell, Dashwood, and Morier live upstairs. Poor Lady Macdonald is all alone at Babelsberg, and very solitary, as the Royal family live together, and do not see anyone in the morning. Yesterday we drove out to the Pfingstberg, and admired the views; the evening was lovely. I sat next the Princess Royal, who is looking well, and was very kind and amiable, and said she was very glad to hear you were better. After dinner we went out on the terrace, and it was so pleasant, like an Italian evening without the mosquitos! The drive home was very nice, and all was so except the atmosphere of the apartments. They were magnificently lighted, and the effect was splendid from the outside. The Royal British ensign

is flying on the Castle, and the hours we keep would make one fancy oneself at Windsor ! Breakfast at nine ; luncheon at two ; dinner at eight ! What must the Germans say ! but it is not the Queen's doing, as Her Majesty proposed to follow the usages of the Prussian Court as to meals ; but it is a great blessing that we have not done so, or the whole day would have gone.

Potsdam, August 15, 1858.—We have had a tremendous storm of rain, but the air is not much cooled by it. The parade ground, moreover, is a mass of water, so that one can breathe a wee bit. Old Baron Humboldt was here to-day, and is gone to lunch with the Queen at Babelsberg. He charged me with many messages for you ; he says he is getting weak, and he certainly does not look as he used, though I do not observe any remarkable change.

[Alexander von Humboldt was born at Berlin on September 14, 1769, and died on May 6, 1859. As a young man he was soon immersed in the study of botany, chemistry, geology, and other physical sciences. He began his travels in Italy in 1797, and in July 1799 he landed on American soil near Cumana. On June 23, 1802, he climbed Chimborazo to a height greater than any that had till then been reached, viz., 19,300 feet, a performance he was very proud of, and often alluded to, calling himself 'le vieux de la montagne.' In 1826 he took up his residence in Berlin, and engaged in political life, enjoying the most intimate intercourse with the King of Prussia, at whose table he was always a welcome guest ; and though he occasionally travelled, Berlin was his home, where for many years he was the centre of literary and scientific circles. I had the great pleasure and privilege of knowing Baron Humboldt intimately. I first made his acquaintance at Windsor, when he came with the King of Prussia to attend the Prince of Wales's christening in February 1842. During my long residence at Berlin I had frequent opportunities of seeing Baron Humboldt, who was always particularly kind and friendly to us, and I believe the very last time he dined out was to celebrate my birthday on April 13, 1859. He was then so weak he could scarcely rise off his chair, but his mind was perfectly clear, and he made very particular inquiries about his friend the Marquis of Bristol, Bishop of Derry, who was taken prisoner during the French war. His speech had become very indistinct, and his voice was so feeble I had great difficulty in keeping up conversation ; but he was very tenacious on that point, and liked talking himself. He was short in stature, and a small made man, with an exceedingly sharp, intelligent, and satirical countenance ; but I hardly ever heard him speak unkindly of anyone, and he was always willing to use his influence in forwarding the interests of those whom he considered worthy of his protection. His memory was wonderful, and I was particularly struck by it one day when I called upon him with Lord Bloomfield, who wished to speak to him about Schlagentweit, the traveller, who was missing in Africa. Lord Bloomfield could not remember the name of one of the African Roman Catholic Bishops who, he thought, might be able to give information. Humboldt, though suffering at the time, mentioned it immediately. I several times heard him speak of having been at Warren Hastings' trial, and heard a debate in which Burke, Pitt, and Fox took part ! He never spoke on matters of religion, but once when he was speaking of the King's illness, which affected him deeply, he sighed and said the failure of *such* a mind was a great mystery, but was ordered and permitted by God, and that therefore we should submit to such trials humbly.]

Yesterday we had a large dinner at Babelsberg. The evening was delicious, and the Queen and all the Royalties sat out on the terrace. The sky was cloudless, the atmosphere still, and the music of the 1st Life Guards admirable. The Queen seems very well, and all is going off well—it is a pleasure to see the whole Royal family so happy, and joy is depicted on every countenance. The Princess Royal looks rather pale and tired, and on my telling her I wished she could manage to rest a little more, she said, ' When the mind is perpetually at work, there can be no rest for the body.' She has always a quaint original way of expressing herself.

Potsdam, August 18, 1858.—The Review yesterday was extremely pretty on the square of the Palace. The Queen was in an open carriage with the Princess of Prussia, the Princess Royal with Princess Charles. They first drove round the line, and then the troops defiled past Her Majesty, whose manner was quite perfect on the occasion. This evening after a dinner at the Marshal's table, we are all to go to the Pfauen Insel. If the evening is as fine as the morning, it will be extremely pleasant. There never was anything like the care taken of everybody of the Queen's suite.

Potsdam, August 21, 1858.—Yesterday the day was passed sight-seeing at Berlin, but Lord Malmesbury and I departed from the Court and lunched with Baron Manteuffel and some members of the Corps Diplomatique. Lord Malmesbury is very amusing, and the easiest man in the world to get on with. I must say I never saw a Minister for Foreign Affairs more desirous than he is to put the right man in the right place, and promote good public servants without giving any consideration to their political creed.

Potsdam, August 22, 1858.—I have just heard that Lord Malmesbury has submitted my name to the Queen for a G.C.B., so you will soon see me with a broad red ribbon, which will, I hope, be a source of gratification to you. I hope to have an opportunity of thanking Her Majesty for her gracious intention. There was divine service yesterday in the Round Room, and Mr. Belson came down for the occasion, and did the service very well. Some of the Dom choir were ordered down, and we had some English hymns. I presented Mr. Belson afterwards to the Queen. I have just been writing to the Consul at Cologne to say that the Queen wishes to have divine service at the Hotel Deutz next Sunday, but begs not to interfere with the usual service at the English Chapel.

Belle Vue Hotel, Deutz, August 28.—I have only time to say we arrived here at ten o'clock.

We leave on Monday, and the Queen will see the Cathedral to-morrow at one. It will be brilliantly illuminated at 9 P.M., but Her Majesty declines any other demonstration. Phipps has just told me that the Queen will probably land at Dover, and that I am to accompany Her Majesty and cross over in the yacht. I hope to reach London on Tuesday.

The Princess Royal was confined of a son on January 27, 1859, and it was a very anxious moment. Lord Bloomfield was sent for about noon, and kept sending me messages to say the Princess was very ill ; and therefore it was an inexpressible relief when the welcome news came that all was happily over, but at first it was supposed the baby was dead, and it was only by the doctors inflating his lungs that he was brought round. An accident happened which might have cost the Princess her life ! She was to be attended by Dr. Martin, as well as her own household doctor. About 8 A.M. the latter wrote to Dr. Martin to say his services were required immediately, but the servant to whom the letter was entrusted, instead of taking it, put it into the post; the consequence was it never reached Dr. Martin till past 1 P.M., and when he arrived at the Palace he found it was too late to do what ought to have been done hours before; he was very much alarmed, but the Princess and her child were both saved.

I saw the baby a few hours later—he was a pretty little child, and was sleeping very contentedly in the nurse's arms. When the Princess was so ill she kept begging those present to pray for her, and she looked up to her husband, who held her in his arms the whole time, and asked him to forgive her for being impatient. Countess Blücher who was present told me she never expected the Princess would have strength to get through her confinement, and one of the doctors told her he thought she would die and the baby too. It was a terrible moment for poor Countess Blücher, who was a great personal friend of the Queen's and the Princess of Prussia, and an extremely nice person.

I had a most charming letter from the Queen a few days after. Her Majesty, after saying how much she had gone through, wrote, 'but thank God, in spite of severe sufferings and some anxiety for our dear little grandson, whom we are very proud of, though he has conferred this somewhat ancient dignity on us at the age of thirty-nine (I think *my* dear Prince is one of the youngest grandfathers in existence), all has gone off satisfactorily, and we are extremely satisfied and pleased.'

The child had forty-two godfathers and godmothers, of all kinds of creeds, from the Emperor of Russia to the Emperor of Austria! I could not help thinking the poor baby's religion would be a sort of political *pot-pourri* in consequence!

The Prince and Princess Royal moved into their own Palace for the Princess's birthday, where they received us most kindly, on November 24, in a handsome room hung with dark blue damask; the furniture and picture frames were in silver. Prince Frederick William drew our attention especially to the frame of the looking-glass, which had been designed by the Princess, of which he seemed very proud. The staircase was handsome and hung with family portraits, but the rooms were not well proportioned.

I was much amused one night at a concert at the Prince Regent's, where I was placed on a sofa among the Prussian ladies, one of them a very bitter politician of the ex-ministerial party. I was hardly seated when the new Minister for Foreign Affairs, M. de Schleinitz, came and sat down by me, and as he was a very agreeable man we chatted pleasantly for a long time, in spite of the angry glances which were shot at me by the Prussians, who no doubt were confirmed in their preconceived opinion that I was a most dangerous *intriguante.* The 'Kreuz Zeitung' party were in despair, and talked as if we were on the verge of destruction, or what they considered worse, a Red Republic. On our return from England we found the poor King's malady had increased so much, the Prince of Prussia was appointed Regent. A new ministry came in. Prussian politics took a turn for the better; our position improved greatly, and things seemed much more hopeful. I heard a pretty anecdote of the young Duchess of Malakoff before she was married. She was walking in the garden when she saw the Duke approaching, and at that moment she picked a beautiful rose. The Duke inquired, 'Cette rose est-elle pour moi, Mademoiselle ?' to which she answered, ' Non, Monsieur, pour vous j'aurais ceuilli des lauriers.'

We gave a ball to the Prince of Wales, which was attended by the Royal family, and which was opened by the Prince of Wales and Princess Frederick Charles. I danced with Prince Frederick William as their *vis-à-vis.* It was rather a curious coincidence that my first waiting was at the time of the Prince of Wales's christening, and his first ball seventeen years after was in my house. He seemed very much amused with his first cotillon, and had a thoroughly amiable unaffected manner.

My friend, Countess B——, gave me a most amusing account of Naples at this time. When the King heard that the French and English fleets were going to leave Naples, he only remarked 'tanto meglio,' and he wished all the other foreigners would go too! The Queen was such a bigot she would not allow her children to hear or read the word 'amour,' as she considered it immoral, but she carried her idea so far that wherever the word appeared it was changed to *tambour*, so the Royal children were taught to say, 'le tambour du bon Dieu!'

I was talking one day to Dr. Vehsemeyer about his experience as a medical man. He told me one of the most curious cases was that of a servant of the King of Prussia's, whom he attended on his death-bed. The man invariably spoke of himself as his own father, and used to remark that 'the poor fellow's cough has been very distressing,' or that he had had a very bad night; but he *never* spoke in the first person. One day when the doctor called he found the room darkened, and on approaching the bed he saw his patient laid out, so he thought he was dead, and was leaving the room, when a voice called out very gently, ' Doctor, Doctor !' He therefore went back to the bed, when his patient said, ' The old man was so ill last night he will be dead by six o'clock, so I thought I would lay him out,' and he had actually laid himself out like a corpse, and remained in that position till six o'clock, when he died.

General Sir Henry Bentinck, G.C.B., who came to Berlin in the month of May, told me the following curious detail relating to the battle of Inkermann, which, though he commanded the Guards at that battle, he was unaware of till the circumstance was related to him by Baron von Usedom, who heard it from General Todleben, the celebrated Russian engineer, who made such a magnificent defence at Sebastopol. When the Russians attacked the English army on the plateau of Inkermann, they posted, unknown to the English, a considerable force of artillery in a valley which borders the plateau, with the intention of bringing it up as a reserve in the middle of the battle. An aide-de-camp was accordingly despatched from the Russian head-quarters to order up the guns after the battle had been raging on the plateau for about three hours, but when he reached the valley not a single gun could be moved ! The English shot and shell passing over the plateau had fallen so thickly upon the unfortunate Russian artillery, that scarcely a man or horse was left alive.

Sir Henry also related an anecdote proving the courage of the men he commanded. He said that in the thickest of the fight, when not more than 6,000 English had to withstand the whole force of the Russian army, he saw a Guardsman coolly step out of the ranks, and on inquiring why he did so, the man answered that having observed at the battle of Alma that the wounded Russians often shot at their enemies, he was determined this should not happen again, so he quietly broke the stocks of the guns of all the Russians who were lying within his reach, and then joined the ranks again just as if he was attending a review in Hyde Park.

Mr. Carlyle, the historian, came to Berlin before he began writing his history of Frederick the Great, and he paid us a visit the day he had been to Potsdam, so I asked him what he thought of the place. His answer was very characteristic. He said, in his broad Scotch, 'Well, I thought it a queer sort of an amphibious place, and that I had never seen Neptune coming out of duckweed before,' referring to one of the old fountains. I expressed a hope that he had found the materials he required for his work, upon which he said, ' I shall have to sift through a very cartload of rubbish, and may be I shall find the materials I require ; if I do, I will write my book, and if I don't I hope God will give me grace to leave it alone ! '

London, November 12.—I had a very agreeable visit from Henry Taylor, who was an old friend of mine. He talked about Carlyle, whom he knows intimately, but considers one of the strangest men he ever met. Once Carlyle was staying with the Taylors when there was a most beautiful appearance of a meteor in the sky, which every one admired extremely. Carlyle merely observed, ' Oh, I believe it is nothing but some phosphoric oxygen, or some rubbish of that sort.' Taylor said he called his head ' Wormwood Scrubs,' because what comes out of his mouth is so bitter.

We met the young Maharajah Duleep Singh at Windsor, whose dress, half European and half Eastern, struck me very much. On his head he wore a turban made of grey and gold stripes, fastened on the left side by a most magnificent aigrette of diamonds and several strings of fine pearls. His dark blue velvet frock coat was embroidered with gold and pearls, and under it he wore a yellow tunic fitting tight, also embroidered. Dark trowsers with gold stripes, very large gold earrings with a huge emerald fastening, and six rows of pearls round his neck, each as big as a hazel nut, and an emerald ornament the size of half a crown. The Queen introduced me to him, and he was very chatty and agreeable.

M. Aristarchi Bey, Chargé d'Affaires at Berlin, told me that he was at Ispahan with our minister, Colonel Shiel, and Dolgorouky, the Russian minister.

On New Year's Day it is customary for the Shah to appear before his subjects on the balcony of his palace, and they are made aware, by the colour of his robe, what temper he is in; when he wears green, it is a sign of gentleness and good-will, but when he appears in scarlet it is certain some deed of cruelty is in contemplation. Mrs. Shiel proposed accompanying her husband and the two gentlemen named above when they walked to the square opposite the palace, but Colonel Shiel, not knowing what might occur, advised her not; and it was fortunate he did so, for on arriving before the balcony, to their horror the Shah appeared clad in bright scarlet, and at a given signal fifty unhappy prisoners were dragged forward, bound hand and foot, and in one moment their fifty heads flew off, and—the Shah retired.

Whenever he travels in Persia, the ladies of every town he passes through assemble to select the most beautiful girl in the place, who is presented to the Shah on his arrival with a request that he will accept her for his harem.

I have heard Lord Bloomfield say that he read a despatch from Persia whilst he was at St. Petersburg which stated that the Shah had invented a new torture for some political offenders, and had ordered their own teeth to be drawn out, and then hammered one by one into their own skulls!

I had a long visit from Prince D—— whom I had met at Moscow in 1847, at which time he was in a kind of exile, and not allowed to come to St. Petersburg, as he had written a book displeasing to the Emperor Nicholas. He was a man of liberal opinions, fond of literature, and spoke quite openly about the faults and failures of the Russian Government. In the course of conversation I happened to remark that I thought the Emperor Alexander had shown considerable moral courage in making peace after the Crimean War, contrary to the general feeling in Russia, and Prince D—— gave me the following curious details of what occurred on that occasion, which he said had been related to him by one of the ministers present.   The Emperor called a council of war at St. Petersburg, which was composed of the following members : Prince Dolgorouky, Minister of War; the Grand Duke Constantine, Minister of Marine ; M. de Broek, Minister of Finance ; Count Bloudoff, Prince Woronzow, and, I think, M. Lapouchine, Minister of the Interior. The Emperor first called on the Minister of War to report on the state of the army, and he said the resources were exhausted, that more recruiting was almost impossible, and that he did not see how the war could be continued.   The Emperor next addressed himself to his brother, who, together with Count Bloudoff, was in favour of continuing hostilities at all risks.   The Emperor asked what was the state of the navy?   The Grand Duke answered, 'Sire, we have a fleet in the Baltic, and another in the Black Sea.'   The Emperor acquiesced, but added, ' True, but those fleets have never left our harbours.   Are they fit to oppose the English and French fleets ? '   The Grand Duke was obliged to reply in the negative. ' Then,' said the Emperor, ' it appears we have no army and no fleet.'   The Grand Duke sighed, looked down, but made no answer.   The Emperor next addressed the Minister of Finance, and asked what report he could give. He said, ' Sire, we have just made one disadvantageous loan, upon conditions imposed upon us at Hamburg, and I believe another to be impossible.' The Emperor then addressed the Council and said, ' Gentlemen, it appears from what we have just heard that we have neither army, navy, nor money ; how, then, is it possible for me to continue the war ? ' Count Bloudoff then stepped forward and said, with deep emotion, ' Sire, after the report we have just heard, it is clear that your Majesty is forced to make peace, but at the same time you must dismiss your incompetent ministers, who have not known how to serve either your father or yourself, " renvoyez nous tous." ' The consternation of the other members of the Council at this outburst was great, but—peace was signed forthwith.

I heard another curious illustration of the frauds practised by Russian officials during the war. The Government was charged a large sum of money for oxen, for the use of the army, which, however, were never purchased. At the end of a certain period another large bill was brought in for feeding these said oxen, and the General at the head of the Commissariat inquired whether they were to be killed and salted. The Government answered in the affirmative, and a number of cases were accordingly forwarded to the Crimea, but when they were opened the contents were so completely rotten they were totally unfit for use, having been originally filled with refuse instead of good meat ; but first and last the sum paid and pocketed by the officials was fabulous.

Prince D—— informed me that he was a member of the committee in the Government of Toula, which had been called together to discuss the question of the emancipation of the serfs. About 400 members met in the Town Hall at Toula, but the moujiks, isvoschieks (coachmen), and peasants knew perfectly the opinion of the different members ; and one day, coming away from the meeting, the Prince's coachman was asleep, and did not answer to his name. A moujik woke him up rudely saying, ' What business have *you* to be asleep, Ivan Ivanowitch, when you know that *your* master is in favour of emancipation ? '

I was very intimate at Berlin with Marie de la Motte Fouqué, the daughter of the author of ' Ondine,' whose mother married secondly M. de Rochow. Her son was minister to King Frederick William III., and another son was General Rochow, afterwards Prussian Minister at Petersburg. Marie de la Motte Fonqué had very delicate health, and lived at Berlin with her half-brother. One day he came home from the palace and told her that great excitement prevailed there in consequence of the apparition of the white lady. The lady-in-waiting, on coming out of the Queen's apartments, found the sentinel on guard in a dead faint. She immediately called the officers-in-waiting, and when the sentinel came to himself he declared he had seen the white lady, and Monsieur de Rochow told his sister the circumstance, adding that it had caused great alarm. The following Sunday a small party was given to the Royal family by Prince Albrecht of Prussia, to which Monsieur de Rochow, in his capacity of Prime Minister, was invited. In the course of the evening the King complained of feeling ill, and told M. de Rochow that he felt so unwell he must return home, and indeed that he never should have come out that evening had he not been unwilling to disappoint his son, who had arranged the family gathering for him. The King took to his bed that evening, and never left it again ; he died very shortly afterwards.

Once whilst we were at Potsdam we heard that the sentinel on guard at the Neue Palais declared he had seen a funeral procession pass by and go towards the Garnison Kirche. We were not aware of any member of the Royal family being ill, but the next day the news arrived of the sudden and unexpected death of Princess Charlotte of Meiningen, the King's niece.

Some private theatricals were successfully got up for a charitable purpose, in which the Attachés took part.   The plays were acted in a great room attached to the theatre, and the young men who had to be rouged and dressed for their respective parts dressed at the theatre, where ' Marie Stuart ' was being acted.   Mr. J., who was to represent an Italian brigand, lost his way in the intricacies of the theatre, and as nearly as possible found himself appearing before the audience who had come to see the tragedy.   He had only just time to fall back : the effect, had he suddenly appeared on the stage, would have been too absurd !   Then we heard that three of the young men dressed as brigands met a wretched little ballet dancer in one of the passages, who was so terrified at their ruffianly appearance that she fell down in a fit of hysterics !

We dined the other day at Prince Frederick William's, and I had a pleasant chat with him after dinner.   He told me that when he was only seventeen he stood at the window of the Queen's room when the first shot was fired during the revolution of 1848, from the bridge opposite the Palace, and that had found an echo in his heart which no time could ever silence ; he only hoped to God he might never live to witness such a scene again. He laughed at the reports which have been circulated of his marriage being un-happy and of his illtreating his wife, and cer-tainly it would not be possible to see a happier couple.

My dear husband received the kindest possible letter from the Prince Regent, saying he had greatly wished to give him a public mark of esteem, in the shape of a decoration ; but as that is contrary to the rule of our diplomatic service, he could not refuse himself the pleasure of giving us a souvenir of the interesting and important events we had witnessed at Berlin, and therefore he had ordered two large china vases to be painted, to commemorate them, which he hopes we shall like and value.

At this time a Parisian *bon mot* went the round of the diplomatic society at Berlin, which caused great amusement. It was said that when Count Pourtales heard the Emperor's speech at the opening of the Chambers, he felt as if 'il avait reçu un coup d'épée aux reins !' Some months afterwards, Lord Clarendon met Count Perponcher

at Windsor, and they were discussing the attitude
of France at that moment. Count Perponcher
observed that either Prussia or England ought
to interfere, upon which Lord Clarendon, with
his usual happy way of turning the tables, said,
' Oui ! et nous avec cette courtoisie qui nous est
habituelle serons heureux de vous céder le pas.'

I left Berlin in May, and never returned
there.

Extracts of Letters from my Husband.

Danzig, August 19, 1860.—Here I am, after
a very good journey. . . . I met old General
Gröben in the train, who awakened me from my
slumbers about 4 o'clock A.M., and was as much
surprised to see me as I was to see him. What,
think you, he is longing to do ? To go and slay
the Druses and Turks in Syria ! His Christian
blood is boiling within him, and he is seriously
bent on revenge. He is a wonderful talker, and
went on without stopping till he left the train
at 9.30. I wanted to sleep, but it was useless
thinking of it. The Berlin papers having announced my intention of visiting Danzig, of
course our Consul-General Plaw came to the
station to meet me, and asked me to go and dine
with him in the country. He has a charming

place—Oliva, a sort of Royal residence lent to him by the King.

Well, no sooner had I done luncheon than the Vice-Consul walked in; so I have not had a quiet moment. As far as I have seen the town, it is a most curious, quaint place; but, oh! such an ugly journey to reach it. The only nice-looking places along the line are the stations, which are charmingly kept. The bridge across the Vistula at Dirschau is a splendid work. There are such beautiful old wardrobes in the hall of this hotel. You would, I am sure, be tempted to purchase them.

Danzig, August 20, 1860.—You will be glad to hear that the weather is fine, which is an immense boon when one is sight-seeing; and I am just returned from a trip to the Fairwater, which is the entrance to the harbour, and rather an interesting trip in a steamer. There seems a deal of trade going on, and the masses of floating timber from Poland are enormous. I have not as yet had time to see the town in detail. The impression of the quaint old houses and architecture is that one is suddenly transported to Venice, only there are no canals and no gondoliers. (This reminded me of an anecdote of Whately, the Archbishop of Dublin, when an enthusiastic lady remarked that the entrance of the Bay of Dublin reminded her of Switzerland; the Archbishop immediately rejoined, 'Yes, ma'am; only in Switzerland there is no sea, and here there are no Alps!')

You would be delighted with the architecture of Danzig, and could find hundreds of subjects for sketching. The market-boats on the river are so picturesque, and the Exchange is a most curious place. This hotel was formerly the English factory, and our countrymen are great favourites in Danzig.

Yesterday, at two o'clock, we drove to Oliva, formerly the residence of the Abbot of the same name, and now turned into a Royal Palace, which has been kindly lent by the King and the Regent to Mr. Plaw. Nice gardens, good timber, and charming walks, which we inspected before dinner. We had a most sumptuous dinner, and a variety of choice wines, all of which I would gladly have dispensed with. After tea we drove into town, a distance of about seven miles; and I was very glad to go to bed, and had a very comfortable, quiet room.

Lord Bloomfield was suddenly recalled to Berlin, by the death of the Grand Duke of Mecklenburg Strelitz, as he was ordered to attend the funeral as the Queen's representative. Before that sad ceremony he accompanied Mr. Paget to Count Hohenthal's place, Knauthayn, near Leipsic, from which place he wrote me the following letters :—

Knauthayn, August 27, 1860.—We have fallen into most comfortable quarters, and Paget (who was then engaged to be married to Countess Wally Hohenthal, a maid of honour of the Crown Princess's) is quite *l'enfant de la maison*, and all seem delighted with him. This is an immense château in a village through which one drives from the main road, but of which one knows nothing at the house. The country is as flat as a pancake; but there is some nice vegetation, a garden with good flowers, and a pleasure ground well kept, a pond in front of my window on which two swans are disporting themselves; and altogether it is exactly the sort of place one sees represented on Meissen plates and dishes.

This house is remarkably well furnished and handsome, but not gaudy—altogether the sort of place where one might lead a very comfortable existence. I have a capital bedroom, beautifully clean. I got to Leipsic at five yesterday, where I found Hohenthal's carriage; and Crowe, our Consul, came to meet me, and drove part of the way with me. It is about a nine miles drive. We are a family party, with the exception of an old M. Küster, the wise man of this neighbourhood. After breakfast, the Countess read, as she does every day, a short sermon, at which we all assisted; but not the servants. She is very kind to her poor people, and very thoughtful about them.

The day is lovely; and, oh! such a moon as we had last night. Wally looks very well indeed, and seems supremely happy.

Knauthayn, August 28, 1860.—Yesterday was a fearfully oppressive day till about six o'clock, when we returned from a drive and walk to Count Hohenthal's model farm, which is a most magnificent and extensive concern. A fine building, with some forty cows, and lots of pigs, &c. &c.; but he says it brings in nothing. We drove in a sort of *char-à-bancs* and four horses, through a nice wood, in which there were some good oaks; deer and roe are said to be there, but we saw none. I thought we should have been literally devoured with gnats, which, owing to the great floods that have prevailed, have increased fearfully; but, happily, they have not invaded the house, so there we are in comparative peace.

The hours would just suit you. On being asked on Sunday, by the hostess, what were the habits in England, I told her it was usual to breakfast at 9.30 or 10, lunch at 2, and dine at 8; and so it was arranged. But what I did not approve of was having to sit up gossiping till 1 o'clock this morning. The Budbergs are expected to-day; but the weather has changed, and there was an awful storm of wind, thunder, and lightning about seven o'clock, and some hailstones of gigantic dimensions that had fallen two miles from here were brought to the house. They had, of course, much diminished in size when I saw them; but they were then the size of half-a-crown, and so thick that Hohenthal declares if they had fallen on the house every window would have been smashed.

Knauthayn, August 29, 1860.—There are fearful accounts of the damage done to houses and people by the hailstorm of Monday afternoon, and serious damage has been caused to the picture gallery at Leipsic: a large and very valuable picture of Napoleon I. has been, they say, irremediably injured by the hail, which, after breaking the thick skylight, came like grape-shot through the canvas, and all the collection has suffered more or less. Countess Hohenthal has just taken us over the house—such a sight of house linen as I have seen, and all in such perfect order!

Nothing could be cleaner or nicer than the house, and one might eat one's dinner off the floor of any of the rooms, master's and servants'.   It is all so deliciously sweet—the air nearer perfection than anything I have felt in Germany.   The Countess desires me to tell you she should so much like to see you here, and hopes she may do so some day.   She has just been playing on a capital harmonium, made at Leipsic, which you would like to have for choral music.   She plays the instrument well, and hopes her boy will take to it in course of time.

Knauthayn, August 30, 1860.—Such dreadful accounts of the hailstorm ! Fancy hailstones as big as eggs and billiard balls ! People and animals have suffered as well as houses.   Countess Hohenthal (Dölken), with whom we dined yesterday, and who lives about twelve miles off, said that all the tiles on the roof of her husband's house at Leipsic have been destroyed.   The papers give an account of the serious damage done to the Palace of Gotha ; but, happily, this is false.   Fire caught in the guard-room, but was soon put out ; and so the newspapers, having nothing to write about, declared that everything was destroyed, and the progress of the flames was only arrested by the firing of cannon !

Dölken is a fine place—such oaks! We had a very good dinner, and then went out on the lake. I start for Berlin this evening.

Berlin, September 3, 1860.—Things look very bad all over Europe; but still I hope that nothing serious will come out of it all this year—at least, that we shall escape a general war; though in Italy events are progressing so rapidly that one may expect Venetia to be attacked any day, after the Roman people have upset the existing government; and we are already told that Victor Emanuel is no longer master of the situation. . . . Austria is in a frightful mess, in consequence of the Italian troubles, and the Hungarians and Kossuth are ready to respond to the movement. All these things naturally make me suppose that a complication in the affairs of Europe may be expected any day or hour; and the state of Turkey in Europe and Asia is such that there also one may look for bad work.

I have had a most agreeable conversation with Prince William of Baden, who was with me for nearly an hour. He is, I am sorry to say about to take leave of the Prussian service.

Berlin, September 12, 1860.—Just returned from my melancholy mission to Strelitz. Fortunately the weather was extremely fine for the funeral, or I know not what would have happened to us all, in open carriages, travelling fourteen miles over deep sand. At nine on Thursday morning I went to the Palace, and saw the two Grand Duchesses and the young Grand Duke, who were most amiable—the poor widow much touched at the Queen having ordered me to attend the funeral. The King of Hanover and his son, the Prince Regent of Prussia, Prince Charles, and the Prince of Hesse were there. I drove to Mirow, the church, with the Grand Duchess and King of Hanover, and back with the two poor blind sovereigns, which was sad.

I am going to meet the Queen at Aix-la-Chapelle next week. All along the road to Strelitz, through Prussia, there were triumphal arches and garlands to welcome the Prince Regent, and a display of Prussian and English flags; and the instant we entered the frontier town of Fürstenberg, all was dark—black flags from the houses, and everyone in deep mourning for the late Grand Duke, who was universally beloved and respected. Mirow, where the funeral took place, is a small Palace, where I believe Queen Charlotte was born.

Berlin, September 26, 1860.—I have just returned from Verviers. The weather was per-

fectly lovely—like summer; in fact, I believe
that Monday last was the first fine day that
the royal party have seen in the course of
this year. We were in a fuss, as news arrived
of the dangerous illness of Prince Albert's step-
mother, and probability of her death. The Prince
Regent reached Aix-la-Chapelle at half-past ten,
and was uncertain what to expect. He asked
me what I thought, and I answered that the
Queen is not in the habit of changing her plans;
and so it proved.

The news of the Duchess Dowager of
Coburg's death reached Her Majesty between
Liège and Verviers. The blinds were down as
the train drove up; but all went on as had been
previously arranged. The Queen and Prince
were very kind and gracious, but there was no
time for conversation. At Coblenz I surrendered
my rights to Sir A. Malet. The Princess of
Prussia and the Duke and Duchess of Baden
came to meet the Queen at Frankfort. I dined
with the household, and returned here.

Berlin, October 2, 1860.—The Macdonald
affair is very disagreeable, and may lead to
unpleasant complications. I have just been
penning a note to Schleinitz, in plain, strong
terms. I am sure he would willingly do anything

in his power, but is not supported by the other members of the Cabinet.[1]

I think it is lucky I am not at Coburg; for my absence at this moment might have been detrimental to the interests of our countrymen at Bonn.

The Prince Consort was run away with in a carriage, on his return from the chase, and jumped out. What a mercy His Royal Highness was not seriously injured by this accident!

Berlin, October 3, 1860.—The Macdonald affair takes up my whole time. The Ministers here are furious with me for the tone I have been compelled to use in my communications with the Prussian Government, which is very different from that of all my former letters; but the case is becoming an interesting and exciting one, though it is not pleasant to have to lay it bare. I have shown the correspondence to Lord Wensleydale, and asked his advice. He cannot give any, as he does not understand Prussian law; but he says such a thing could not possibly happen in England.

[1] On September 12, 1860, Capt. Macdonald was committed to prison at Bonn for resisting the railway authorities. The English residents appealed and were also censured. A correspondence ensued between the Prussian Government and the British Foreign Secretary; and strong language was uttered in the House of Commons and in the Prussian Chambers.— See Haydn's *Dictionary of Dates.*

You will be glad to know that I have just received by telegraph Lord John Russell's entire approbation of the note I addressed yesterday to Schleinitz on this odious Macdonald affair.

The English at Bonn, who signed the protest, did a most imprudent thing, and will get into trouble; for their proceeding was unquestionably illegal and in opposition to the Prussian laws, but their English patriotic feelings at hearing their nation abused in open court got the better of their prudence. If they had not printed the abuse of the Prussian Prosecutor, we should have had a better cause against Müller. It is a most disagreeable business.

Cologne, October 10, 1860.—The Queen comes down the Rhine in the ' Fairy ' to-morrow from Mayence to Coblenz; Saturday, to Cologne and Brussels.

Coblenz, October 11, 1860.—What a kind, civil, thoughtful person is the Princess of Prussia! I arrived at the station here at 5.15 yesterday, and met Her Royal Highness there, who had come to receive the Grand Duke and Grand Duchess of Baden. She said a few kind words to me, and desired me to come and dine with her at six; so I bustled off to dress, and luckily arrived at the Palace in time. The dinner was soon over, and the Princess told me to come back to tea at nine; but as all the guests had had long journeys we were dismissed early.

The Queen is expected this afternoon at four. Unfortunately the rain has been falling rapidly; but it is clearing a little, and I hope it will not rain when Her Majesty comes.

We are to keep the same hours as at Babelsberg; and the Princess of Prussia has got some artistes to enliven the evenings by music.

Coblenz, October 12, 1860.—The weather is bitter; to-day we had a hailstorm, and it was not pleasant for a drive to Stolzenfels in an open carriage, with Sir Charles Phipps and the ladies in waiting. The royalty went before, and it was, oh! so bitterly cold up there; but we had some fine glimpses of the rocks and Rhine, and the sun peeped forth and lighted up the scene, which would have been lovely in other weather. Not satisfied with this drive, we were taken over the Moselle to a distant fort. Lord John Russell, like a sensible man, left us and walked home. Conceive that after reading my correspondence on the Macdonald affair. Lord Palmerston marked on the despatches, 'If we don't get satisfaction the whole Mission should be recalled from Berlin'! But it won't go so far as this, I hope.

The yacht was sent home to-day, and the Queen leaves at 10.30 to-morrow, reaches Aix-la-Chapelle at 2.15 ; and I hope to return to Berlin immediately. I spoke to Lord John about leave ; and he will give it to me, but not at this moment. He said, ' This is not pleasant weather for travelling ;' as much as to say, are you not better at home ? He is the most cheery little man that ever was, and kept us all in roars of laughter in the railroad carriage. He and Schleinitz got on capitally, and the latter is much pleased with Lord John ; so I hope we shall pull well for some time to come, and their meeting has done good. The Paget marriage is fixed for Saturday, the 20th, and will take place at the Legation. The Princess Royal will attend.

CHAPTER XV.

Extracts of Letters from Lord Bloomfield.

Berlin, October 26, 1860.—I have a startling communication to make to you. . . I wish you were with me to decide and settle what answer I must send to a most gracious proposal from Lord John Russell that my name should be submitted to the Queen for the post of Ambassador at Vienna. I will transcribe Lord John's letter :—

' The question of your coming home on leave of absence brings me to treat of another matter of considerable importance.

' The Queen has approved of my opening at Vienna and St. Petersburg the conversion of these two missions into embassies. But if this is done

I shall think it but due to your long and meritorious services to propose you to Her Majesty as her Ambassador at Vienna. You are fully entitled to that distinction, and it will be a fit climax to your diplomatic career. Of course I do not enter into the question of your private and domestic arrangements; I am only solicitous to show you that consideration which the Foreign Secretary is bound to show to one who has served so long, so well, and so honourably as yourself.'

I know not when I have been so taken by surprise as by this news. It is certainly very flattering; and if I am to serve a while longer, it is perhaps as well I should do so in a capacity which will give me the highest rank in my profession. But I do not like the undertaking or the change to a new post where I shall have to begin life over again—a serious matter when one is verging on fifty-eight. At the same time, Vienna is a pleasant residence, the country about is pretty and enjoyable, there are nice summer residences to be had in the neighbourhood, and though the climate is severe in winter, the spring, summer, and autumn are extremely pleasant.

What shall you say to all this? and how shall I answer Lord John? for of course I cannot accept the offer unless I know that you will be disposed to share my fate—I must have my ambassadress with me !

Of course, though I was in very bad health at that time, and quite unequal to the fatigues of diplomatic life, I could only express gratification at my dear husband's promotion ; and accordingly he was officially appointed Ambassador Extra-ordinary and Plenipotentiary to the Court of Vienna, and came to England to get his letters of credence. We were invited to Windsor, and that was the last time I had the honour of seeing the Prince Consort. On that occasion I sat next the Prince at dinner, and had a most interesting conversation with him. He said his great object through life had been to learn as much as possible, not with a view of doing much himself—as, he observed, any branch of study or art required a lifetime—but simply for the sake of appreciating the works of others ; for he added quite simply and without any self-consciousness or vanity, ' No one knows the difficulties of a thing till they have tried to do it themselves ; and it was with this idea that I learnt oil painting, water-colour, etching, fresco painting, chalks, and lithography, and in music I studied the organ, pianoforte, and violin, thorough bass, and singing.'

What a noble view this was of the duties of

his position! and how well it agreed with the modest, unselfish, and studious character of that remarkable man.

I had a very dangerous illness, which prevented my leaving England with Lord Bloomfield when he went to present his letters of recall at Berlin. He arrived there just as King Frederick William IV. died; and the following letters were written during our separation, which lasted for some months :—

Extracts of Letters from Lord Bloomfield.

Berlin, January 6, 1861.—I received a telegram ordering me to convey the Queen's condolence on the death of King Frederick William; so I went to Potsdam yesterday in uniform, and to Sans-Souci, where all the royal family are living. The Princess of Prussia excused herself; but the Prince—now King—received me at once, and was most kind : very much affected at first, and I shall be glad when to-morrow's ceremony is over, on his account. We conversed for some time, and then in came the Grand Duke Nicholas of Russia, who seemed pleased to see me again. I paid my respects to the Crown Prince and Princess at 3.30. The Princess was well; the Crown Prince looked ill and fatigued. Half the sovereigns of Germany are coming to the funeral.

Berlin, January 7, 1861.—The sad ceremony at Potsdam is over, and it would have been difficult to select a colder day in Russia for the removal of the body to its last earthly home: there were upwards of 20 degrees of frost, Réaumur, last night. We got off about half-past nine, accompanied by a mass of cavalry, and whilst we were waiting at the station for their disembarkation, we heard a whistle, and shortly afterwards another train came hard against us, but fortunately did us no serious harm beyond a severe shake. Then we proceeded, partly in a carriage and partly on foot, to the Friedenskirche, where we found apartments for us to wait in that were fortunately well warmed. We waited a full hour in the Church; for the procession only moved at half-past twelve. The King conducted the poor Queen Dowager, and all the royal family were deeply affected. The service was performed by Dr. Heym, and everything went off well, considering the weather. I believe all walked from the Palace of Sans-Souci, and it will be wonderful if there are not many deaths in consequence. It is quite providential that you did not undertake the journey to Berlin, for the cold would have been unbearable to you. I have felt nothing so like Russia since we left that country.

Berlin, January 23, 1861.—I am most thankful for the good accounts of your progress towards recovery, and it was not necessary to remind me to think of you in Church; I have been praying for you constantly, and have returned my poor thanks to the Almighty for His great mercy under your present severe illness. He has dealt very graciously with both of us, and I am ever mindful of his goodness, and pray that I may be worthy of it.

You may judge of the great kindness of the King and Queen of Prussia yesterday when I took leave of their Majesties. Both were quite touching about you as well as about myself. The King again expressed his sorrow not to give me his Order, and promised me his picture. Both His Majesty and the Queen spoke with such unfeigned kindness of the services I have rendered here during my long residence, that I begin to fancy I have done more than is the case; for after all I have only been guided by the endeavour conscientiously to discharge my duties, and certainly the great desire I have always had has been to keep matters straight between the two countries.

The Princess Royal was so kind, and seems really sorry to lose us. She said I had always spoilt her! She has given us a charming bust of her little boy, in plaster, made by her own hands, and handsome medallions of herself and the Prince. That branch of the royal family seem to look upon our residence here as an epoch in their history, and to consider us identified with so many of their sad and happy days. God grant that the events of coming years may leave an equally happy impression !

The weather is not bad, but the frost has returned, not however with intensity ; and I hope not to suffer from cold on my journey to Vienna.

Vienna, January 26, 1861.—I arrived here safely last night ; the journey was not too disagreeable as to weather, and when I got here it felt comparatively mild. The streets are very well kept and clean ; it is a great blessing, moreover, to have good pavement for one's feet and horses, and no *open* drains. On arriving at the Austrian frontier I found orders had been given to facilitate my progress, and I had a splendid saloon carriage with tables and chairs—very comfortable—in fact, I was received with all the honours. At Berlin the Attachés saw me off, and seemed low at parting 'with their ancient chief. Here I was met by Julian Fane, and all the members of the Chancery, with joy depicted on their countenances ; and I must say one seldom sees a nicer lot of young men than Lytton, Antrobus, Kennedy, and Dillon.

Count Rechberg has just returned my visit, and announced to me that the Emperor will receive me to-morrow at 10 o'clock.

Vienna, January 30, 1861.—The day was very fine. At half-past twelve soldiers marched to the house, court footmen, and state carriages. The Introducer of Ambassadors came in proper time, and put me into my carriage. He preceded me in his carriage ; two state chariots ; a third followed with Fane and Lytton, and a fourth with the others ; and a handsome lot they were. The carriages were peculiar, very rich and hand-some ; and such fine cream-coloured horses ! There were cavalry to escort me, and all the world in the streets saluted and uncovered their heads as I drove by. The young men declared they heard cheering amongst the crowd : I cannot say that such sounds reached my ears ; but the restoration of the Embassy is most popular. The guard at the Burg turned out, and there was a whole lot of household troops and the Palace guards, who lined the way up to the audience

room.   The Grand Chamberlain, Count Lans-
karonsky (an old acquaintance) received me and
announced my arrival to the Emperor.   The
folding doors were opened, and I made my best
bow to His Imperial Majesty, who was very
gracious and dignified, and has made a most
agreeable impression upon me.   He is not handsome; but he has a fine figure, a good countenance, and a great deal of beard, which is, I
should think, an improvement.   The Emperor
asked about you, and wanted to know when you
are coming to Vienna.   He kept me a quarter of
an hour, and then I retired *à reculons*, and brought
in the gentlemen of the Embassy, whom I presented one after the other.   We returned home
in the same order ; and I am very glad the
ceremony is over.

Vienna, February 5, 1861.—I have found
many acquaintances here ; one and all were most
kind, and seem to be resolved to be on the most
friendly terms with us.

I have paved the way for our future existence,
and it is pleasant to see how the Austrians recollect an acquaintance of years ago ![1]   My house
is besieged with visitors.   The ladies look nice,

[1] Lord Bloomfield began his diplomatic career at Vienna in
1818 as an Attaché.

and how they *do* dance and amuse themselves. The Viennese manners are very different from those in North Germany, and there is an absence of stiffness in them which strikes one. Old Prince Paul Esterhazy has just been here, and I delivered your message by reading him the part of your letter which referred to himself; he is wonderfully kind and most friendly.

February 7, 1861.—We had a splendid dinner last night at Rothschild's—people are so very civil ; but then just now I am a lion, and this will wear off! I went to a great Magyar ball last night— the men wore their national costume, and some of them were very handsome. The national dance was rather amusing, very wild, Hungarian music, and the dancing something between a jig, a reel, and a mazurka! very hard work I should think. All the great Hungarians were there, and I made the acquaintance of the Chancellor Vay and Count Scéczen, two of the leading characters of the day.

Vienna, February 9, 1861.—Yesterday I had an audience of the Archduke Francis Charles (the Emperor's father), and his wife, the Archduchess Sophie. They were so gracious that I was de tained at the Burg for nearly an hour, and the Master of the Ceremonies said usually these audiences are terminated in five minutes! There is no mistake as to the reactionary politics of this Court, and there is no concealment of their sentiments, which are also general throughout the mass of the society here. Last night I called at Princess Schönburg's, *née* Schwarzenberg. She lives in the Faubourg, and is a very agreeable person. Her sister-in-law, Princess Lori Schwarzenberg, is the leader of society in Vienna. She is not young now, having attended the Queen's coronation, but she is still good-looking and amusing. These two ladies are types of the society of this place, and their salons the principal resource of Vienna.

Do you remember Bela Szécheny, a young Hungarian who came to our ball at Berlin, and who has been a great deal in England. He came from Pesth this morning, and wore his national costume. He is intelligent and very good-looking, and knows a great deal of what is passing now in his own country. I do not see how the Hungarians are to be satisfied with less than the restoration of everything they obtained in '48, and the establishment of a mere personal union with Austria under the same sovereign, as is the case between Norway and Sweden. I believe, though it sounds strange, that the Hungarians are among the most loyal of all the Emperor's subjects;

but they wont hear of him except as their King, and the difficulty is to discover some mode of representation for them here. They want to have their King and Court at Pesth, and a little personal concession on this point would be very useful!

Vienna, February 27, 1861.—To-day we are very busy translating this tremendous constitution for the Empire. I cannot yet form any opinion on the subject, and am here too short a time to be justified in having one; but I fear it will not give satisfaction to either party. It goes too far for some and of course not half far enough for others; and the Hungarians will never consent to send, as it is intended, a mass of representatives to the Lower House which shall have any right of decision in the affairs of the kingdom!

I joined my husband at Vienna in the spring of 1861. I arrived just as the Schmerling Government was formed and the Constitution proclaimed. The Emperor opened Parliament in person, and I was amused to hear that some of the remoter Provinces of the Austrian Dominion, such as the Buckowina, selected peasants as their representatives, who could neither read, write, nor understand a word of German! And when they voted in a way disapproved of by their constituents, they were flogged by them on their return home.

The Empress was absent in Madeira when I arrived, but I was presented to the Emperor and Archduchesses, and then held my receptions, which were rather formidable. One of the ladies of high rank at Court, Countess Buquoy, was appointed to introduce the Vienna society to me. I sat in full Court dress upon a sofa in the middle of the drawing-room at the Embassy, and the person of highest rank present, after being introduced, sat down next to me till a lady of still higher rank arrived, when she immediately got up and gave up her place. This went on till all the society had been introduced to me, and lasted for three evenings ; everyone being in Court dress. One of the Chamberlains presented the gentlemen, and after my receptions were over, I was expected to return the visits. The Empress returned at the end of May, and received me shortly after.

She was very beautiful, tall, and had the greatest profusion of rich brown hair, which hung in curls down her back. She wore a magenta coloured satin train, and when the folding doors were thrown wide open, and I saw Her Majesty, for the first time, she appeared like a beautiful vision. We were a considerable distance from each other, as the Empress stood in one room,

I in another, and there was a large empty room between us. No one was present; when the folding doors were opened we curtsied to one another, then each advanced a few steps, curtsied again, and finally we met in the centre of the middle room. Her eyes were very fine, her complexion brilliant, and altogether she was most striking. She spoke in English, which she informed me she learnt from her father's grooms! She was passionately fond of dogs and horses, rode splendidly, and sometimes drove a four-in-hand.

We spent a pleasant summer at Hietzing, visited the environs, which are exceedingly pretty, and went one day to the convent of Heiligen Kreuz, near the Brühl. The frescoes there represent the life of St. Bernard, and one of them amused me exceedingly. It represented the saint as a young man tempted by a lovely female, so he threw her headlong into a fountain full of ice, but is represented sitting warmly clad upon a bench contemplating her struggles. This curious episode reminded me of an anecdote of the late Lord Alvanley, the famous wit. Gunter, the confectioner, was run away with in the hunting field, and nearly ran over Lord Alvanley. The next day he apologised saying, ' Really, my Lord, I was very sorry, but my 'orse was so 'ot I couldn't

'old him.' Lord Alvanley immediately rejoined,
' Ice him, Gunter, ice him !'

Mr. Bonamy Price dined with us, and was a
great talker but very amusing. He came to
Vienna to collect materials for a political pam-
phlet. Among other anecdotes he told one of
Whately, the Archbishop of Dublin, who asked
a young man ' how it happened that truth, which
everyone is by way of seeking after, is so rarely
found ? ' When the youth demurred answering,
the Archbishop said, ' I'll tell you why—because
men always prefer getting truth on their side to
being on the side of truth.'

Count Rechberg, who was Minister for Foreign
Affairs when we went to Vienna in 1861, gave me
the following interesting details of Prince and Princess Metternich's flight from Vienna in March 1848.
The Prince's longer residence in Vienna had become
extremely dangerous—the mob was exasperated
against him, the town was in a state of revolution, and the streets full of barricades. Prince
and Princess Metternich were, therefore, unable to
start from their own house, and when Count
Rechberg called to take leave, the Prince begged
him, as an old and intimate friend, to come and
see the Princess at a friend's house, from which
she and the Prince intended starting in a *fiacre*

for Felsberg, a country house belonging to Prince Lichtenstein, about thirty leagues from Vienna, leaving their children to follow by railway. About five o'clock in the afternoon Count Rechberg accordingly went to see the Princess. He found her terribly anxious, for the gentleman upon whom they had depended to escort their children failed them at the last minute, so they asked Count Rechberg whether he would undertake the responsibility. Not a moment was to be lost, the mob was getting more and more violent, and any delay might have proved fatal ; so all unprepared as he was Count Rechberg put the Prince and Princess into their *fiacre*, and then gave his arm to their eldest unmarried daughter, Princess Mélanie, the present Countess Zichy, and accompanied by Princess Herminie, who was lame, and her two brothers, they started to walk through the street as best they could, Count Rechberg having ordered his *fiacre* to meet them just outside the Rothethurm Gate, on the banks of the Danube. Unfortunately just before they reached that gate they were recognised by the mob, who with ferocious yells and shrieks attacked the Princesses and threatened to tear them to pieces. Count Rechberg contrived to place them against a wall and defend them, when, unable to resist the great pressure of the crowd, there was a sudden move, and they were all carried on through the gate. There they were recognised by the drivers of the *fiacres* who, seeing their danger, flogged the horses into a gallop, and drove at the crowd, which dispersed for a moment, so that the fugitives escaped, and drove off to the railroad station near the Prater. But they found to their consternation that they must wait three hours, a train with troops, having been delayed, blocked up the line. A citizen of Vienna who recognised the party told Count Rechberg he might depend upon him, that he would keep near, and in case of need come to their assistance. The students having got wind of the Prince's intended departure came to the station to watch for him, and every five minutes kept going up and down among the passengers, requiring their passports ; but luckily an official took the fugitives under his protection, showed his passport, and said they belonged to his party, so they escaped detection and started for Lunenburg. On arriving there, on a cold winter's night, they found the station was some miles from Felsberg, and there were no conveyances to take them on, so they went to the small inn, but had scarcely arrived when a mob assembled and required the innkeeper to give them up. He in the meanwhile pushed the whole party through a back door and locked it, and they found themselves upon a narrow back staircase, or rather ladder, which communicated with the stables. They found a one-horse carriage, into which they all got, and drove off at the back of the inn, whilst the mob was besieging the front. They arrived at Felsberg, where they found Prince and Princess Metternich, but they hadn't a change of linen, or any sort of comfort, were wet to the skin, and the house was uninhabited. They remained there, however, three days, and in the meantime Count Rechberg returned to Vienna with instructions from Prince Metternich to Count Ficquelmont, who succeeded him as Minister for Foreign Affairs, and also in order to procure money and the means of continuing the journey. On leaving Vienna for Felsberg he had desired his servant to follow him with his luggage, &c. &c., but the man missed the train, so Count Rechberg started without him, but brought Princess Schandor back with him, who had entreated him to allow her to accompany him to see her father. They arrived at Felsberg at three o'clock in the morning, and Princess Metternich was waiting for them on the staircase. She told them that their retreat had been discovered, the house had been surrounded, and the mob had declared that if they did not leave the place immediately it should be burnt down over their heads! Nothing, therefore, remained but instant flight, and the Princess asked Count Rechberg whether he would undertake to escort them to Olmütz, where the Prince had a friend he thought he might rely upon, to whose house they intended going. After a little reflection, Count Rechberg said he could only undertake the responsibility of escorting them on one condition, viz., that they should separate from their children, and send them back to Vienna, with their sister, Princess Schandor. This Princess Metternich at first positively refused to do, but seeing that resistance was hopeless, she took leave of her children, and pale and trembling with emotion, the tears rolling down her cheeks, she took Count Rechberg's arm, and followed by her husband they started. As soon as they entered the carriage the poor Princess threw herself into her husband's arms, and said she felt she had given way and shown great weakness, but that from that moment she should never do so again; and truly, in spite of being in very delicate health, she never wavered, but went through fatigue and anxiety with the greatest courage and cheerfulness, whenever Prince Metternich was present, watching him with the utmost tenderness and devotion, and attending to all his wants and wishes, but at nights when alone, she used to break down and weep bitterly. When the party reached Olmütz they found a message from the gentleman to whose house they were going declining to receive them, and an order from the governor of the town forbidding them to enter it! They were recognised by a mob, who had intimation of their expected arrival, and who with yells and hisses attacked Prince Metternich, tore his coat, and would probably have ill-treated him had not Count Rechberg dragged him back to the railway carriage, just as the train was starting.

They found themselves seated in the same compartment as one of the Polish revolutionary agents, who a few days previously had made a most inflammatory speech before the Foreign Office at Vienna. The Prince was in the habit of wearing a peculiar hat, and Count Rechberg implored him to exchange it for a cap, but he positively declined doing so, saying he would not make himself look like a mad Englishman (ein verrückter Engländer), and he was much more annoyed at being unable to light his cigar, because his lucifer-match would not burn, than he was with his torn and muddy garments. They had no money and no tickets, and were in the greatest dilemma, when Count Rechberg found one of the directors in the next carriage, who was a well-intentioned man, so he applied to him. He said it would be fatal for them to attempt going to Prague, as nothing could be worse than the state of political feeling there, and that the only chance of their escaping would be by stopping the train suddenly in the middle of a field, where the fugitives must alight as quickly as possible, and be left behind before the other passengers were aware of their escape; for at all the stations the other passengers got out and surrounded the Prince's carriage, abusing him in the most offensive language and threatening his life.

Accordingly, a few miles from Prague, the train stopped suddenly, the Prince, Princess, and Count Rechberg alighted, and before the other passengers knew what was happening the train went on again. The ground was covered with snow, and it was bitterly cold; the fugitives, however, managed to reach the next village, and, avoiding Prague, arrived at Dresden, where they could not remain; but Mr. Forbes, the English Minister, met them and took them under his protection, accompanying them to Leipsic. From thence they reached Arnheim in safety; but whilst they were dining there the waiter began talking very violently, and saying he understood the famous Prince Metternich was coming ; but he had better not, for if he dared show his face nothing would give him (the waiter) greater pleasure than to murder him. The poor Princess was much alarmed and wished to decamp immediately, but the Prince assured her that it never was the person who brags most loudly of committing murder who did the act ; and not long after the Municipal Authorities arrived at the inn, and desired to be shown up to Prince Metternich's room, whereupon the same waiter came in, pale and trembling, to announce them, and during the remainder of the Prince's stay at Arnheim, he waited upon them with the utmost attention and respect ! The Prince and Princess proceeded from Holland to England, where they were joined by their children, and thus ended one of the most adventurous and perilous escapes recorded in history.

In July, Victor Williamson and I made a charming tour in Upper Austria, which I enjoyed exceedingly. The following letters were written to my husband at that time :—

Adler Hotel, Gmunden, July 10, 1861.—You will be glad to hear that we arrived here safely, and are charmed with this place : the view is lovely.

The Stockhausens (Baron S. was Hanoverian Minister at Vienna) met us at the station. The view is quite worth coming to see ; the mountains are such a beautiful shape—very different to those we have been used to lately, which are like 'one's knees under the counterpane,' as my brother Thomas used to describe Cheviot. Victor is a charming companion. We travelled with Countess Kolonitz and her daughter, and another lady who got out half-way ; she had just come from Russia, and amused herself by performing gymnastic exercises with her lower jaw and false teeth ! We have been to the falls of the Traun, where I sketched.

Ischl, Tuesday, July 16, 1861.—We left pretty Gmunden by the one o'clock boat, and had a nice trip to Ebensee, where we found a small carriage which took us to Landbadsee. Such a wild, though narrow, gorge, and fine views ! The lake itself is very pretty, and I sat and sketched whilst Victor walked up to the second lake.

We dined at a small inn half-way between Ebensee and Landbadsee, where we were accosted by a Protestant pastor from Buda, who has come to these regions for his health. He looked very ill ; but had an intelligent countenance. I asked him how he thought things were going on in

Hungary; and he said, he hoped better, and that the Moderate party would get the ascendency. We had an excellent dinner; got back to Ebensee a quarter before seven, and had a most lovely drive here in the cool of the evening. The road is excellent—nearly flat, as it follows the course of the Traun all the way—and I saw *such* subjects; but it was too late to sketch much.

I slept badly, and suffered from one of the *fire* panics, which I sometimes get when I am lodged at the top of a large hotel with a wooden staircase. I lay awake for hours thinking what we *should* do if the house caught fire. (N.B.—The hotel, the ' Kaiserin Elizabeth,' *was* burnt to the ground not very long after that.) I think one reason I am subject to these fancies is that when I was a girl I saw the awful fire in Dover Street which destroyed Raggett's Hotel. I had been at a party at Lady Jersey's with my sister Lady Normanby, who was then residing in Dover Street. When we got to her house, we observed a great crowd in the street, and did not know what it was; so my sister bade me get out of the carriage, and we ran upstairs, threw open the drawing-room window, and then saw that a house a few doors down was burning. Lady Mulgrave was expecting her first confinement.

and my sister was afraid of her being alarmed, and went gently to wake her up, and wrap her in a dressing-gown previous to taking her to Percy's Cross in my father's carriage. My sister then proceeded to put all the valuables she could collect into the pillow cases, and we started in about ten minutes; but by that time the fire had got such hold that the house was completely gutted, and presented a frightful appearance as we drove through Berkeley Square. Alas! seven people lost their lives, among them Mrs. Round, who had just returned from the Opera. During the night, her sons, in great alarm, knocked at every door in Dover Street, asking whether their mother had been seen; but she was never found, and must have perished. A gentleman whose infant was sleeping at the top of the house rushed up to take it. The nurse said, 'Let me dress it first;' but he answered, 'Good God! woman, the house is on fire: follow me.' When he reached the top of the staircase he saw it was burning; but he thought he should get down, which he did with difficulty—the baby's eyebrows were singed, but it was saved. The nurse, who stayed behind to put on some clothes, perished.

Ischl is a regular fashionable watering-place, with people parading about in smart dresses, and villas in all directions. Very nice, I dare say, for those who like this sort of thing; but not *nearly* as beautiful as Gmunden. We got a view of a snow mountain (the Dachstein) last night.

Archduke Charles Hotel, Salzburg, July 19, 1861.—The weather looks very settled and fine, and we are going on to Golling this morning; it is only three hours' drive from here. To-morrow we hope to arrive at Lend, and stay there on Sunday. The sunset last night was splendid, and the views lovely.

Golling, July 20, 1861.—After finishing my letter yesterday I went out sketching. I walked into a private garden, where I thought there *must* be a beautiful view. A lady was sitting before her villa; so I said who I was, and asked leave to sketch. She was extremely civil and amiable, granted my request, and, when the sun got too hot, took me up into her drawing-room whence there was a lovely view of the fortress and the beautiful mountains round Salzburg! We dined at three, started soon after four, and arrived here about seven, when we got an *Einspänner* (or one-horse carriage) and drove up to see the waterfall, which is beautiful. The drive last night was quite lovely all the way, and the Alpenglühn at sunset glorious.

Lend, Saturday Evening, July 20, 1861.—
You will be glad to hear that we have had a
most beautiful day for seeing some of the grandest
scenery I ever beheld.   We left Golling at nine;
and the Pass Leug is magnificent.   There are
perpendicular rocks on each side of the road, and
the river Salza roars down between them!   We
reached Werfen at 11.15, and rested quietly there
in a delightfully clean, cool room till four.   The
morning was very hot; I walked through part
of the Pass.   We dined at 3.30, and came on
here, along a very pretty road, but comparatively
tame after the Pass Leug.   The position of the
Castle of Werfen is very fine, with mountains
above it and the river running below.   This is
quite a country inn; but kept by the brother of
M. Staudiger, the great hotel-keeper at Gastein.
We have got clean, comfortable rooms, with the
river running just under our windows; and I
think we could not have found a better *gîte* for
spending a quiet Sunday.   The Klamm Pass
begins here.

Lend, Sunday Evening, July 21, 1861.—This
has been a sultry day, and there must have been
a thunder-storm somewhere, as we heard it
rumbling a long way off, and a few drops of
rain fell about three o'clock. Victor and I walked

up to see the Klamm Pass, which runs up a narrow gorge just above this inn, with a torrent rushing down and tumbling over rocks and precipices. It was very hot whilst we were walking.

We have been exceedingly comfortable here; such a clean, tidy house, and the food very fair indeed! The situation is pretty, but not nearly so fine as some of the other places we have seen. I tried to make a little sketch to-day; but the colouring was monotonous, and the river that cold, grey, muddy colour of the snow-water, very different to the beautiful bright Traun. Altogether I think Gmunden quite as beautiful as anything I have seen since I left it, though the mountains about Salzburg and the Pass Leug are higher.

Lend, Monday Evening, July 22, 1861.—We have had a most successful expedition to Gastein, and have enjoyed our day very much. We started at 9 A.M., and reached Bad-Gastein about 12.30. The Pass Klamm is very, very wild and awful, the road very narrow, in parts shelved out of the rock, with a tremendous precipice and roaring torrent below. The Boothbys were waiting for us, and we went first to their lodging, and had not been there long when Prince Windischgrätz arrived, and sat a long time with me, and invited us all to dine with him at three. Before dinner I took a little walk to see the waterfall, which is very fine indeed. Such a body of water, falling almost perpendicularly, roaring and foaming most tremendously! At dinner I met Baron Meyendorf and his son, old Marshal Walmoden, the Prince's A.D.C., and his son. I was very glad to see Meyendorf again; his wife is staying with her brother, Count Buol, at the Brühl. After dinner, Meyendorf and I walked up to call on old Marshal Wrangel, and you never saw anything more affectionate than our meeting. He opened his arms wide and embraced me on the high-road, to the great astonishment and amusement of the many passers-by; and then he took me to his house, and would hardly let me go again—he wanted me to stay. We then all drove to a Swiss châlet, where Marshal Windischgrätz and a large party were assembled, and where we heard some very pretty Tyrolese music. I was presented to several charming Austrian ladies. To-morrow we travel on to St. Johann and Saalfelden. I walked back the last two miles down the Pass as it was getting so dark. The next day we had a very pretty drive to Saalfelden, and then over the Hirschbühl to Berchtesgaden. I was very sleepy and tired, and much annoyed when, at Saalfelden, some builders began knocking at daybreak. My room was only divided from Victor's by a thin partition ; and, to my great disgust, when the knocking began I heard him cry out 'All right!' as he thought the servant was calling him to get up. 'All right!' said I, in a growling tone of voice: '*I* should say it's all wrong.'

The Hirschbühl is a very high mountain, and we lunched at the top, where we met a priest with whom I had some conversation. I told him how much struck and distressed I had been at seeing the terrible *goîtres* nearly all the women suffer from in those regions, and I asked him whether there were no remedies to prevent their growth. To my extreme astonishment, he answered, 'Oh, dear, yes! they can easily be cured in the first instance ; but here the peasants admire them, and think them ornamental. Just as in your country people admire fine hair, here the *goître* is considered national, and the people would not on any account destroy them.' I thought to myself there is no accounting for taste. The *rhododendron hirsutum* was in full bloom as we passed over the Hirschbühl, and I never saw anything more lovely than the 'Alpine rose,' as it is commonly called. The weather changed suddenly, and, after ten days of very fine settled weather, it began to pour when we reached Berchtesgaden ; so, instead of sleeping there as we intended, we drove on to Salzburg, arriving there unexpectedly late at night. The hotel was quite full, and to my extreme surprise and annoyance the landlord told me he had not got a room. It was nearly midnight, and we were very tired and knew not what to do ; so after some parleying the landlord said there was a house in the town where he sometimes sent people in an emergency, and that, if we would wait in the carriage, he would send there and see whether any rooms were to be had.

In course of time the messenger came back, and said we could have beds ; so, accordingly, we drove into one of the old narrow streets near the river, and stopped under an archway. We were shown up a stone staircase three stories high, where at last we found two clean vaulted rooms, which we were too thankful to get, and go to bed. The beds were straw, and very hard, but clean. The next morning Victor knocked at my door, and called out, 'Aunt Georgy, do you know where you are ?' To his great amusement it turned out that we had been sleeping in the ' Brauerei zur Hölle,' or ' Hell Brewery '— *not* a very aristocratic *gîte* for an Ambassadress, who was, nevertheless, very thankful to have had it.

That day I returned to Hietzing, having enjoyed a most delightful trip, to which I often look back with pleasure.

Extracts of Letters from my Husband during my absence from Vienna.

Vienna, July 19, 1861.—We are rather in a state of excitement at the resignation of Vay and Széczen, and at the expectation that other Hungarian *employés* will follow their example. The actual deduction from these facts is that the Austrian Government are bent on adopting more stringent measures towards Hungary, and cease temporising with the Diet, and to endeavour to re-establish the Emperor's authority by putting an end, *by force*, to the horrors which are committed by the local authorities on those who pay their taxes. It is said that the whole Diet of Pesth will retire and leave Austria in possession, and that they will continue their system of passive resistance and refuse to pay anything. Schmerling has carried the day, at all events, *versus* the Nationalities, and all I hope is that he will not have sown the seeds of disaffection elsewhere than in Hungary.

Vienna, July 23, 1861.—I went to the Herren House to-day to hear the Rescript to the Hungarian Diet read by Schmerling. It is a tremendously long affair, and has been ill received at Pesth. There was no demonstration in either Chamber, because the Government desired that there should be none; but in the Lords there would no doubt have otherwise been cheering. There was not a sound to be heard but the three everlasting 'Hochs!'

It is believed that on Saturday something will be done at Pesth; but what, nobody knows. I suspect there will be an answer, and another Rescript; then the Reichsrath must meet and vote the money next month, with or without the Hungarians; and 'les absens ont toujours tort' is a principle that may be applied to the present case.

I went to Princess Auersperg's last night, and the Germans were all enchanted at the indications of a change of policy towards Hungary.

Vienna, December 18, 1861.—On the 14th we dined with Prince Paul Esterhazy. The papers had mentioned the Prince Consort's indisposition; but we were not at all alarmed, and therefore I was dreadfully shocked when my husband hurried into my room on Sunday morning, the 15th, and informed me that the accounts of the Prince were so bad they caused him (Lord Bloomfield) the deepest anxiety. We attended morning service in the private chapel of the Embassy, and hardly had we returned to our apartments when Prince Augustus of Saxe Coburg brought the terrible news which plunged us into the profoundest grief —grief which was shared by our whole nation.   I felt completely stunned, and for many days could think of nothing but our beloved Queen and her afflicted family, and pray God to support and comfort them, as He alone can. We received great sympathy in our distress ; but such a blow seemed to shake the very ground under our feet, and to bring home the solemn truth that man's life is indeed like the flower of the field—' in the morning it is green and groweth up, in the evening it is cut down, dried up, and withered.'

CHAPTER XVI.

LORD BLOOMFIELD and I left Vienna on March 14
for Pesth. We were lodged in a nice apartment
in the Hôtel de l'Europe, overlooking the Danube,
immediately opposite the fine suspension bridge
which separates Pesth from the old town of Buda,
which rises very finely above the river, the hill
being crowned with the King's Palace. The
full moon was shining brightly, and the aspect
of the town was very striking. Soon after our
arrival we had a visit from Count Béla Széchényi
and Count Henri Zichy, who very kindly placed
themselves at our disposal during our visit to
Hungary, offering to act as our cicerone. The
weather on Saturday, the 15th, was beautiful, and
quite warm. We walked through the Weiler
Strasse (one of the gayest and most fashionable

streets in Pesth) to the Museum, which is a very fine building situated in a garden, with a handsome portico and a flight of stone steps. In 1861 the Lower House of Representatives sat in one of the large halls of the Museum, and the empty benches were still there. The proportions of the building are fine, but it is perfectly plain, as the town is too poor to expend any money upon it, so the fittings were all of the commonest kind.

The collection of jewellery and coins was interesting. Most of the former had been found in tombs in different parts of Hungary, and was more curious than beautiful; though some of the shapes were very classical, and reminded me of the ornaments found at Pompeii. I was also struck by a collection of dark red terra cotta, like that found in Italy; the shapes were very pretty and graceful. Count Széchényi pointed out to us a cane which had belonged to Lord Nelson, which he was in the habit of using when he came to Vienna. A Hungarian nobleman, a friend of Count Széchényi's father, called upon Lord Nelson, who admired a very handsome cane he held in his hand; upon which the Hungarian nobleman said he would most willingly exchange it to have the honour of possessing the stick Lord Nelson was using; so accordingly the exchange was made, and the owner afterwards made a present of the interesting relic to Count Stephan Széchényi, and his son presented it to the Museum, where it is carefully locked up in a glass case.

From the Museum we drove up to the Palace at Buda, which commands a magnificent view of the Danube and the town of Pesth, but the country on the Pesth side of the river is flat, bare, and ugly. There are pretty hills between Buda and Gran, and quantities of villas and vineyards; but after Gran the whole line of railway to Vienna, with the exception of Presburg, is flat and ugly, but richly cultivated. The palace is small, and not remarkable. The park belonging to the town is large, but ill kept, and in order to reach it we had to drive through the Jews' quarter, which was very close and dirty. There are fine trees in the park, and the views of hills in the distance were very pretty. The air felt milder than at Vienna, but the dust was awful; and, as Count Zichy remarked to me, one swallows more dust there in a day than one does in two years in England. I had a long and interesting conversation with Count Széchényi about the state of Hungary, then in opposition to the Government at Vienna, as the dual system of government introduced some years later by Count Beust, and which has tended so much to the reconciliation of the two countries, was not contemplated in 1862 ; and the Hungarians were determined not to give up their ancient rights and privileges. Although they did not desire a separation from Austria, they insisted upon having their own Diet, the rights of voting taxes and regulating the size of the army, which privileges were not compatible with the Constitution given by the Emperor Francis Joseph in 1861. The taxation in Hungary was very heavy ; but Count Széchényi informed me it could ·be borne were it more equally divided. He remarked that 'a strong horse could easily carry seventeen or eighteen stone if properly saddled and weighted ; but if the saddle did not fit, the animal's back got sore, and then every step caused pain ; and this he said described the condition of Hungary at that time.

On Sunday afternoon we took a drive along the Danube, and the views were beautiful. The quays were lined with the most picturesque boats and figures. The former have not changed their shape for centuries ; they have immense, heavy oars, like the ancient Roman galleys, and are filled with merchandise. Some were laden with crockery, others with wooden utensils from Upper Austria ; and I was told that in the summer the quantity of fruit, especially melons, is marvellous. A fair was being held during our stay at Pesth, and the variety of costumes was amusing and interesting.

What struck me very much was seeing the whole population, male and female, wearing the national dress, which consisted for the men of a braided coat buttoned at the top, showing the waistcoat, which was likewise braided, tight-fitting pantaloons, long boots and spurs, and a low crowned hat. The women wore small round hats, braided cloaks generally slung over their shoulders, hussar fashion, with the sleeves hanging loose, and always black. The Slavacks look *very* wild in large white cloaks and broad-brimmed hats, long black hair and beards, loose full trousers, and legs and feet in linen sandals like the Italian peasants.

The horse fair was a curious sight, very Eastern in character, which reminded me more of the scenes described in the ' Arabian Nights ' than anything I had ever seen in Europe. We did not see many fine horses ; but a motley crew of Slavacks, gipsies, and Transylvanians, and the booths with their smoking cauldrons, brimming flagons, and the bright head-dresses of the women, formed subjects which any artist would be glad to contemplate. Much did I long for the pencil of Rosa Bonheur to commemorate the scene. We dined with Count Zichy, and met Count George Apponyi, who was at that time considered the leader of the Hungarian party.

In the autumn of 1868 we paid Count and Countess Waldstein a pleasant visit at Sčisčo, near Raab. Hungary generally is flat, richly cultivated, but uninteresting. I believe there is beautiful scenery in the Carpathians, but I never visited them. I shall never forget one beautiful scene I saw at Sčisčo. The vintage was going on, and we drove one fine bright afternoon to a large vineyard where the peasants, men and women, in their picturesque national costume, were plucking the grapes. Large baskets full of beautiful black and white fruit were piled up ready for transport; the rich autumn tints were glorious, and the evening lights heightened the whole scene, when suddenly a band arrived, the peasants left their work, and began dancing their tchzardashes with all their might. It was the prettiest ballet scene I ever witnessed, and one which would have delighted an artist's eye.

Baden Baden, May 18, 1862.—I arrived here this afternoon, and Countess Blücher met me at the station, bringing a most kind message from the Queen of Prussia, and an invitation to dinner at five, which I declined on the plea of fatigue, and not having my trunks unpacked; but I went to Her Majesty at eight, and she received me as cordially as ever, and was most kind, friendly, and agreeable, especially in all she said about you. The Queen is thinner, and very pale. I am to accompany her to church to-morrow at 11.30, and dine with Her Majesty at five.

Countess Blücher told me the accounts of our dear Queen are very sad. She is so weak, and when Countess Blücher was last at Windsor, her pulse could hardly be felt at all. She says the Queen is resigned to God's will, and speaks constantly about His knowing best; but she is quite broken-hearted. She wrote at the bottom of a photograph I saw of herself sitting on a sofa, with Prince Alfred standing by her, Princess Alice kneeling, the Princess Royal stooping over her, and the bust of the Prince Consort with a garland round it, ' Day is turned into night.'

Baden Baden, May 21, 1862.—I was above an hour with the Queen of Prussia yesterday, and drove and walked with Her Majesty after dinner ; and certainly I am more than ever struck with her. Depend upon it some day she will be appreciated as she never has been hitherto. Hers is too noble a character to be understood by the great majority, but she is 'eine edle ausgezeichnete Frau ; ' and if she never meets her reward in this world, she undoubtedly will in a better place. I have been so touched by all the proofs of confidence and affection I have received from Her Majesty. You know I do not attach much importance to mere phrases, but it has given me real and heartfelt pleasure to find my preconceived ideas more than realised, and I am so glad I came here.

Nancy, May 22, 1862.—When I took leave of the Queen of Prussia yesterday, she took off a gold pin she was wearing, with a medal of the King and herself, and gave it to me, saying : ' Now mind you never forget me, my dear ; and whenever you can, whenever you have an opportunity, come and see me, I have been so happy to see you again.'

Countess Blücher told me the Queen had said to her that it was a long time since she had

had such a real pleasure. I certainly am very deeply attached to Her Majesty, and always feel so thoroughly at my ease with her that I can talk *à cœur ouvert*, which I suppose she is not used to, as her position necessarily isolates her from people in general.

44 *Belgrave Square, June* 4, 1862.—I have just come back from seeing the International Exhibition, which is beautiful and very interesting. I devoted myself chiefly to the pictures; and the English and Belgian schools are decidedly the best, with the exceptions of the Ary Scheffers and Paul de la Roche.

The building is endless, and the only plan is to look at the specialities which interest chiefly, as every one must suit their own taste. I was particularly taken up with the china and pottery. They are wonderfully good, and only inferior to the old in the glaze.

Hatchlands, June 23, 1862. — Thank God England is beginning to have its usual good effect upon me, and I feel much better than I did when I arrived. I am charmed with the beauty of this country. I had no idea there was so much unreclaimed land in England as there is about here, and we have been driving through miles and miles of the most lovely old forest, with the thorns and furze in full blossom, perfuming the whole atmosphere, backed by such noble beech and yews, the blue distance stretching out as far as the eye can reach.

I have been much pained to hear of Lord Canning's death, which is indeed most sad; and what a lesson! but I do not pity him. His work was well and nobly done; and he is gone to her whose loss would never have been made up to him in this world. He leaves an honoured and respected name behind him, which will always mark in the history of his country; and probably, had he lived, he would have suffered much, as all his vital organs were more or less affected. He died of abscess on the brain.

Vienna, July 4, 1863.—Monsieur Thiers came to dine with us, and I sat next him. He is now past sixty, and looks old for his age; short and stout, with small black sharp eyes, and is a complete type of a clever, intelligent, French *bourgeois.* I think his personal appearance tallies with his writings and character; full of talent, but entirely wanting in dignity; his conversation (which he carried on in a quick, low tone of voice which was rather difficult to follow) was full of anecdotes, and amusing. He was asked by Mr. Fane whether Napoleon I. was in the habit of giving his orders on the field of battle verbally or in writing. He answered almost invariably the former, but that he was so particular about being rightly understood that he used to make his aides-de-camps repeat the order two or three times, and that very often if they were at all excited or flurried he would tell them to speak more distinctly and slower ; when assured that the command had been rightly understood, he nodded and said, ' Partez.'   M. Thiers told me that he was first initiated into the horrors of war at Marseilles, when part of the Army of the Nile landed there, and was so ill received by the inhabitants that there was a regular battle in the streets, and blood was shed in considerable quantities. 'Mais,' added he, 'on s'habitue à tout! L'année 1848 j'étois membre du gouvernement provisoire dans les terribles journées de Juin! Nous siégions en permanence à la chambre des Députés, parce que les généraux ne voulaient point agir sans que quelques ministres partageassent leur responsabilité.   Nous sommes donc restés 8 ou 10 jours sans bouger, nous mangions ce qu'on nous apportait et nous étions couchés sur la paille. Le cannon était placé entre chaque colonne de la chambre des Députés, vis-à-vis du pont et de la place Carrousel ; notre vie étoit dans le plus grand danger! Eh bien ! le temps passait, je mangeais du pain noir, et je riais avec les soldats!' So true is it that present dangers never appear so important as past ones, and therefore also the great events which mark most in history pass by us almost unheeded, and even often unknown.

Brussels, October 26, 1863.—I spent two days at Coblentz with the Queen of Prussia, who was kindness itself to me. We drove to see a very fine view from the fortress above Coblentz, and she took me all over the palace, and showed me her own rooms and things, saying: ' Je vous montre tout cela parce que vous vous intéressez à tout.' I dined and spent the evening with Her Majesty, and when I was coming away she took off a brooch with a crown of pearls on it and gave it to me. I had some interesting conversation with M. de Bacourt, who was very clever and agreeable.

Windsor, November 3, 1863.—I arrived soon after five, my first visit since the death of the Prince Consort. Lady Augusta Bruce came and sat a long time with me. Just as I had begun to dress for dinner the Queen sent for me. I went with a beating heart to the little audience chamber, and I can never forget my feelings when first I saw my beloved mistress. I thought I must have choked, and all I could do was to kneel and kiss her hand. We neither of us spoke for some minutes, but the Queen was so kind. Her countenance has quite changed, but she had the sweetest, gentlest, and most benevolent smile I ever saw. There was something in her expression I cannot describe, but it was most touching ; and even when the tears rolled down her cheeks she tried to smile. Her Majesty expressed pleasure at seeing me again, and asked most kindly after you and my sisters by name. I think I must have been with her for three-quarters of an hour.

I cannot express what coming back to Windsor was to me. Everything so exactly the same, and yet it seemed as if a great black pall was over the place, such a weight of sorrow pervaded it.

I sat next Sir Charles Phipps at dinner, who gave me some more sad details of the Prince's illness. He was taken ill in his dressing-room, which was a small room next the Queen's ; and he would not be moved for some days, as he said the bells rang to his various servants ; but one night he desired another room to be got ready, and walked there. He remarked when he got into bed, 'Ah ! this is the room George IV. and William IV. died in ;' and it is a curious fact that the only night the Queen slept in that room was the night the Duchess of Kent died. Her Majesty's own rooms were being painted, so that one was got ready for her. The Prince told Sir Charles Phipps in very early days that he was sure he should not recover ; and when General Phipps said he hoped he would soon be better, he said, ' Look at my tongue ; ' and it was so bad that from that moment he had very little hope.

The Queen wrote my sister Lady Normanby such a beautiful letter after Normanby's death, saying that having drunk the dregs of the cup of grief herself, she knew how to sympathise with others ; but little thought the last time she saw Lady Normanby in April that she too would so soon belong to the sad sisterhood of those who have lost the joy of their life on earth ; but, she added, though every day makes her feel her loss more keenly, each day brings us nearer our real home.

London, November 12, 1863.—I went to a small party at Cambridge House last night, and very pleasant it was. I met Lady de Grey, Lord Clarendon, Charles Villiers, Charles Grenville, Lady Tankerville, Evelyn Ashley, the Cardwells, and a few others. I had long, interesting talks with Lord Palmerston and Lord Clarendon, and

all they said about Austria was most satisfactory
and gratifying. Lord Clarendon said he had done
the Austrians a good turn at Paris, where he had
a long audience of the Emperor, who told him
that Austria was quite ready to consider the
question of the reconstitution of Poland, not according to the treaties of 1815, but 'la vieille
Pologne de 1775 ;' so Lord Clarendon answered
very plainly and curtly that it was the first he
had heard of this, and that he simply *didn't believe
it*.   Upon which the Emperor looked very much
surprised, and said : ' Comment vous doutez donc
de la parole d'un ministre ?'   Lord Clarendon
replied : ' Oui, sire, parce que tout dépend *qui* dit
une chose, à qui on la dit, comment c'est dit, et à
quelle occasion.   Or comme la réconstitution
de la Pologne entraîneroit infailliblement une
guerre avec la Russie, et la cession de la Gallicie,
je ne puis croire que l'Autriche puisse la désirer.'
Then he told me of a very interesting conversation he had with the Crown Prince of Prussia at
Coburg, relative to what passed between his father
and the Emperor of Austria at Gastein.   It
struck me, from all I heard yesterday, that the
question of a Congress is considered impracticable
at this moment, though, as you say, it sounds
plausible.   Clarendon told the Crown Prince

after the coronation at Königsberg that he hoped the King would not take tickets by the same railway which led Charles X. and Louis Philippe to the Waterloo Bridge terminus, and which unfortunately were not return tickets.

London, November 25, 1863.—The Danish question seems to get more complicated every day. I think the only possible solution of it would be to follow the example of the late Lord Enniskillen, who was much respected in Ireland as a magistrate. He was a great foxhunter, and used to hear cases early in the morning when ready dressed for hunting. After hearing the plaintiff, he got up and horsewhipped the defendant, asking him how he could behave in such a blackguard manner. The poor man then opened *his* case; and after hearing that, Lord Enniskillen attacked the plaintiff and horsewhipped him, after which both parties left his presence *perfectly satisfied*, each saying that his opponent had been horsewhipped by his Honour. If the plaintiffs and defendants in the Sleswig-Holstein affair could all be horsewhipped morally, perhaps it might bring them to reason.

London, November 18, 1863.—I dined at the Russells' last night, a small but very pleasant party, with the Argyles, Mr. Gladstone, Robert

Meade, and Lord Amberley, who seems a very intelligent youth. Lord Russell appeared quite satisfied with the state of affairs at Vienna, and talked of Julian Fane soon being Chargé d'Affaires there, so I hope you will soon get leave. I went afterwards to see old Lady Jersey, who seemed delighted to see me and have a talk about Vienna. There was quite a party there; the Spencer Ponsonbys, Henry Greville, Lord Vane, Lord Claude Hamilton, Wimpffen, and a young Prince Gortchakoff. The old lady looked well, was dressed in all the colours of the rainbow; but she is a wonderful person for her age, and I cannot help liking her. She has always been very good-natured to me, and I was so fond of her two charming daughters, Sarah, Princess Esterhazy, and Clementina Villiers, who died unmarried.

I dined with the Apponyis last night, and tried to get some news for you ; but Apponyi declared he had not had a line from Vienna, and had not heard of a second candidate for the Duchies. He was delighted at our refusing to attend the Congress, and hopes the whole affair will end in smoke—not, however, that from the cannon's mouth, which I fear seems probable.

I went yesterday to call on Mrs. Blomfield, the Bishop's widow, at Richmond, where she has a charming old-fashioned house overlooking the river, and the view was lovely. She was delighted to see me, and says she feels as if every one had forgotten her now. I always feel for people who have been in a prominent position when they lose it, for the world soon ceases to care for those who cannot be of use to it. Mrs. Blomfield seems comfortably off. I believe the Bishop insured his life, but always spent his full income. It is said he gave away 250,000*l.* in charity during his twenty-eight years' episcopacy.

London, December 10, 1863.—My brother-in-law, Captain Trotter, gave me some very interesting details about Lord Lyndhurst, whom he visited constantly during his last illness, reading the Bible with him regularly every week for a year and a half before he died. Trotter said at first it was alarming, for Lord Lyndhurst's mind was so wonderfully bright and vigorous : he always bowed to the authority of Scripture, and accepted readily any doctrine founded on that. He died a humble but most sincere Christian.

Wimpole, January 5, 1864.—To judge from yesterday's ' Times,' the King of Prussia is in a greater fix than ever, but he seems to be behaving much better than his Chambers about adhering to the Treaty of 1852.

Kossuth's Proclamation is plain enough; but how, with the example of Poland before their eyes, the so-called Hungarian patriots can try the same game as their unfortunate neighbours is indeed inexplicable! However, it would seem that nations, like individuals, never profit by the experience of others, and that it is a law of nature each must gain their own.

London, January 9, 1864.—The guns have been firing to announce the birth of the Prince of Wales's son. The servants are clapping their hands, and every one is delighted. It seems Her Royal Highness was on the ice when the first symptoms of the approaching event showed themselves, so she had to hurry home, and the wags have called the infant 'All but on the ice!' Lady Macclesfield, who was fortunately in waiting, had to play the part of Mrs. Clarke, the monthly nurse, and no preparations had been made for the infant, who had to be wrapped up in wadding!

The news to-day is so bad, I fear we must expect hostilities to break out soon, as there seems no hope of the Sleswig-Holstein question being settled without war.

London, January 30, 1864.—Last night rumours were rife of a change of Government. One thing is certain, viz., that Lord Derby went to Osborne after Lord Russell's visit, and it is said he and Disraeli will attack the Ministers at the opening of the session of Parliament, and there is a split in the Cabinet on our foreign policy. As far as I can learn there is no war party in England, but a very general feeling that the Danes have been ill used, and that in the event of hostilities England ought to support them, as it was chiefly owing to her advice that the Danes gave up Holstein ; but the meeting of Parliament will decide the question as far as we are concerned.

London, January 12, 1864.—The Prince de la Tour d'Auvergne (the French ambassador in London) was a most agreeable, charming man, and a great friend of mine. I had an interesting conversation with him, and he said he had been much gratified by his reception in England, and had found both Lord Palmerston and Lord Russell most amiable, conciliatory, and satisfactory to deal with.

The Prince regretted the manner in which we refused the proposal of a Congress, and said that had left a feeling of soreness at Paris he was labouring to remove, and he sincerely hoped Sir Henry Bulwer's visit might tend to the same end. He saw Lord Russell two days ago, who spoke very kindly about Lord Bloomfield, and regretted his inability to give him leave.

London, January 21, 1864. — My brother Augustus has just returned from Osborne, where he heard the following curious story which was related at the Queen's table by Lord William Paulet :—Two soldiers were cleaning their accoutrements at Portsmouth, when one asked the other to lend him a piece of soap, as his was used up. The man said, he had not got any ; upon which his comrade said that was not true, as he had seen him put a piece in his pocket. The soldier, upon this, exclaimed, ' God Almighty strike me dumb if I did!' and he *was* struck dumb at that moment. When taken to the hospital, he made signs that he wanted to write, and he wrote ' Struck dumb by the visitation of God.'

London, February 2, 1864.—I hear that the Queen has declared that she won't go against Prussia, and accordingly she sent for Lord Derby, but found he was more Danish than the present Government. The Prince of Wales is very Danish, and in the meanwhile Gladstone insists on a reduction of our army, beginning with the artillery; the Duke of Cambridge is furious, and one cannot wonder at it! The public feeling is decidedly Danish, and people are grumbling at the Government for holding strong language without being prepared to support it. I had a very interesting talk with Lord Russell on Sunday, and he told me I must not return to Vienna at present, as he thought it most probable you would have to come home for a few weeks, so I am just waiting to see what happens when Parliament meets. Sir Hamilton Seymour is very anxious about the state of the Austrian finances, and thinks she is mad to go to war, but supposes her rivalry with Prussia would not admit of her allowing Prussia to attack the Danes alone.

February 4, 1864.—I called on Lady Palmerston yesterday, and she kindly said she thought it might interest me to come in after their great political dinner to-night and hear what is going on; so I went and had some very interesting conversation with the Premier (Lord Palmerston), Charles Villiers, Lord Clarendon, Azeglio, &c. I think, from what I culled, there is not much likelihood of an immediate rupture, but we shall know more after this evening's debate; apparently there is a great feeling of sympathy in this country for the Danes, and the Germans are much blamed, however people differ as to the line of policy England ought to adopt.   Lord Palmerston seems still to believe that the Allies only wish to keep Sleswig as a material guarantee for the fulfilment of the convention, and that in spite of the war they will consider themselves bound by the Treaty of 1852. I own I can hardly believe this, because I fear that the same force which has brought on the war in spite of the better judgment of the Governments of Prussia and Austria will prevent their ever restoring Sleswig to Denmark after they have conquered it at the price of so much blood and money! At present it does not seem as if we were going to take any active part against the Allies, so I hope nothing will delay my return to Vienna. I am anxious to get back to you as soon as possible, and am weary of all this uncertainty and prolonged separation. Last night Lord Clarendon was, as usual, very funny and agreeable.   He certainly is a charming man, though he chaffed me about wishing to return to Vienna, and said it was all nonsense, and I had much better stay at home! When I asked him to tell me what is likely to happen he looked very sly, and said he could only answer as

Prince Metternich did when he was over here in 1848—'Tout le monde me demande ce qui va arriver, et moi, avec cette franchise qui me caractérise, je leur réponds je n'en sais rien.' Sir Henry Lytton-Bulwer was at the Palmerstons' last night; he came mooning in just as I was leaving, and I think he did not remember me, so I did not speak to him. It amuses me sometimes to see people look, when I bow to them, as if they had seen me many years ago in a dream; but considering how long I have been away from London it is not astonishing.

London, February 5, 1864.—The debate in the House of Lords last night was very interesting, though I cannot say it has enlightened me much, except that I think it is clear that we shall not take any active part in the war at present. Lord Sligo moved the Address, and was very unintelligible; the seconder even more so; so it was a relief when Lord Derby got up and spoke, as he always does, distinctly and fluently: but he was too flippant, and his allusion to Bottom the weaver was, I thought, in bad taste, though of course it sent the House into roars of laughter. Lord Russell was dignified and clear, but seemed very nervous, and I cannot say I thought he answered Lord Derby's attack, but rather passed

over it. I left Lord Grey speaking, as I could
not hear him and was tired. I saw my brothers
Henry and Hardwicke as I was coming away, and
they both seemed to think the debate unfruitful.
The Duchess of Cambridge, the Grand Duchess
of Mecklenburg-Strelitz, and Princess Mary were
in the Peeresses' gallery, and the Prince of Wales
and the Duke of Cambridge sat on the cross
benches. The Prince of Wales looked well and
dignified; he kept his hat on all the while, and
seemed very attentive.

Paris, February 12, 1864.—William Grey has
just been here, and tells me the carnage in this
wretched Danish war has been frightful. 3,000
Danes sacrificed themselves to save the rest of
the army, and kept the enemy in check for five
hours, but 2,200 were killed and all the officers—
quite another Thermopylæ.

I have seen poor Madame de Roboredo, who
is in a sad state about her country, and asked
whether I really thought England will do nothing.
I said that was a question I was not able to
answer; that I thought it would depend upon the
turn things take, and whether the Germans throw
over the Treaty of 1852 or not; that I believed
the sympathy of England is with the Danes; but
sympathy is one thing, and active assistance

another, all parties at home wishing to avoid war if possible.

Paris, February 14, 1864.—Lady Elgin is here and I have just been paying her a sad visit. We knew each other as girls, and she asked to see me. She has gone through a great deal since last we met, and looks worn and aged. She was tolerably calm, though great tears occasionally rolled down her pale cheeks, and my heart ached for her, for she was devotedly attached to Lord Elgin, and says she was so thankful she was with him and able to nurse him through his last painful struggle, which she told me no one could imagine who had not seen it. He was quite conscious of his danger, and thank God, quite resigned. He died of dropsy and disease of the heart.

I dined with the Cowleys last night, sat next M. Drouyn de Lhuys, and made the acquaintance of the Metternichs and Bassanos. Princess Metternich wore a white net gown embroidered all over with swallows flying, which was *fast*, to say the least of it, and, I thought, remarkably ugly; it was excessively *décolletée*, and she had a bouquet of violets under her arm which looked queer; but then she aims at being a *lionne*, and certainly succeeds.

Some years after this I witnessed a curious scene at Princess Schwarzenberg's at Vienna. Princess Pauline Metternich had acted in some private theatricals at the Auersperg Palace, and the Turkish Ambassador had seen fit to criticise her acting most severely and unjustly, and went about saying that had she acted like that at Paris she would have been pelted, ' avec des pommes cuites.' Princess Schwarzenberg was sitting next me a few evenings afterwards at a party in her own house, when we saw the Turkish Ambassador and Princess Pauline having an altercation in the distance. Princess Schwarzenberg looked at me rather alarmed, and presently afterwards the Ambassador came up to us and said, ' Ma foi ! je savois bien que l'on lui avoit répété ce que j'avois dit, qu'elle avoit si mal joué qu'à Paris on lui auroit jeté des pommes cuites, et comme j'ai le courage de mon opinion je suis allé lui dire la même chose en face !' Princess Schwarzenberg, much annoyed, told him she thought he had acted very uncivilly, and that everyone agreed in saying Princess Pauline had acted remarkably well. In the meantime she herself joined the group, and she said, with great good temper, she thought when people went on the stage they subjected themselves to being criticised, and that the Ambassador was at perfect liberty to find fault with her acting if he liked; but then, turning to him, she asked whether he had seen the piece acted at Paris. He said of course he had; so then she said, ' Eh bien, Monsieur l'Ambassadeur, vous trouvez, n'est-ce pas, que je ne l'ai pas jouée comme Mdlle. —— ?' naming a famous actress. ' Oh, que non, Princesse, si vous aviez joué comme elle, cela auroit été une bien autre affaire.' Thereupon the Princess made him a little curtsy, and said with the greatest dignity, ' Eh bien, Monsieur l'Ambassadeur, je vous remercie, car vous m'avez fait un joli compliment sans le savoir. Si vous m'aviez dit que j'avois joué comme . . . . je me serois sentie humiliée, car, voyez-vous, cela auroit été parfaitement inconvenable ; maintenant je suis tout à fait satisfaite. Ainsi bon soir, au revoir ;' and she walked away. I never, in all my experience of society, saw a better piece of acting than this was, and it did Princess Metternich infinite credit, for she turned the tables against her adversary with immense tact, dignity, and good humour. Princess Schwarzenberg seemed much relieved at the turn things had taken, as really they might have occasioned a very disagreeable scene.

Extracts of Letters from my Husband during the Sleswig-Holstein War.

Vienna, November 7, 1863.—I got back from the Duke (Augustus) of Coburg's last night. I had a most kind and gracious reception. The Princess Clémentine (daughter of Louis Philippe) was particularly amiable and agreeable, and all the family equally so. The weather was not very pleasant, for we had cold heavy rain yesterday, and a good hot luncheon served in the field was not improved by a considerable admixture of rain-water from above, and drippings from one's hat; but it was essential to eat, as the start at 7 A.M. had considerably sharpened our appetites. The afternoon was luckily fine and dry. We killed about 700 hares and a few partridges. The Château ' Ebenthal' is a queer old place—a large courtyard and corridor all round it like a monastery. The rooms very comfortable, and dinner at half-past six, so the evening was not too long, particularly as after dinner we retired to the smoking-room, and then adjourned to the Princess's drawing-room where we had a rubber of whist.

Vienna, November 8, 1863.—We are all on

the *qui vive* at the speech of the Emperor Napoleon, and you may conceive that the allusion to the Treaties of 1815 as being no more, is not a pleasant theme for an Austrian to ponder over. I have had a long interview with Count Rechberg who is *hors de lui.* I know not where you heard that the Archduke Maximilian is to start for Mexico in February. Nothing has passed on the question *here* since the deputation went through, but the Emperor Napoleon seems to consider the affair as arranged. I shall be very anxious to hear what happens on the proposal for a Congress on the Sleswig-Holstein question. Hitherto we have always opposed the idea ; but, query, Isn't a Congress better than a War ?

November 9, 1863.—The great man on the Seine seems bent on bringing matters to a crisis. His speech is certainly the most perfect and artistic thing of the kind I ever read, there is so much plausibility in it ; but what stands behind it ? Black and dismal is the look-out in my humble opinion.

Vienna, November 11, 1863.—I heard yesterday a graphic account of the scene at Prince Metternich's the other night, when the telegram arrived with the Emperor Napoleon's speech. The Princess read it to the evening visitors who were there, amongst whom was the Duc de Gramont who, on the morning of that eventful day, had written to Rechberg to say he had news from Paris, and that he could assure him the speech would be satisfactory to Austria ! Metternich's face grew longer and longer, and Gramont's paler and paler, as the Princess proceeded with the 'lecture,' and things were at their 'comble' when the passage stating the Treaties of 1815 ceased to exist was heard. Here, I must say, the impression is most unfavourable, and there has been a panic on 'change. The value of Austrian paper has fallen alarmingly ; exchange on London has risen in the same ratio. People don't know what to be after ; but after a little time ' les esprits se calment,' and so I hope this will be the case now.

Vienna, November 12, 1863.—I am happy to tell you that England and Austria are very nearly of one mind as to the answer to be sent to Paris. We don't intend to go in for the purpose of ripping up the last remnants of the Treaty of Vienna, and will take existing territorial arrangements as our basis. In fact we cannot admit that the Treaty of Vienna ceases to exist unless we seek to create confusion all over the world. If Napoleon wants war he will not want a Congress to justify it, and he won't like to enter on one without an ally, for that is his happy position at this moment.

Vienna, November 15, 1863.—I am glad to have heard to-day that Prussia is going straight on the Congress question, and I incline to think that all the great Powers, even Russia, will act *correctly*, as is said here. The draft of the answer to Paris is before the Emperor, and its sense will be the same as the Queen's. The French explanation of the letter inviting to a Congress, and the declaration in Napoleon's speech that the Treaties of 1815 have ceased to exist, is, that the latter was calculated as a piece of oratorical effect, nothing else! It has produced a nice effect out of France, and if the Emperor had wished to unite the Sovereigns of Europe against him he has succeeded.

The news of the Augustenberg claim to the Duchies of Sleswig-Holstein will set Europe in a flame, if Prussia don't act with Austria and the great Powers. It seems only *a speck* in itself, but 'tis quite enough to set everybody by the ears. The Emperor of Austria holds to the Protocol of London, and I hope he will run straight, but he is in a minority at Frankfort. What a mess! and just, too, when we hoped the Danish question might be settled.   The new King has aggravated his difficulties with Germany by signing the act of the Constitution, which is tantamount to an incorporation of Sleswig!   What a state of excitement Germany is in at this moment with this Sleswig-Holstein question! The Democratic party seem to me to be going ahead, and the small Governments have completely succumbed to the schemes of the National-Verein.   Austria and Prussia happily are pulling together, and intending to go all right, but they are outvoted at Frankfort.

Vienna, November 27, 1863.—I shall be very anxious to know how the Diet of Frankfort settle the question of the Execution of the Federal occupation of Denmark.   Austria and Prussia are for it being carried out at once, in order to maintain some authority in Holstein, where the King-Duke's has nearly ceased in consequence of the *employés* having refused to take the oath of allegiance.   How will the occupation of the Duchies take place?   Will it be in the interests of Denmark or of the House of Augustenberg?   That is the question.   Here the Government have no notion of allowing the Treaty of London 1852 to be a dead letter.   Matters are very lively I do assure you, and our Queen must be in an anxious state with the different interests that are at stake in Germany. We shall see, I think, the smaller States all adopting a different course from the two great Powers, which will be a novelty if nothing else.

Vienna, December 1, 1863.—How very sad it is about Lord Elgin's death ! First of all, the loss to his family and his poor wife, who positively adored him, is irreparable. To the country his loss will be very sensible, for I believe few men were so capable of directing our affairs in India as Lord Elgin. He was laborious, full of resource and firm as a rock, and had, further, an intimate knowledge of the character of the Easterns. The Government will have difficulty in replacing him, and the Queen was personally attached to him and his whole family, so that it will be to Her Majesty another source of grief.

What a comical creature my dear mother is ! My carpets being put down I thought a very prosaic proceeding, and she immediately remarked she supposed I have grave matters 'sur le tapis.'

[The revolution in Poland was headed by Langewicz, and much encouraged by democratic meetings in England, which led the unfortunate Poles to believe Lord Palmerston would give them active support. This opinion Lord Bloomfield tried in vain to combat : the Poles at Vienna would not believe him when he said public meetings were one thing, armed intervention another.]

I had a visit from Adam Potocki yesterday, who gives a most deplorable account of the state of things in Poland. The feeling is unsubdued, and is likely to go on through the winter ; Galicia as bad as can be. Roebuck is here looking fresh and well ; he came to see me, and was very amusing, but very bitter. He told me he had been nearly poisoned in London by the drains, and got an attack of vertigo which almost killed him, only his wife doctored him with champagne, and brought him round.

Vienna, December 4, 1863.—I had a visit this morning from Dr. Hitschfeldt, who has brought me the model you wished for of the boxes in which the sick are moved to the hospitals here. It will show exactly what they want to know in London, and is a much better and more practical explanation than any drawing or measurement. The bearers of these machines belong to the hospitals, and their sole business is conveying the sick and dead from their wards to the chapel or dead-room, as may be ; the body being always left there three hours before it is removed. These bearers have, however, nothing to do with the funeral arrangements, which are under another department. There must be a great number at the Allgemeine Krankenhaus (the principal hospital at Vienna), as the average number of patients in that establishment is 2,000 ; the average number of deaths daily is forty-five.

To-day Count Rechberg gives his explanation on the Sleswig-Holstein affair in the Lower House. Austria and Prussia have made up their minds not to be governed by a majority at the Diet, and a circular to the small German Courts, which goes off to-day, will not be very gratifying to their feelings. They are completely under the influence of the National-Verein at this moment, and it is impossible to foresee what their proceedings will lead to. Whether Austria and Prussia will be able to pull through or not is very doubtful, for they literally stand alone, and have not one German ally with them. Reform of the Bund certainly was, and is, necessary. . . . What astonished me is the perfect understanding between Austria and Prussia which is established, and which has been a simple consequence of the action of the small Courts.

Vienna, December 5, 1863.—Count Rechberg made his statement to the Reichsrath yesterday on the Sleswig-Holstein affairs, and I admire him for his pluck in facing public opinion on the subject. The House and a large party are for joining the national cause to any length, and walking into Holstein and proclaiming the Prince of Augustenberg without asking with your leave or by your leave. The Germans are so violent that one knows not whether the two great Powers may not be forced from their present policy. If the Danes won't give in, I do not see how the matter can end without war. Lord Wodehouse goes to Copenhagen to congratulate the King of Denmark on his accession, and if he carries good advice it may be listened to. We are in a fearful diplomatic crisis.

I was at Princess Schönburg's last night, and passed a pleasant time there with her and Princess Bretzenheim. I like Princess Schönburg very much ; and if one goes to see her once a week or once a year, she is always the same, and never wishes you to suppose that she has been neglected!

Vienna, December 6, 1863.—Things are looking very bad I fear ; and I do not see, when the blood of two nations is roused as it now is in Germany and Denmark, how the matter can end without coming to blows.

General von Gablenz, who has lately commanded a division at Vienna, a Saxon by birth, a young and intelligent officer, is selected for the command of the Austrian contingent of the federal army of occupation in Holstein--25,000 men. I saw him last night at the Casino.

Vienna, December 7, 1863.—To-day I have seen Count Rechberg and Baron Werther (the Prussian Ministers). The news is that a Danish Admiral who was sent here with letters announcing King Christian IX.'s accession was not received at Berlin by the King, and here they will not receive him officially. I am sorry that he should have been thus treated, as it will make bad blood. It is by way of exercising pressure at Copenhagen, and of gaining popularity in Germany. Under these circumstances, General Bülow (the Danish Minister) will have no chance of presenting his new credentials. I think Germany is resolved to go to war on the Sleswig-Holstein affair, and to finish it once for all.

Vienna, December 9, 1863.—The unfortunate Danish Special Envoy has just been to see me, and is gone away frightfully vexed at this Court and that of Berlin having turned a cold shoulder towards his King. There has certainly been a great want of courtesy towards the poor Admiral, who seems a good, honest, straightforward man, and not understanding why, when he is charged with a polite communication, it can be refused. He don't enter into the importance of the fact that his letter being received implies a recognition of the succession in Holstein. Count Rechberg told him that he hoped times would soon change, and that he would come back to Vienna. The old Dane answered with dignity that his impressions of Vienna were not of that agreeable nature which would give him the least wish to return!

This Danish visit is the only little incident of the last days, and in its way it is not devoid of importance; but if Austria and Prussia did not choose to receive the letter notifying the King's accession it would have been more polite and considerate to have saved the Admiral the trouble of the journey. I should much like to have leave for a while to see my dear mother; but I dare not look forward to this pleasure for some time to come, and you know I am not one of those who make plans for months beforehand.

Vienna, December 17, 1863.—The result of the departure of the Danish Admiral is that the affairs of the Legation are to be given over to *me*. This is, I think, hard, but it is so. I thought I had plenty to do before, and this will add to my work and my responsibilities. Bülow knows not when the fatal day will come, but he expects that he will have orders to declare his mission over as soon as the federal troops enter Holstein, and that will be in the course of next week. You seem to hope matters may calm down. Alas! I have no such expectation. What Wodehouse may succeed in effecting I cannot guess, but I am sure he will effect all that a man can do. The rest must be left to Him who disposes of all things here below, and who will bring peace or war as he thinks best for us poor mortals at this crisis.

Vienna, December 19, 1863.—You ask if there is a question of Schmerling's resigning—not at present. There are troubles in this Cabinet as in others, and Hungary is the point to which the attention of the Austrian Government has been seriously directed for some time past, and Schmerling is a hard man to deal with on this question. He uselessly considers his original programme may be carried out as to Hungary, and he is decidedly wrong. I hope for the best, and that he may yet remain in office, because one knows that he is honest in seeking to establish the Constitutional system in the Empire.

Vienna, December 20, 1863.—You ask me what the dissension is in the Austrian Cabinet.

I believe a little of everything—Hungary, the Concordat, and Sleswig-Holstein; but up to the present moment I have no reason to suppose that it is leading to any change. Schmerling is decidedly a Liberal in religious matters; and I don't believe that any of his colleagues, except perhaps Degenfels (Minister of War), partake of these same opinions.

Vienna, December 22, 1863.—War may not be this week; but I will answer for nothing after January 1, unless the Danes revoke the new Constitution, and that Austria and Prussia are able to face the torrent of unpopularity which would follow to their holding to the Treaty of London in regard to the succession in the Duchies. I do not think people in England are aware of the excitement prevailing in Germany on this subject at the present moment. We are in the habit of holding to the faith of treaties, but other countries seem to think it as easy to *sidle* out of them as it is for their Princes to consider themselves emancipated from the obligations contracted by their fathers. The long and short of the whole business is, that the Germans are determined that they, and not the Danes, shall have the port of Kiel; but they forget that the Emperor of Russia has a prior claim to the Duke of

Augustenberg, and that it was with a view to put aside all other claims that the Treaty of London was signed. Things are in a great mess, and it will be a miracle if blood is not shed within a month.

Vienna, December 29, 1863.—Matters are certainly no better than they were in the political world ; but we hear from France that there is no wish for war in that country at all events, only Louis Napoleon knows very well what he is about. He will make a pacific speech, no doubt, on New Year's Day ; but I hear that he declined a Conference on the Danish question, and that his representative at Constantinople declined also meeting his colleagues to consider the proceedings of the Moldo-Wallachian Government in the case of Prince Couza's sequestration of the revenue of the dedicated convents. If we don't choose to go to Paris, I suppose Louis Napoleon will not confer with the Powers.

The placarding some insurrectionary appeals in a few towns in Hungary has turned out a complete fiasco ; but the attempt indicates a foreign hand, and the work is evidently not native—of course here it is supposed to be Italian. All I hear of Poland is that the spirit of the Poles is the same as ever, but that the insurrection is being gradually put down by Berg. It would seem that the peasantry take little part in the movement, and that it is all the townspeople, the women, and the priests.

Vienna, January 6, 1864.—Matters are growing very serious indeed, and I am sure, with all the disturbing elements about, I do not see how war can possibly be averted. The Germans won't give in, and the Danes have been counting too hastily on foreign aid and on the Treaty of London. For Germany I must say, as far as the question of the Duchies of Sleswig and Holstein is concerned, that she has been consistent in her determination to obtain the fulfilment of promises made to her by Denmark . . . All is confusion in the distance, and no outlet is visible.

Vienna, January 13, 1864.—The cold has increased and is now intense. *We* don't care much for this, for the houses are warm and comfortable ; but I am always thinking of the long, cold journey you have before you, and I know not what to advise under the circumstances. At Baden Baden the cold is bitter ; there has been no warming the houses there. At Venice the gondoliers have been obliged to break the ice to get along, at Trieste there has been fearful frost, and the streets were so slippery it was impossible to move out.

I go about as I used at St. Petersburg, and do not find my furs at all too much. I am expecting an official visit from Baron Henri Gagern, the new Minister from Hesse Darmstadt. He is a very shrewd and remarkable man.

Vienna, January 16, 1864.—Last night was so bitterly cold I am sure you would have suffered horridly on the road; and the frost is so hard it kept me awake for several hours thinking what I should do between my desire to have you here, and my fear that the journey would do you harm. By this time you will have received my telegram written under the impression of 9° Réaumur in this sheltered yard and a rising barometer. You could not travel with impunity in such weather, so I shall let you know when the frost becomes bearable; but people here say no change is to be expected, and that the frost will continue in the ascendant till February.

I was with Count Rechberg, and had to telegraph before dinner to London as usual. Things are in a queer state in Germany. Austria and Prussia have taken the bull by the horns; and I think, though their proceedings are far from regular, we shall have a better chance of coming to an understanding with Denmark than if we were dependent on that motley crew at Frankfort.

Everything must be hard frozen in Sleswig, so the German troops will have no difficulty to contend with in the way of inundations, and I do hope that the King of Denmark will find some means of avoiding a collision. If he does, and can submit to the temporary occupation of Sleswig by the troops of Austria and Prussia, I shall not be afraid of the result of negotiations, and the horrors of war might be averted.

Vienna, January 17, 1864.—I am almost glad to find you have decided to wait a little longer in England.

I suppose the Austrian and Prussian Ministers will leave Copenhagen to-morrow; and if the troops of Austria and Prussia, destined to act upon Sleswig, are on the frontier in a fortnight, it will be the earliest date at which they can arrive. Between this and then the Danes must decide to revoke the Constitution, or to leave the Duchy occupied. I hope they won't resist. Their cause would be all the better if they took up their position in Denmark proper pending negotiations. If we can get into Conference I shall not despair.

Vienna, January 19, 1864.—There are 14° and 15° of frost every morning, and I must congratulate you on being away from this horrid cold. The great Danube is hard and fast to Presburg, and all up the river it was a marvellous sight. When there *is* a thaw, it will be awful, and all sorts of preparations are being made to meet the expected inundation. Skating is the order of the day, and there is not much fear of the ice breaking through. The Emperor received some regiments under orders for Holstein yesterday, and the poor fellows are much to be pitied in having to move in such weather. There will be no end of men frostbitten and general illness amongst them. The Danes don't seem in the least inclined to yield, and if they don't make room for the invading Germans, God knows what the consequences may not be.

I see no indication that the reactionary party is getting ahead in Austria. Rechberg and Schmerling are pulling better together, but it is impossible to say whether they will get ten millions of florins out of the Chambers for the Sleswig-Holstein army, as the Liberals want the Government to go with Frankfort and not against it.

I expect war on the Eider. Had the Danes made up their minds to yield a month ago, it might have been avoided—now it is too late.

Vienna, January 23, 1864.—There is a road established across the Danube, which is all fixed and fast. The Bülows (the Danish Minister) are preparing for a start, and I suppose will be off as soon as the Eider is crossed.

What is to happen in the spring I cannot pretend to say; for the moment we are only looking to the Dano-German difficulty.

The Danes would gain nothing by opposing a fruitless resistance to the German armies on the Eider, except the ill-will of Austria and Prussia, who still desire to maintain the Treaty of London, and of course if there is actual war, they will declare to Denmark that they are absolved from it. I hope there is a more conciliatory state of feeling produced at Copenhagen by the pressure that has been exercised, but . . 'tis all too late now.

As to my stay here in the event of a general complication, I can say nothing. Of course if we fought with the Danes against Austria and Prussia, my Embassy would soon come to an end, but things are not sufficiently advanced yet awhile to form an opinion.

There is a serious debate going on just now in the Lower House on the ten millions for the army. The Government are quite uncertain whether they will carry it, but I suspect they will somehow or other.

Vienna, January 27, 1864.—With regard to your idea of postponing your departure till after the meeting of Parliament, I have nothing to say against it except that we shall be so much longer separated. There is no doubt Lord Derby is preparing a serious onslaught on the foreign policy of the Government, but I hardly think Ministers will not be able to defend themselves. Of course if there is a strong war party in England there may be serious complications, but people will think twice before taking a serious decision on the question at issue. There is nothing new here except that Russia has now joined the coalition in favour of giving Denmark more time—six weeks—to revoke her constitution, but all Germany is violent on the Sleswig-Holstein question ; the small states are beyond all treatment, the large states doing what they can to stop a revolutionary movement.

Vienna, January 30, 1864.—The weather has turned cold again, so I strongly advise your not being in any hurry. There was a strong frost last night. The vote for money for the Sleswig-Holstein expedition has not passed, but I suppose the debate to-day will be over, and will turn out unfavourably to the Government. but it has enabled them to make declarations as to their intentions which are so far satisfactory, but I do not see how they can stem the torrent that is working against them.   If that is the case here, what will it not be in Prussia ?   Those poor Danes are sadly to be pitied, but they have much to answer for in their long refusal to listen to advice.   The Government of the day may have been unable to do so owing to the strong state of public feeling, but it never showed the least disposition to enter into negotiations in a sense that could lead to an amicable settlement of the matter, and always counted on support from abroad to carry it through its difficulties.

It does not seem to me there is the least chance of stopping the Germans from entering Sleswig ; they are determined to fight.

We had a hot crowded party last night at Count Rechberg's, which was very solemn and dull, and what between the debate and the movement of troops, always an ominous business, the Viennese who *do* think are not happy in their minds.   But still pleasures go on as usual, and the young people care for nothing else.   The distress in Hungary is growing serious, and of course discontent will follow.   The news, too, from Galicia is not one bit better than it was, and nearly all the revenues that ought to go to the landed proprietors are paid now to the national fund by the farmers and agents, who dare not do otherwise. All these things should be a warning to Austria to keep out of war I think, and not to go and seek it in Sleswig.

Vienna, February 5, 1864.—I can judge of nothing at present. I live in hope, and shall do so to the last, that we may not be involved in active work out of my sphere, but things look very dark.

The Queen's Speech and the mention of the Treaty of 1852, with the details, shows that we are resolved to maintain it if possible. In a few days we shall see what turn Parliament is disposed to give to the whole affair, and I am riding quietly at single anchor. My idea is that we shall do nothing serious till the Danes are obliged to fall back from Sleswig, and then we *must* speak out, but in what way we shall act I really do not know, as we should have to go against the popular craze for nationalities, and stand up for the faith of treaties. The troops are already suffering much from bivouacking, and I should think half the Germans will be in hospital before long. I have had a visit from General Bülow, who starts next week.

How surprised you must have been at a visit

from the Secretary of State.[1] I hope he will be able to make a good fight in Parliament. I suspect there is a serious cry getting up in favour of Denmark. It will be the old story, ' We must stand by the weak.' I think the last diplomatic move will have served Denmark well ; before then she was to a certain degree in the wrong, but the gallant defence she is sure to make will soon set her right with our public.

Rechberg asked me when you are coming. I said as soon as the weather improved. He replied he should be very glad to see you back here ; it would be ' un bon signal.' People here are very anxious.

Vienna, February 7, 1864.—Never was anything more unexpected than the news which arrived last night that the Danes had evacuated the Danewerk. I am delighted. In the first place there will be less bloodshed, the Danes will save their brave little army, and negotiations will be opened under more favourable circumstances than if it had been destroyed. The papers here this morning call it an Anglo-Danish intrigue, and I have no doubt call us as well as the Danes a race of perfidious islanders. It is amusing to think that the Austrian regiments

[1] Earl Russell, Minister for Foreign Affairs.

who occupied the Königsberg and made a brilliant fight had not a single German soldier in them. I think it is a sensible arrangement made here to send no Germans to the north.

Of course this news caused great excitement, and was the great topic of conversation at the ball at the Burg. The Emperor was more pleased than I can describe. He and the Empress made tender inquiries about you and the period of your return, and, in fact, that has become a subject of political importance. I said I hoped you would soon be here—this week, perhaps, as the weather had got milder. Perhaps this may not be, but I suppose the taking of the Danewerk will be followed by an early resumption of negotiations.

I have just finished the debate in our House of Lords. Lord Derby made, as he always does, a spirited and plausible attack, but I think Lord John demolished him, and if parties were not so nicely poised, I do not think much value could be placed on the attack.

The Germans are beginning to shout and grumble at the embargo on their ships and goods ordered by the Danish Government.

Vienna, February 8, 1864.—We are at this moment undergoing a tremendous fall of snow. It is not cold, but it may be the precursor of a return of winter, and I should think at all events the railways will be blocked up for a few days.

I have been greatly distressed to hear of this fresh combat, but I suppose one must always expect a retreating enemy to be attacked if possible, though I think it was an unnecessary encounter, and that the Danish army might have been allowed to retire to its strongholds without unnecessary bloodshed. The Austrians appear to have been up and at the enemy with great vigour, but again they have to deplore a severe loss, and that of one of the best Colonels in the army, a prince of Würtemberg, who distinguished himself in Italy. He is not dead, but so badly wounded I am told his life is in great danger. I dined yesterday with the Bille Brahes and a few of the neutral Ministers. Those poor Danes are sadly broken down by the retreat from their stronghold, but the manœuvre was the best they could have made, and I am only sorry they did not start earlier, for they might then have saved more of their men. The Count Gröben, killed at Missunde, was a nephew, not a son, of our old friend.

You must have had an amusing party at Lady Palmerston's, and it would have been very wrong of you to have missed the chance of seeing so many interesting people, and picking up a little news. I have just returned from Count Rechberg's, but there is no news from the army. The headquarters are beyond reach of electric wires. The Emperor has made the Prince of Würtemberg a General.

Vienna, February 9, 1864.—I have just found your telegram announcing your intended departure, and I am so glad, but I do trust the weather will not be severe ; it was very miserable at the Nordbahn Station when I saw the poor Bülows depart. Several members of the Corps Diplomatique were there—the neutrals of course. The Danes are making a gallant retreat, and I hope they will save a considerable force for the defence of their position in the Island of Alsen ; but the Austrians have shown much intelligence in their movements, and they have got a clever youthful general who is trying to prove his worth in case of his services being required elsewhere on more important business to the true interests of Austria than this miserable war in Sleswig. I wish so much bravery had been called forth on her part in a better cause. Last night I heard that the Prince of Würtemberg is badly wounded in the leg, but that there were hopes of saving him. He is a most gallant and brilliant officer ; I hope he may be restored to health and efficiency. The Austrian losses have been heavy, and I am sorry to hear poor Prokesch's son has been killed. There will be endless deaths, no doubt, and the loss of officers seems to me unaccountable, and makes one fancy that the men were not as willing to advance as might have been expected. I hear but one opinion here, regret at the loss of life on both sides, for nobody at Vienna, except some few members of the Reichsrath who want to make political capital out of the war, say an ill word of the Danes ; on the contrary they all wonder why they are plunged into this bloody war. I fear the same feeling will not, however, prevail at Berlin.

Lord Derby's speech was not one of his best, and there was an absence of dignity at the opening of it which was unworthy of the occasion. I do not think a hole has yet been made in the hard skin of the Government, but the great fight will be when the Blue Book comes down, and I hope that we shall soon get an armistice, and then I suppose matters will rest for a while. Here they are ready for one, but not so at Berlin.

Vienna, February 10, 1864.—I am not happy at the state of the weather. The cold is not what we at Vienna call severe, though it is still freezing hard. Yesterday all the sledges in the town turned out for a *corso* in the Prater, and I hear it was rather pretty, but I did not see it, and contented myself with a drive to the Nordbahn to see the Bülows depart. The trains are all late on account of the snow. I have no news. The Kammer ball at Court was put off last night in consequence of the war, and the number of killed and wounded, and the Vienna public were consequently obliged to pass a somewhat sober evening on Shrove Tuesday compared with their habits on that day. I went to the Casino, and found half of the males of the town there going off to a great ball at the Redoute, where they were going to finish their Carnival. All are full of the war, but the electric wires being out of order, and the headquarters not having a stoker man at hand, there is little certainty in the reports.

It was supposed that the Prussians had by a quick and unexpected movement from Glücksburg cut off the retreat of the Danes upon Alsen, but this news is not confirmed, and if it had taken place the poor Danes would have been annihilated or forced to lay down their arms. I should like to see the Danish report of the proceedings ; they are making a very gallant retreat at all events. The losses are very great on both sides, and I should fear the hospitals will soon be filling with sick as well as wounded men, for bivouacking night after night at this season in Sleswig cannot be pleasant. There appears to have been an awful fight in and about Flensburg. The carnage is horrible, and I have no doubt the Danes, who can ill afford such losses, will have suffered proportionately more than the Germans.

CHAPTER XVII.

I visit Munich and England—M. de Berg—Lord Rosse—Dr. Goulburn—Lady Palmerston—Matinée musicale—Mrs. Sartoris —Extracts of Letters from Lord Bloomfield during the Austro-Prussian War.

Munich, April 18, 1866.—I went with Sir Henry and Lady Howard yesterday to see the Aretinische Museum, which was begun eleven years ago by the late King Louis for a collection of Bavarian antiquities. M. Aretine, the collector, showed us over it, and it was most interesting. The lower story is full of sculptures, tombs, altar-pieces, carvings, &c. &c., collected in the various old castles and churches in Bavaria from the eleventh century. On the first floor there are 246 frescoes by modern artists representing all the principal events in the history of Bavaria. The doors and ceilings are old and quite beautiful. When finished it will be one of the most complete and instructive collections extant.

London, June 5.—I grieve to hear that all idea of a Conference is given up, for, though it was not likely to do much good, it seemed, as Julian Fane said, 'the last peg to hang the hope of peace upon,' and now we can only look forward to a fearful war! I don't think Austria is to blame *now*, but she is reaping the bitter fruit of her mistaken policy two years ago! It comforts me to think that *you* are free from blame, for you certainly did all you could to warn Count Rechberg of danger ahead, and if your advice had been followed things would not be as they are.

I was invited to breakfast at 10 A.M. at the Archbishop of Dublin's, to meet the Bishop of Oxford, and it was a most delightful party. I sat next the Archbishop, and met Count Strelecky, Lord Wentworth, Mr. Kennaway, two Misses Trench, my old friend Lord Richard Cavendish, and Richmond the artist. The conversation was very animated and extremely entertaining, and the Bishop of Oxford told very amusing stories. It seems that some time ago he preached a sermon which was much commented on and found fault with, on which one of his admirers, an undergraduate at Oxford, took up the cudgels in his defence, and said, ' Poor beggar, he did not mean what he said ; do not be so hard upon him.' The Bishop recounted this with great glee. Then he told us that as a young man he went with his father to pay old

Gurney a visit, and being obliged to leave early in the morning he was wishing his Quaker host good-bye, when Mr. Gurney said, ' I'm sorry, brother, thou must go, for I thought the Spirit might move me to-morrow morning to address thee and thy family.' The Bishop said he answered rather maliciously that if he was *sure* of that he would stay. On which Mr. Gurney remarked, ' Nay, but thou oughtest to have the moral certainty !'

London, May 18, 1866.—I had rather a curious conversation with M. de Berg, the Russian Consul whom I met at Percy's Cross. He said, ' Voyez-vous, avec une Italie, une Allemagne, une France, il faudra bien aussi un empire d'Orient, et que les Turques soient chassés de l'Europe !' ' Oh,' said I, ' c'est là votre idée.' Upon which he corrected himself and said, ' Oui, oui, mais vous savez, je parle surtout de Napoleon, c'est *lui* qui voudra s'emparer de Constantinople'. I laughed and said, ' Oh, oui, je comprends parfaitement, ce sont les Français surtout qui ont toujours désiré posséder Constantinople !' He laughed at this, and we parted very good friends.

Azeglio told me at Holdernesse House that there is a question of a Conference on the grounds of the cession of Venetia, the Principalities, and the Duchies I said I was sure Austria would not cede Venetia without a war, and that if she did the Italians would then want the Italian Tyrol, Trieste, &c. &c. Upon which he said, ' Oh no—*we* only want Venice, which we *must* have ; the other countries you have mentioned want us, and of course we could not refuse their wish.' Bernstorff then joined us, and told us the Austrians had refused the Conference, and looking at me and smiling, he added, ' Les Autrichiens sont *si* belliqueux, il n'y a pas moyen de les contenter nous autres sommes pacifiques.'

Lord Rosse told me a delightful story about the Fenians.　It seems there was an apothecary's boy at Birr who was an active Fenian agent, and he wrote to headquarters to say he was getting on so well he knew the cause would soon be triumphant, so he was looking about for a dwelling, and as Birr Castle would probably be pounded to pieces, he thought he should prefer Castle Bernard, and as then he should want a wife, he was hesitating between Miss Westenra and Miss Darby (two of the handsomest young ladies in the neighbourhood), and thought he should prefer the latter.　This was counting his chickens before they were hatched with a vengeance !

London, May 19, 1866.—I heard Dr. Goulburn preach such a very fine sermon on the doctrine of the Holy Trinity. He began by saying that as the Church appointed the first lesson from the first chapter in the Bible, and the Epistle from the last book, the Revelation, she intended thereby to teach us that the doctrines taught throughout the Bible, or *the* Book, are all inspired by one and the self-same Spirit, which, like the sun shining through the different colours of a painted glass window, are expressed in different ways. So God permits the human element in the character of the different writers in Scripture to appear; and therefore the Psalms are quite different to the Proverbs, the books of Moses to the Prophets, and the writings of St. Paul to those of St. John, though they were all members of the self-same body; just as the eye and ear, the hand and the foot, are different, and yet united under one head, actuated by one soul. So when one leaves a cathedral one sees the pure, bright, tintless light which shone through the coloured glass and threw such various tints upon the pavement. He said he thought the difficult subject of the Trinity in Unity beautifully exemplified by the different parts of Scripture, the doctrine of the Father being chiefly taught in the Old Testament, that of the Son in the Gospels, and that of the Holy Spirit in the Epistles.

Some days later Dr. Goulburn came to see me, and I happened to remark I thought nowadays people gave themselves no time to think. He said, ' Oh, and what is worse, they give themselves no time to feel !'

> ' He that lacks time to mourn lacks time to mend.
> Eternity mourns that.'

London, May 20, 1866.—I called yesterday on poor old Lady Palmerston, who is living at Breadalbane House, Park Lane. She received me most kindly, and looks pretty well, in spite of a very severe attack of bronchitis she has been suffering from.

She said she was much grieved at the turn affairs have taken since Lord Palmerston's death, and at all the Radical measures the Government have brought forward, which are contrary to *his* opinions. She referred to the estrangement which had taken place between Normanby and Lord Palmerston, but added, as if she wished to feel at peace with every one now, ' I always had a great respect for your sister, so pray when you see her again give her my love, and say I should be very glad if she would call upon me.'

I heard such a very funny anecdote of ——— , which is so characteristic of him ! It seems he is an immense admirer of Miss ———, the actress, and the other day he went behind the scenes to pay her a visit, which it seems is contrary to rule He found her door locked, so he began knocking at it with his stick. One of the managers came up and said, 'What are you doing here, sir? You must go away.' —— growled out, 'You be quiet,' and went on knocking. The man, very much astonished, said, 'Sir, I must insist upon your leaving, as you have no business here, and it is contrary to the regulations. So if you don't desist, I must call a policeman!' —— growled again and went on knocking. The manager, furious, rushed off to call a policeman, but in the meanwhile Miss —— opened her door. —— entered, and was sitting quietly chatting with her when the manager returned with a policeman, who said, 'Sir, I arrest you.' —— quietly said, 'You great fool, you don't know what you are doing. Be quiet!' Miss ——, in fits of laughter, had to explain that he was a Peer, and her intimate friend, upon which the manager and his companion beat a hasty retreat, very much disconcerted!

London, June 14, 1866.—I had the most delightful musical party this afternoon; Ella, Jaell the pianiste, Wianewsky, Agneta Yorke, Mr. Wade, and Adelaide Sartoris, whose singing was the most beautiful and dramatic I ever heard.

Her whole face lighted up, and she looked like the tragic muse.

She was very much *en train*, and sang several ballads so touchingly I fairly broke down. Her enunciation was wonderful, and she has such a grand face, and so much expression, though it *can* be satirical. She has the sweetest smile imaginable, and is as gentle as a dove.

June 15.—I dined at Montagu House last night, and had the pleasure of meeting the Bishop of Oxford (Samuel Wilberforce). I was told a funny story about him the other day, viz., that when he was dining with a large party, a poor curate who was deploring the large family he had to educate with a very small income, said, ' Do you know, my lord, I have nineteen children ! ' Upon which a very red-faced woman with a squeaky voice exclaimed, ' Only fourteen by me, Mr. Jones ! '

I regret to see that the diplomatic relations between Austria and Prussia have been suspended, so Werther's *Leiden* have come to an end at Vienna for the present. (He was Prussian Minister there when the war commenced).

June 19.—Monday's news of the rapid advance of the Prussian army is very alarming, and every one wonders that they have been allowed to march on unchecked. I hope the Austrians will not follow the fatal policy of delay which has so often been disastrous to them. It must be a great advantage to the Prussians carrying the war into the enemy's country. I grieve to think that all your efforts have failed, and that you are now likely to be shut up in Vienna for a long time to come. I was glad to hear that the Austrians had a decided victory at Custozza, and that the Italians had to retreat across the Mincio. I trust this will raise the spirits of the Austrian troops. I was sorry to hear from the Duchess of Cambridge yesterday that the Duc d'Aumale's son, the Prince de Condé, died of typhus fever at Sydney—a terrible blow, as he was a fine young man of twenty-one.

Penmaenmawr, July 4.—The news of the Prussian advance makes me very anxious, for unless Benedek, with an inferior force, succeeds in stopping them, there is nothing to prevent their marching to Prague, and even Vienna, as the Austrians have no army of reserve. The accounts of the devastation in Bohemia are heartrending, and I feel almost ashamed of the peace I am enjoying at this lovely place, which is as beautiful as any place I ever saw abroad.

I was much amused at the following article,

which appeared a few days ago, 'The true Cause
of Austria's Reverses.' In the church of the
Jesuits at Vienna, Father Klinkowström declared
in the pulpit that if the Austrian army was beaten,
her reverses were not to be attributed to the de
fective combinations of its chiefs, the needle-gun,
or the skill of the Prussian Generals, but solely
to the will of Providence, who has thus punished
Austria for having confided the chief command to
Benedek, *a Protestant*, and an enemy of true
religion. The reverend gentleman, however, appeared to have forgotten to explain how and why
Providence, having permitted a Protestant to be
defeated, had, at the same time, allowed two
princes of the same religion to be victorious !

*Extracts from Lord Bloomfield's Letters during
the Austrian and Prussian War.*

Vienna, April 18, 1866.—I am going to see
Count Mensdorff, and am somewhat hopeful that I
may do good, but matters are just on the 'wende
Punct,' and much will depend on the course
decided on here in the next twenty-four hours.

Vienna, April 19, 1866.—I was very busy all
day yesterday, and in the evening went to
Countess Mensdorff's, where there were very few

people. Mensdorff had hurt his leg and did not appear, but the worst is staved off for the time being, and there will be a simultaneous disarmament, and as Prussia will have it so, Austria will announce her intentions one day before Prussia does the same ! In the meantime, Austria has been put to vast trouble and expense to gratify the *amour propre* of the Prussian Minister (Bismarck).

Vienna, April 20, 1866.—I am going to see Mensdorff, and hope to hear good news, for by this time it is possible there may be some understanding as to the disarmament. Had this been agreed upon a fortnight ago, Austria might have economised the price of a host of artillerymen, but it is part and parcel of Bismarck's policy and love to establish union in Germany, to try and ruin this country's finances. What is being established I look upon merely as a truce, for no lasting understanding will be possible so long as the Duchy question is not settled, and Bismarck continues to rule in Prussia.

There has been a tremendous hubbub in the press here, by an apocryphal despatch published at Stuttgart, attributed to Mensdorff, and addressed to England, in answer to a condition of peace which we are supposed to have made. If

Mensdorff would write something in the sense of this *apocryph*, and thereby reassume the position at Frankfort which he ought to occupy, matters would soon be changed, and things brought to a point.

Pray give my love to dear Julian Fane, and tell him that I miss him every day, but am glad he is out of the way of these horrid winds, which never fail at Vienna.

Vienna, April 21, 1866.—I cannot tell you how the last communication to Berlin has been received. It is hoped it will produce the desired disarmament.

Vienna, May 5, 1866.—Things are looking worse each day. Yesterday I reported the intended issue of Bank notes to the amount of one hundred and fifty millions, to-day I hear the whole Austrian army is to be placed on the war footing in consequence of the mobilisation in Prussia, and the placing of the Prussian army corps at Görlitz and Erfurth to watch the Saxons, and I suppose prevent their slipping away. The Archduke Albert goes off to-morrow to Venetia, so things are looking very serious.

Poor old Prince Paul Esterhazy is dying.

Vienna, May 8, 1866.—Things are in a shocking state, both countries still arming, but still I will not give up all hope, because the Government in Prussia have learnt, within the last few days, that the Liberals at home and in Germany will not support the warlike policy of the Berlin Cabinet; but now that things have so far advanced it will be very difficult to know how to creep back again.

The Austrians are preparing vigorously for the fight. On the 18th the army in Venetia will be complete, one hundred and twenty thousand men, and in a month they will have an overwhelming force to defend themselves with in the north, or to attack, if necessary. But may God grant all these horrors may be avoided, and that before it is too late the King of Prussia will allow the question in dispute to take the less expensive and more Christian course of negotiation. Prussia wants a loan, and nobody will give it to her, so that if she goes to war she will soon find herself in the financial condition of Austria; all her savings will soon go for nothing.

Vienna, May 11, 1866.—There is nothing particularly new in the situation except the vote of the Frankfort Diet, which improves the position of this country and gives her strength, but I do not suppose Prussia cares for anything or anybody at this moment, and she, I mean her

Government, seems perfectly reckless as to the responsibility of producing a bloody war. She has had warning enough, but she is resolved at any price to support her policy by recourse to arms. In the meantime Austria and Germany are preparing, and we must wait to see which is the strongest. Part of the Vienna garrison has left, and the rest is going north in a few days, and we are to have some Gränzers, I believe, to take care of us. I saw young Prince Philip of Coburg the other day, who was to start in a few hours for his regiment, also ordered north, and seemed in great spirits at the prospect of a fight; and I must say there is but one feeling here on the subject, that if war breaks out Austria is on the side of justice, and marches to defend a righteous cause. However, all this will soon be forgotten if once the dogs of war are let loose, and I will yet cling to the hope that at the last moment Europe may be saved from the carnage which threatens her. I have had a visit this morning from young Baron Pfeil. He came to take leave, and marches in a few days to the north. His regiment has now four complete battalions, upwards of 4,000 men. I hear a fifth battalion is to be formed for each regiment, which looks very serious.

There is the greatest enthusiasm here for war,

but none for defence against Italy. Free corps are being formed all over the Empire, and if the fever lasts there will be no lack of soldiers for the fight, but where is the money to come from ? The army already costs one million of florins a day. It is curious that a war should be popular here, and not so in Prussia, where they will soon have a big national debt like Austria.

Vienna, May 22, 1866.—To-day the telegraph announces the arrival in Roumania of Prince Charles of Hohenzollern.

Things are getting into a terrible mess, and alas ! I see no chance of quiet but after *large* blood-letting. A severe remedy, no doubt, and in that case we shall have revolution with all its horrors ! Maurice Esterhazy has just told me there is a black cloud in every direction. Famine, war, cholera. The latter, however, don't appear to have got yet to Vienna, and perhaps we may be mercifully spared that visitation. There will be no wine and no fruit this year ; a fearful loss for this country.[1]

Vienna, May 29, 1866.—Things continue in a very unsettled state, and there is so much excitement in favour of war, that it would be next to

---

[1] One of our friends, who had large estates in Bohemia, generally derived an income of 60,000 florins (6,000*l.*) from the sale of his plums alone !

impossible to stop it now, unless Prussia were to give way, which is not to be expected. If the Ministers for Foreign Affairs attend a Congress at Paris Mensdorff will go, and there is a question of his being accompanied to Paris ; Mensdorff would prefer not to go to Paris, but the Emperor has too much confidence in his good sense and honesty to allow him to resign, and I highly applaud him for so just an opinion of the superior qualifications of this Minister.

This escapade of the young Hohenzollern is a fresh complication. I suppose *we* shall be very angry and yet bow to the accomplished fact ! And then . . . where are all our achievements resulting from the Crimean War, and all the blood and treasure which we spent there ?

Vienna, June 17, 1866.—I drove out yester-day to Dornbach, where we spent a pleasant evening. As we entered the drawing-room, which looks towards Vienna, there was the most beautiful effect of light I ever saw. There were very few ladies, however ; nearly all have left ; but I met our old friends the Arembergs, Princess Mathilde Windischgrätz, Princess Auersperg, and pretty Madame De Jongh, the wife of the Belgian Minister, who seems a great favourite with every-body. The great sight of the evening was

Karolyi, who is looking well, and not at all like poor Werther before he left this. He seems happy to have got home, but speaks very calmly and dispassionately about Prussia. He says the Prussian army is numerically stronger than the Austrian army opposed to it ; but here there is a great feeling in the justice of the cause, but hardly any of enthusiasm in the army, though I doubt not that it will do its duty. Politically, Prussia must feel annoyed by the desertion of her cause by all Germany, except, as appears in to-day's paper, by Coburg. I do pity Hanover, Saxony, Brunswick, and Hesse Cassel, for they must be at once overrun, and can make no resistance to the superior power of their adversary. It is neck or nothing with them, and as these small states have no desire to become simple vassals of Prussia, there remained nothing for them but to stand by Austria. The small states were foolish in not having made greater military preparation, but Saxony was the only country ready to march its army towards Austria.[1]

[1] On June 7 there was a meeting of the Federal Diet at Frankfort. The demobilisation of the Prussian army was proposed by Austria, and voted for by Bavaria, Saxony, Hanover, Hesse Cassel, Nassau, and others. Prussia declared the Germanic Confederation to be dissolved. June 14, Prince Alexander of Hesse was appointed to command the Federal army. The Prussians declared war against Hanover and Saxony. June 15, justificatory manifestos were issued by Austria and Prussia. June 17, Prussia declared war.

The Emperor has addressed a manifesto to his people, and it is moderate and truthful. I hope that his renewed assurances of his intention to go back to constitutional government will do good and show other countries in Germany that Austria is in the right way of improvement. I suppose we shall have fighting next week in poor Saxony. 'Tis there, no doubt, that the great struggle will begin, and where it will be decided whether Germany is to be free.

Vienna, June 20, 1866.—The Austrian armies have not yet massed, and are waiting to be attacked, but as yet there seem to be no symptoms of any such intention as immediate, and Mensdorff tells me we must wait for at least another week; in the meantime the Prussians are consolidating themselves in Saxony and elsewhere, and raising contributions according to the old system which they adopted in Sleswig-Holstein on the occasion of the first war in 1848. We are anxious to know the fate of the King of Hanover and his small band, and hope he will escape with it to join the Hessians under Prince Alexander.

I cannot help admiring the conduct of the Elector of Hesse in sending away his successor, Prince Frederick, with the army, and remaining alone without a guard. The Prussians will be puzzled to know how to treat him, but they will devise some means of evading the difficulty. The confidence here in the cause of Austria and Germany is unbounded, and there is reason to expect that the Italians will not be very firm in their attack on the Austrian lines.

I dined on Monday with the Mensdorffs. Karolyi, and Chotek from Berlin were there, and Alphonse Mensdorff, the Count's military elder brother, who is raising a body of Alpenjägers, and hopes to enlist Garibaldi.

Karolyi, Chotek, and Bray (the Bavarian Minister) dined with me yesterday, and in the evening we all adjourned to the Volksgarten, where we met the Schwarzenbergs. Princess Schwarzenberg had come in from Dornbach about some hospital arrangements for the poor sick and wounded soldiers, at which all are working in this country. Really the feeling shown in all classes towards the army and the sufferers from the war is admirable here ; but they expect also much from them.

I know nothing of the Stockhausens, except that of course they will have to leave Berlin, as all the other German Ministers have done except the Mecklenburgers and Hamburgers. What a lively place Berlin must be just now !

Vienna, June 21, 1866.—I went to see Knesebeck (the Hanoverian Minister) yesterday, whom I found at home, but without news of the King. Amongst other visitors I hear we are likely to have the Prince of Augustenburg at Vienna. He has got away from the Prussians, leaving his wife and children at Kiel in the safe keeping of the Prussian Admiral Jackmann, who will, I have no doubt, take very good care of them. To be sure these are terrible times for the small kings and princes of Germany, and whatever turn the war may take I should think a good number of them will be mediatised—perhaps the best thing that can happen in their own interests and those of their people. Nobody here knows anything about Benedek's movements, except that his army is marching on; but so long as his headquarters continue at Olmütz *we* cannot expect anything of importance. I hear the Prussians say, that when they have polished off the Austrians they will march to Paris, and therefore those who have had no chance against the Austrians look to one against the French.

The Berlin newspapers have published an address of Benedek's to his army written for the amusement of the Berliners, and which is so absurd it ought not to take in anybody. It is written too in the *Prussian* lingo, to the great amusement of the people here. The telegraph has just brought a piece of uncomfortable news as to our Government at home. It will be an unfortunate complication in the affairs of Europe if we are to have a new Minister for Foreign Affairs ; but if the Government cling to their Reform Bill, they must, I suppose, resign or dissolve.[1]

The Americans appear to have behaved uncommonly well about the Fenians. I hope we shall have no more serious trouble at the present time about them.

Vienna, June 22, 1866.—The Italians and Prussians have now declared war against Austria, and Benedek has marched on his headquarters to the junction of the railways. The whole army is marching north, and we shall hear of bloody work in a few days.

St. John Foley is superseded by Colonel Crealock, who arrives here to-morrow. He was Military Secretary to Lord Elgin in China, and is a capital draughtsman. He has been Military Attaché in Russia.

There was a ' Volksfest ' yesterday for pa-

[1] New Reform Bill introduced by Mr. Gladstone. The Government was defeated on it on June 18. The third Derby Cabinet formed. Lord Stanley succeeded Lord Clarendon as Minister for Foreign Affairs.

triotic purposes, and the Männer-Gesangverein sang well. There were fireworks afterwards. Pray tell Lord Richard Cavendish that there is no probability of the road from Strasburg to Munich being interfered with.

Vienna, June 24, 1866.—I was last night at Princess Schwarzenberg's at Dornbach, where I found the Archduke Louis Victor, who was full of his visits to the King of Saxony at Prague, where he said the enthusiasm for him was boundless. The poor Queen is low and her eyes tearful, the King full of dignity and firmness. The Archduke remains here as Civil Adlatus to the Emperor for receptions and so forth, as the Archduke Charles Louis is gone to the field. We shall hear what happens soon. I confess I see nothing certain in the distance but the most cruel bloodshedding and misery north and south! The Prussians and Italians, I believe, hope to shake hands at Vienna in a month!

I send you an account from the newspapers to-day, which will show you what the ladies of Vienna are doing for the poor wounded soldiers that will be! and the sacrifices of all kinds that are being made in Austria by all classes is worthy of admiration and example in other countries. Princess Schwarzenberg showed me a letter she had got from the young Crown Prince Rudolph, written by himself, sending her 200 florins out of his ' Sparkasse ' for her charities, and thanking her so nicely for all her exertions in endeavouring to provide for the comfort and relief of the army of Austria. It is all very, *very* sad, and what will it end in ?

I have no news to tell you of the least importance, but next week will be a momentous one north and south, I suspect; and perhaps before this reaches you the telegraph will have reported a battle in Italy. The Federal army seems to be advancing. As the Rhine Province has hardly a soldier, it would seem as if Prince Bismarck could not hold it, and would try and consolidate the monarchy by rounding off its frontiers in another direction. He is playing a great game, and at present we can form no calculations as to the result; but with 33 millions of Austrians and more than 10 millions of Germans opposed to a Prussia of 18 millions, he ought not to succeed but for the alliance with Italy.

I should deplore our Government leaving office at this critical moment, for Europe is not in its normal condition.

Vienna, June 25, 1866.—I have heard of

Stockhausen, who is Acting Grand Master to the Queen of Hanover at Herrenhausen, the King's country palace, close to Hanover. The bad news has just arrived that the King has been taken prisoner by the Prussians!

Vienna, June 27, 1866.—To-day we shall have the official details of the battle of Custozza. The Italian prisoners will be at Comorn to-morrow, I understand. Quick work! The Italian papers say they have got 600 Austrian prisoners, but how they can say their army was obliged to yield to a superior force, when they were two to one, I do not know—history must clear up that point. I fear the King of Hanover will go to Prussia! If the Bavarians had shown a little vigour, they were in a position to save him and his little army; but they are much more intent on carrying out their own policy and watching their own particular interests, than those of Germany and Austria.

I had Mr. Russell, the ' Times ' Correspondent, to dinner yesterday, who is off to Benedek's headquarters to-night. He is a very amusing, clever Irishman. He goes armed with letters, and hopes Benedek won't send him away. He is well disposed, and I think the Austrians ought to be thankful to have such a man to write the history of the war, and he will do nothing likely to divulge the secrets of the army which might be of advantage to the enemy. Lumley[1] is in somewhat of a difficulty, and I do not know what will be the result of his application for instructions, for I cannot learn that any of the foreign Ministers formerly at Dresden are gone to Prague. The King of Saxony was to go to the head-quarters of his army to-day.

Vienna, June 22, 1866.—I hear Lord Stanley is to go to the Foreign Office. He is very clever, but inexperienced in diplomatic affairs and habits, and we shall have some queer work after a while, only I suppose his papa (Lord Derby) will guide him. He has made speeches favourable to Bismarck's political system for Germany, and I should think his appointment to the Foreign Office will frighten the small states. Bismarck has nearly done for them. The 'Times' of yesterday will no doubt have informed you that there was fighting along the whole Bohemian and Silesian frontiers. The Prussians came on, and as far as we are informed, have been repulsed. It is impossible to form much of an opinion as to the intentions of Prussia, but it would appear that they

---

[1] Mr. John Savile Lumley had just been appointed British Minister at Dresden

have extended their line.   Benedek has kept his army together.   The Austrian artillery is good, and the Prussian needle-gun has not terrorised the Austrians, as was expected, but it is horrid work ! We heard of the fighting in the middle of the day, and of the repulse in the afternoon, but it is only this morning that we have the detailed telegram.   The Italian reports have arrived, and one cannot help admiring the modest expressions of the Archduke's final telegrams. 4,000 prisoners and 14 guns.   By-the-bye I must tell a funny story.   Some volunteer Chasseurs *des Gamins de Vienne*, were enlisted a month ago.   These fellows took one of the guns and were allowed to bring it to Vienna and present it to the Emperor.   Yesterday morning they arrived, and went back again to Verona last night.   If the whole army is composed of such chaps the Italians and Prussians will not have a pleasant time of it ! Lumley is gone in a private capacity to see Beust at Prague.   The King of Saxony is with the army, which was engaged yesterday at Münchengrätz.

Vienna, June 29, 1866.—Just got a telegram from Princess Mary, who will be received here as a Princess of England, and treated with all due honours.

There has been very heavy fighting in Bohemia. The Austrians have been advancing steadily into the position they wanted, and have, I believe with great loss, obtained what they intended, but in a day or two there will probably be a great battle, and if Benedek succeeds he will get in between the two great Prussian armies like a wedge, and secure a good position for carrying on the war. The Austrian losses in Italy have been sensible. 4,182 Italian prisoners have already passed to Comorn, and there are upwards of 2,000 wounded men in Venetia. The Italian losses at Custozza are estimated at 2,000 men.

We drove last evening to Schönbrunn, and I saw the poor Archduchess Sophie, who is in a great state of agitation. Her sister, the Dowager Queen Mary of Saxony, is at Dresden. I wonder how long the Prussians will hold Saxony. We hear to-day that the Bavarians have entered that kingdom. The Saxons fought admirably; they are in Count Clam Gallas' army corps, and have had two or three days' continued fighting, and it is evident the Prussians want to force him back towards Prague. On my way homewards from the Volksgarten I saw a great crowd looking at some chasseurs, Tyrolese volunteers, who had formed the guard of honour at the Theatre, where the play, 'Andreas Hofer,' was given. It is a curious fact that the chief of this volunteer corps is the grandson of the original man. The enthusiasm here is great, and we cannot but admire the way the Emperor's cause has become that of the many nations he rules over. The Hungarians, about whom the newspapers abroad talk such nonsense, are sending daily 100 men for the army. I saw Princess Khevenhüller last night, who told me the ladies had already got above 6,000*l.* for the wounded, and they have accommodation for 200; but what is that for the mass of suffering which has been brought on the world. I saw Wimpffen at the Casino, who said the defeat of the Italians was complete. They, however, fought well, and it is to be regretted that General Cialdini did not come on, as the Archduke would have had a good chance of defeating him. It seems the Italian regiments have generally moved; composed of Piedmontese, Neapolitans, Romans, and Tuscans; and they were so completely disorganised by the thrashing they got, that the Archduke don't expect them back very soon. You will have seen the account in the papers of the three Austrian wounded soldiers who were hung up by the Italians. Really one had hoped they had been more civilised, and I fear the account will create a bad impression and produce retaliating measures on this side. The Austrians and Prussians seem to be fighting like perfect gentlemen.

Vienna, July 1, 1866.—There has been a deal of fighting in all directions. Prince Frederick Charles's army is advancing from Reichenberg to the Austrian position, and that of the Crown Prince of Prussia from Glatz. Benedek is taking up a position near the two fortresses of Josefstadt and *Königgrätz*, and in that direction may be fought any day the battle that must have a deciding effect on the war. If Benedek is defeated it will be a bad business. He has not more than 230,000 men to oppose to 300,000 of the enemy, better armed, and with more cavalry than he has. His chances are not so good as the Archduke's in Italy, but we must soon know something more on the subject. In the meantime all traffic between this and Prague is stopped, except the army transport of fresh troops, and wounded being brought back. All the Vienna garrison has gone to guard the railways, and try and prevent the wires being cut and their communications with the capital being cut off. Vitzthum called on me yesterday. He is going to see his King, and is in very low spirits about everything, and well he may be. I do not know whether you have seen

in the papers the proceedings of a Prussian lieutenant in Saxony. Being stationed somewhere
near Pilnitz he found out the villa of Baron Beust,
the first Minister of the King of Saxony. He
asked if any of the family were at home, and on
being informed not, he ordered some of his men
into the house, and broke open everything, destroyed all the furniture, and when he had completed this work of devastation he left his card.
I and others thought this was a *blague*, and I
understand so did Baron Beust himself, and he
only discovered the truth of this villanous proceeding from his wife who has just joined him at
Prague. This on one side, and the hanging up of
the wounded Austrians by the Italians, are credit-
able little incidents in this horrid war.

Vienna, July 2, 1866.—The events of the
war are telling, and if Benedek has no more luck in
resisting the Prussians than his generals have had
up to the present time, it is impossible to say
where we may be next week. There must be a de-
cisive battle very soon, and people here are in very
low spirits, as you may imagine, and so few details
about anything are known, that the very silence
creates an increase of alarm. Prague may be
occupied at any moment, and I suspect we may
be cut off from all telegraphic communications

with the army, for the Prussians seem fully to appreciate the value of railways and telegraphic communications. There have been all sorts of reports of poor General Clam Gallas, but all I know for certain is that he and the Saxon corps have been completely defeated. The Archduke Leopold, to whom the other corps d'armée was confided, has failed, and is reported to be very ill. The situation is full of doubt and anxiety, and notwithstanding the great bravery and devotion of the Austrian army, it would seem that they are likely to be overpowered by the numbers of their adversaries and the superiority of the small arms. Those needle-guns have proved murderous weapons. The King of Saxony was at Pardubitz the other day. He had better retreat, or he will be caught. To be sure, what vigour the Prussians have shown, and how powerfully Bismarck has supported his policy!

I am going to sign a protocol on commercial matters at twelve o'clock to day. Nice time for such negotiations, is it not? Poor Austria is the victim of weak and uncertain allies, and two powerful rivals both leagued to despoil her of her property and her dominions.

Vienna, July 4, 1866.—A most fearful disaster appears to have befallen the Austrian arms. The great battle yesterday ended in the complete success of the Prussians. We have no details beyond the fact of the repulse of the Austrian left wing, and of Benedek's headquarters being in the rear of his fortresses, cut off, I think, from his retreat by rail to Olmütz. It is an awful business for poor Austria. I hear the Empress has just gone off to meet the Archduke William, who has been wounded in the head; I am glad he was not taken prisoner also. Poor General Tassilo Festeticz, a gallant hussar whom you may recollect, and who commanded a corps d'armée has lost his leg. There must have been fearful carnage, and it quite sickens me to think of it all. Had the Bavarians done what was asked of them, and what was agreed on, much of this would have been avoided. I hear Prince Teck has come here to offer his services, but I have not seen him. It was too sad to see Mensdorff on Monday evening when we signed the protocol for the adjournment of the Conferences, and I think he had a presentiment of what was about to happen. The Austrians appear to have fought like lions up to the present time, but the army must be greatly discouraged.

Vienna, July 5, 1866.—There is no further news of the army, the remains of which appears to be retreating towards Olmütz, and to have been so far unmolested by the Prussians.

Poor Mensdorff will have a painful business and time of it at headquarters, and no one seems capable of taking the command with a prospect of success at this moment. I think the best thing to do would be to send the Archduke Albert. He has been in luck at all events, and his presence might inspire confidence. I believe that never was anything so mismanaged.

I have had inquiries from the Queen about the Archduke Joseph and Prince Philip of Würtemberg. The former had four horses shot under him and received a slight wound in the left hand ; he is otherwise well, and with the army. Prince Philip is quietly at Baden with his wife. The Emperor did not accept his services, and I hear the same of Prince Teck.

All the accounts I hear of the army are most unpromising. The men appear to have done generally well, but latterly the commissariat was ill provided for, and after the defeat many officers came off in the trains prepared for the wounded. If this sort of spirit has got up, where will the demoralisation end? The Prussian claims will go on increasing with their success, and we shall have terrible complications.

Vienna, July 7, 1866.—We are in a most woeful condition here, and I most sincerely hope, in the interests of Austria, that an armistice will be at once concluded, for the army is sadly demoralised and the public very discontented.

Valuables are being sent off to safe places, and in fact everything being prepared as if we really were on the point of having a visit from the Prussians here. I am glad to hear Rudy Kheven-hüller is all right : he was supposed to have been killed, and seen to fall over with his horse, but it seems his horse tumbled in the *mêlée*, and both supposed done for, but after being missing for a day he found his way back to headquarters.

Vienna, July 8, 1866.—We know nothing positively yet as to the terms of an armistice, but it seems it will be concluded, and most sincerely do I hope so, for it is the only thing for this poor country.

Poor people! I do pity them all so much, and they do look so sad and so painfully humbled! George Esterhazy is safe. His regiment does not appear to have been much engaged, and is almost intact, and in fact the cavalry have suffered little in comparison with the infantry. Prince Windisch-grätz (the head of the house) is wounded and a prisoner, but going on well, and at any rate no one can say that the aristocracy of Austria have not done their duty as brave soldiers. Russell, the ' Times' correspondent, came to see me yesterday. He was very interesting, and described the battle (Königgrätz) as the most fearful and tremendous sight imaginable. He saw it all from a high tower near Königgrätz, from whence he could observe everything, and I have no doubt his account, which you will see in the ' Times,' will be most clever, and truthfully done. He describes the effect of the needle guns as something marvellous, and as necessitating a complete change in the system of infantry fighting. It is a curious fact, however, that comparatively few of the wounds from them are mortal, but they are irresistible to an attacking force armed with the old-fashioned gun. I wish our Government would make haste and decide on the alterations, or we shall be as behindhand as these poor Austrians have been if we do not adopt a breech-loader. Captain Brackenbury, of the Artillery, was with Russell and saw all, and I hope he is capable of making a full report of all he saw and of the way of manœuvring of the Prussians, who have shown immense intelligence in all they have done during the last year.

I have not heard anything as yet of Lord

Cowley's successor at Paris. The Government will be puzzled to find anybody at this critical moment, and I hope they will try and keep Cowley, particularly as there will certainly be most important Conferences at Paris on the Italian and German questions.

Vienna, July 9, 1866.—We are still without any certain intelligence as to the armistice and mediation proposed by France, and the Prussians are advancing on Vienna! They were yesterday at Iglau in Moravia, and I suppose their intention is to make peace under these walls! The Italians, too, notwithstanding that Venetia is assured to them, are inclined to continue the war. What is to come of it all I know not. The Austrians have rallied 150,000 men at Olmütz, and I suppose will try to get to the lines at Floridsdorf (close to Vienna), where fortifications are being thrown up, and mean to fight another battle, unless Bismarck gets here first. I hear Gablenz and his corps are on the way from Olmütz, and the Austrians have at all events got the railway in their power. But oh! the frightful devastation of war! I met poor Count Harrach last night. His property was selected for the great battle, and everything, his beautiful house and all, is completely destroyed, all his villages burnt, and the country Russell described to me as resembling the most beautiful parts of Kent, with most wonderful promise of crops, all completely devastated. The drawing-rooms were turned into hospital wards, saturated with chloroform, and the damask curtains cut up for bandages. The Prussians took all Prince Trauttmansdorff's horses from his stud, and all his fine cattle, though it was said private property would be respected. Waldstein's fine place is destroyed. Rothschild is a lucky man not to have had the enemy at his fine place at Schillersdorff. I am grieved to see Lord Lansdowne's death in the papers, three days, too, after I had heard that the Government wished to send him to Paris as Cowley's successor. I do hope the latter will stay on there, but I hear he is determined to go.

I have just seen Count Maurice Esterhazy, who has received good news from Paris. Napoleon has at last used pressure on Victor Emanuel, and his army will not advance to enter into conflict with the Austrians, who are coming north as fast as they can. The Italians have got Venetia, Napoleon will settle at what price, and the Austrian army here will soon be sufficiently strengthened to meet the Prussians, only I fear the latter will be too quick, and perhaps get into this capital. Esterhazy thinks not, and seems hopeful the war can now be prolonged, and that Austria will then find herself in a better position. I do not see what troops there are to defend Vienna, but the Danube is a nice little barrier to pass, and these last rains will render it more difficult than before. I am more hopeful to-day, but the town is not, and there is great fear of the Prussians. Mensdorff has just returned from the army.

Vienna, July 12, 1866.—If the Prussians come here, and they are expected next week, I fear they will cut off all railway communication with the west, and we shall then be in a nice predicament. They are said to be moving down in three columns, one from Prague on Linz by Budweis, and the other two upon Linz and Tulln. How they will cross the Danube is another question, but I do not hear of any adequate arrangements being in course of preparation to prevent their doing so. If therefore the attempts making to arrange an armistice at Pardubitz, where Benedetti and the French General Farissant must now be, fail, the Court will probably move at once, and the Government also, to Pesth.

The treasures and valuables—Kunstkammer, Schatzkammer—are gone. The Archduke Albert arrives to-day, and there will be immediately a council of war to decide on the way of employing the military means at the disposal of the Government, but all is here unfortunately done too late, so that one knows not what to count upon. The weather is variable, and pleasant enough. I could not see Mensdorff yesterday ; he is not well since his journey to the army. I had a few words with her, and she is in an awful state of alarm lest Nikolsburg, her place in Moravia, should be devastated. The Prussians take all live animals everywhere. All Prince Lichtenstein's horses came up last night, and everything is being sent to Hungary.

Vienna, July 12, 1866.—I received a note from Princess . . . ., and thought the best thing I could do would be to go and see her. She is in great alarm, and just starting for . . ., but I have advised her not to remain there. Her son is with the army, happily not hurt, but she was seven long days without hearing from him. There is a frightful panic here to-day, and if the French mediation does not stop the Prussians, I doubt anything else effecting it. Last night I drove out with Morier to the Floridsdorf lines, and it was pretty to see the bivouac fires and some of the pleasant part of warlike preparations. The

General Thun you allude to is not killed, but wounded in the head, and not badly. Festeticz is said to be going on pretty well. I do not apprehend any danger from the Prussian soldiery if they enter Vienna, for of course it will be treated as an open town, but I still hope we shall not have the pleasure of seeing them here, though I dare say the King and Bismarck would not dislike going to Schönbrunn.

What times these are! I saw Count Hartig last night, the son of our old friend, and he says, though there was no opposition, his whole house was ransacked for money, everything broken open, and papers strewed about, and now it is turned into a hospital. His sheep and oxen have been eaten up, and his poor peasants are absolutely penniless. Such are the horrors of war.

Vienna, July 13, 1866.—Grieved as I am at our long and painful separation, I think you are to be congratulated at the distance which separates you from the neighbourhood of this place and the perpetual din and talk of war. I strongly suspect that Louis Napoleon is not going to do much in giving material support to poor Austria, and never was a country more in want of it. The Archduke Albert arrived this morning, and I hope some plan for continuing the war will be decided on.

The Bavarians and Germans are doing nothing, and are disheartened and disorganised, so that, militarily speaking, Prussia has everything nearly her own way. The Prussian army is advancing very slowly, and there are some light divisions of cavalry and horse artillery hovering about, which will not make their march towards Vienna quite so pleasant as that to Königgrätz. There is of course great discontent here and dissatisfaction with everything and everybody, but as yet no appearance of a disturbance, and in fact there are plenty of soldiers to keep the peace. But people are flocking in from Moravia for protection and safety against the Prussians, who behave well in the towns, where they are properly watched by the superior officers, but in the country districts they have taken all live stock everywhere, and as the sheep are generally Merinos, they do not eat them, but send them off to improve the farms in Prussia. Horses of all kinds are taken, and poor Princess Vincent Auersperg is furious because they have taken an old *pensioned* pony of hers, twenty years old. Fancy your favourite Pearly being taken by the Fenians. But such are the little incidents of war. Poor Kinsky has had all his fine English horses taken and his linen plundered. But really I think it very weak of people leaving their movable property.

Princess Schwarzenberg is become quite a Sœur de Charité—shelives amongst the wounded. She has six officers in her house in the Mehl-mārkt, and 200 wounded people put up in the palace in the faubourg, and the ladies' establish-ment on the frontiers of Hungary has 600 inva-lids. The Princess is constant in doing all in her power to mitigate the distress of these poor unfortunates, and what a state of mind she must be in at the condition of affairs!

Vienna, July 14, 1866.—The French media-tion has done no good, and is not likely to do any, and it now remains to be seen whether it will be better for Austria to run the risk of another battle, or to treat behind an army of 250,000 men, as powerful, barring the needle-guns, as Prussia can bring into the field. Bavaria and the German allies appear in so bad a way they will soon knock under. Bismarck is now issuing pro-clamations in Bohemia calling on the Czechs and Moravians to consider their national rights to be like those of Hungary. Absolutist on one side, revolutionary on another!

I hear the Reuss' have come up from Ernst.

brünn. Poor people, what a bore for them! But it is said they heard some cannon-firing in the neighbourhood, and thought it better to come away. The Prussians are at Brünn, and coming on as steadily as they were expected, so I suppose there will be another great battle of Aspern or thereabouts.

1 P.M.—Nothing but people coming in all day, and taking up one's time to speak of their fears of the Prussian invasion, and really we can do nothing for them. But they want to make this Embassy a house of deposit, English people thinking they all have a right to take refuge in the Embassy! I am very sorry for these poor people, but I cannot do all they want.

People are beginning to leave Vienna. The Empress and her children are gone to Pesth. The Emperor will, I believe, go to headquarters of the army somewhere beyond Floridsdorf. Oh! it is very sad when one thinks of all the misery this wretched war has brought on the world! The weather is growing hot again, but the air is not so oppressive as it was. Did I tell you that the young Prince of Coburg, son of Duke Augustus, had *four* shots through his cloak? What an escape!

I have just been giving the cook orders to

lay in stores of flour and dry food, for fear of accidents, and our market being uncomfortable!

Vienna, July 15, 1866.—I have just had a visit from poor old Schloissnig, who left Kissingen the day before the fight between the Prussians and Bavarians.   He is ill and broken-hearted: and his son has come back from the war, not hit, but in dreadful suffering from the wind of a cannon-shot.   He has been fourteen days in bed and is recovering, but it will be a long time before he gets well.   And how many are out in this way.   Young Louis Esterhazy, Nicolas' son, is also wounded, but slightly.

Yesterday there was a communication from the Prussian headquarters, through the French Embassy, on the subject of a truce, but the conditions could not be accepted, so the messenger is gone back.   In the course of next week some decision must be taken, but at present all seems to indicate that another battle must be fought before there will be a chance of peace.

In the midst of it all, Princess Mary wants to come here.   The greatest confusion prevails; all the Archdukes and officers not on active service are requested to leave Vienna and the neighbourhood, and the railways are encumbered with troops both west and south!

The Ayllons and Stackelberg and his boys are flocking into town from the country, as the Prussians have frightened the whole population.

The Prater is full of soldiers, a perfect camp. The army from Italy is coming here, and I suppose, in a very few days, we shall have some more serious collisions. The wounds inflicted by the Prussian needle-gun are very slight generally, and half the wounded soldiers will be shortly in the ranks again. The weather is very oppressive. It must be awful work for the troops, and especially for the Prussians at this moment, who are being a good deal troubled by flying bands of Austrian cavalry.

Vienna, July 1, 1866.—Princess Mary arrived this morning, and having been advised of her intention, I went to meet H.R.H., and put her and her husband into our carriage, in which they went to Munsch's Hotel. The Princess and Prince Teck came to dine with me, and we afterwards took a drive in the Prater to see the camp. They wanted to go to the Opera, but it was so hot they preferred finishing the evening at the Volksgarten. To-day the Princess was to go and pay some Imperial visits, and I am to meet them at dinner at Countess Barth's, who is an old friend of the Teck family. Prince Teck is again trying to get into the army ; perhaps he may succeed, but I hope not. The Princess is very amiable and amusing, but complains of the sad star under which she seems to have been married, and I am not surprised that the miseries of the state of Europe should have made this impression.

We saw some cavalry regiments arrive in the Prater yesterday, which had been acting as part of the flying columns of General Edelsheim. I never saw men and horses look more jaded : it is true they had had a tremendous march on a very hot day. In the evening I met young Herberstein, who told me he had not been in bed for thirty-six nights, nor had any one in his regiment. They will soon pick up if they can have a few days' rest, which I trust will be the case. The news from the Prussian side does not encourage the hope that peace will be made, but Benedetti returns to the headquarters at Brünn, I believe, with some new propositions. If Prussia's demands really are the exclusion of Austria from the Bund, the annexation of Austrian Silesia and part of Bohemia, and the payment of the war expenses, I do not see how Austria could get worse terms after another battle. If this country is to be ruined by

Prussia, she may as well die as live under her dictation. I must now go and see Mensdorff. I have been occupied part of this morning in receiving the visits of poor people who are in dread of an invasion.

Vienna, July 19, 1866.—I can well understand all your feelings about this wretched war, and your anxiety, but I am sure you are better far away from the scenes enacting hereabouts. Yesterday Benedetti went to the Prussian headquarters, which Mensdorff told me are to be at his place, Nikolsburg ; and it is possible the last impressions from Paris and a knowledge of the Austrian terms of arrangement may arrest the progress of Prussia's victorious army. I, however, doubt it. At all events, every day is so much gained for Austria and lost for Prussia. The army of the latter is losing tremendously from sickness, and the further they advance from their reserves the worse it will be for them. Poor Grün's eldest son, who was badly wounded at the last great battle, and at the time close to Benedek with a map in his hand, is dead. But one hears of nothing else but deaths and misery on all sides.

Prince Teck has made a renewed application to the Emperor and the Archduke Albert, who have 'thanked' as they say in this country, and as a last resource, he has applied to the Minister of War, who I hope will confirm the refusal of the other two, and let him go away in peace, with the consciousness of having done all that could be expected of a brave and honourable man.

I dined yesterday with H.R.H. at Countess Barth's, and met there Count Stahrenberg and Madame de Löwenthal. It was an excellent dinner, but the heat was dreadful. There was a thunderstorm, and awful hailstones, which the boys called ' Preussische Kugel' (Prussian balls), but the water was so warm the air has by no means been improved by it. The Princess was to go to tea with an Archduchess, and drive to-day to Liesing. H.R.H. dines with me at six o'clock. She seems to fancy this place.

You ask me if I think it likely we shall follow the Emperor to Pesth ? I do not. The Empress is there, and the Government will follow after a last battle. The Emperor will go to the army if there is to be a fight—otherwise H.I.M. will remain here. The Prussians were said to be at Gänsendorff, and at Korneuburg (very near Vienna), but still the main army must be a long way off.

Plach, the great picture dealer, lent me a beautiful Gian Bellini yesterday, with a request that I would take care of it as long as I like. He is evidently afraid of plunderers, as everybody else is.

Vienna, July 20, 1866.—I have no good news to report as to the progress of negotiations, but I will hope they may succeed. The line of the Danube being defended extends from Linz to Presburg, and it is supposed there is some combination with the Italian advance now thought of at the Prussian headquarters. Nobody trusts Prince Napoleon's mission to Florence, or Benedetti's proceedings, both being as anti-Austrian in their principles as can be.

Princess Mary and Prince Teck dined with me yesterday. Chotek, Falbe, and Colonel Probyn were of the party. It was very pleasant, and the Princess was most amiable and amusing. Nobody can be less *gênant* than she is. She was to go and see the poor King of Hanover to-day, and I must do likewise. The weather has improved after a fearful thunderstorm, and I hope we are going to have it a little cooler.

Vienna, July 21, 1866.—There seems more hope of an armistice, and it would seem that the Prussians are beginning to feel they are less

strong than they were at the commencement of
the war.   If Austria can secure reasonable terms,
I trust she will accept them, and put an end to
this horrible devastation, but her army is recovering, and her position is so strong along the
Danube that I think she need not be in a great
hurry.   I hear that Benedek has brought his
army from Olmütz to Presburg, a point for
which the Prussians were making, in order, I
presume, to attempt the crossing at three different
points, and these points are fortified and prepared
for a serious resistance.   The game on this side
is much better than it was a week ago.   I saw
Baron Bourgoing last night, who had been to the
Prussian headquarters, and had seen the King.
He was full of his journey, and very amusing,
but said it was hard work, no rest, and no food.
He was completely done up.

I wrote my name down yesterday at the King
of Hanover's, who is living at Knesebeck's, and
am invited to dine with H.M. to-day to meet
Princess Mary.   The poor King went to see
Princess Schwarzenberg yesterday evening, and
old General Reischak is named to attend on
H.M., which must be a sorrowful occupation.
The King has determined not to become the
vassal of the King of Prussia, and if he cannot

get fair terms he will live abroad. He is personally rich, and I can understand a proud man refusing the degraded position Prussia is preparing for him.

Vienna, July 22, 1866.—Yesterday I dined with the King of Hanover. There was nobody but his son and his own people, and in the middle of dinner who should call to pay a visit but the Crown Prince of Saxony. So the King and his son went out, and stayed away half an hour. The poor King is fond of talking, and being blind has simply no knowledge of time. He looks well, and was most kind and gracious— asked most tenderly after you and all your family, and sent special kind messages to your brother Augustus.

After dinner H.M. gave me the whole account of his short campaign, and really it is touching to think of the bravery and attachment of his little army, which appears to have fought desperately at Langensalza, notwithstanding the Prussian needle-guns.

Karolyi, Count Degenfeldt (the General and former Minister of War), and Baron Brenner went off to-day to the Prussian headquarters, which are always at Nikolsburg, to treat for preliminaries of peace. I hope these negotiations will succeed, for these people are so unlucky in war that I fear another disaster if it should again come to blows. What they ought to do would be to bring Admiral Tegethoff to the Danube, and see what he could do with his ram ! What a capital fight he has made at Lissa, and I am delighted he has prevented the Italians taking that place. It would have been a serious blow to the maritime frontier of this unfortunate country.

Vienna, July 23, 1866.—Well, I suppose we shall have peace, and that it will be bought at a heavy price, but humiliating as it will be, it was to be seen that Austria could not stand against the despoiling alliance of Prussia and Italy, and I only regret all the more that no arrangement was made last year as to the cession of Venetia, when it could have been effected with advantage.

Before this reaches you the telegraph will probably report what comes of the negotiations, and I need say no more but that I hear the King of Prussia is by no means disposed to make easy terms, and as to the Germans they are so many broken reeds, and will of course carefully avoid doing anything to make their own position worse than it is vis-à-vis of the ruling Power.

The Austrians were having a successful engagement yesterday near Presburg, and had every chance of success, and of completing it by the approach of Colonel Thun's corps d'armée, when intelligence was communicated of the armistice, and they were obliged to stop hostilities.

Vienna, July 26, 1866.—I have no news except a melancholy telegram from Malet, who has returned with the remnants of the Diet to Augsburg, asking me to protest against Manteuffel's threat of giving up Frankfort to pillage and plunder if the town hesitates further to pay the twenty-five million florins of contribution to Prussia. It is a most preposterous proceeding on the part of a general when a town has offered no resistance, and is no doubt done to spite a city which has always had Austrian proclivities.

Vienna, July 27, 1866.—The preliminaries are agreed to, and I hope that Austria will be able to pay the indemnities without delay, so as to put an end to the Prussian occupation. We have martial law declared at Vienna, which is rather a good thing, as it will keep people in order and not affect the quiet and well-disposed. There are loads of intriguing foreigners and spies about who can be easily disposed of by this measure, like our Fenians, and the press will not be allowed to write exciting articles against the Government, which, under present circumstances, cannot act differently to what they have been doing.

As to the poor wounded Austrians, I believe that up to the present time the funds are adequate, for personal charity has been unbounded. The poor soldiers and officers who are really deserving of pity are those left near the field of action, too badly wounded to be moved to the capital. I shan't be surprised if there is more fighting to-day, for the armistice expired at noon, and yesterday no order for its renewal could be issued from here on the Prussian side. I see there are subscriptions being raised at Liverpool, and I will do my best with the money sent me for the relief of the poor soldiers, but I do not wish you to state openly your readiness to receive subscriptions, because we are neutral, and can leave this task to the ladies of England.

Last night I was at a tea at Countess Barth's, and old Madame Hetzingen, the actress, and a very clever one too, was there and declaimed. Princess Mary sang, and altogether it was pleasant and amusing, but the rooms were small and the heat excessive. Prince Teck was nearly stifled.

I hope you will now cease to be so very anxious about the state of things here, and about me in particular. The war may be considered over, and now there will only be some diplomatic work to attend to, and ultimately a Congress, where, I cannot tell, but I hope Paris, though there is a talk of its being at some German town. What a nice little paragraph about the Austrian reverses and Father Klinkowström's opinions! I hear the priests here have been talking a great deal in their pulpits, but not so much in Klinkowström's sense as in attributing the misfortune of this country to the machinations of the devil, who has not done yet with the people in consequence of their irreligious tendencies and more liberal views and heresies.

Vienna, July 29, 1866.—Matters seem inclined to fall rapidly back into peace, but I should think the Italians are still likely to give trouble, for they have been advancing into the Tyrol, and if they do not choose to retire I apprehend they will have to be forced out. Prussia having got everything her own way in Germany will probably not care much about Italy, as it seems the order of the day not to stick to treaties when they happen to be inconvenient. I saw Mensdorff yesterday, but heard nothing more of interest as to the further progress of the negotiations.

Russell, of the 'Times,' Brackenbury, and some others dined with me. Russell had just returned from Presburg, and there is no doubt the Prussians would have got into that town if the armistice had not prevented them. The Austrians, to the number of about 90,000 men, in excellent trim, have taken up their position on the other side of the river, in connection with the projected defence of the Danube, and I think that if the war had continued the Austrians would have had a fair chance, if properly commanded. The army is now quite fresh again, and the Prussians have grown less so, and are fast dwindling down from cholera and other diseases.

To make things more comfortable in Bohemia the masses of dead have been carelessly buried, and putrid fevers are breaking out, so that the Prussians will no doubt be glad to get away as soon as possible.

Vienna, August 2, 1866.—I dined with Princess Mary yesterday at Munsch's Hotel. We had Countess Barth, Madame Löwenstein, Lothair Metternich, and Aldenburg. Her Royal Highness went afterwards to the ballet, and I betook myself to the Motleys, where I had been invited to dine, and found the guests in the garden at croquet, wrapped up in winter garments. Motley is full of the changes in Germany ; thinks a good era has come over this nationality, and that a strong increase in the democratic principle will assuredly result from Bismarck's policy. I think so too : and who knows but we may yet see him at the head of the movement party ? The German diplomatists have some cause to apprehend revolution about everything, and they talk of a German Republic. I think Bismarck will, however, be able to keep them in hand for awhile.

There is a prolonged truce with Italy for another week, and we shall see how the peace negotiations are likely to proceed in that direction. In the meantime a considerable reinforcement of troops has been ordered to the south ; 25,000 are gone, and 80,000 more are under orders, for the Italians have not heeded the truce, and are perpetually advancing, just as the Prussians have been doing against the Bavarians and others, regardless of orders from the superior authority. In fact it has been a reign of Pretorian Guards. There is no post direct to Poland from here, but letters are forwarded through Hungary. If Vienna had been taken by the Prussians communications would probably have been interrupted, but I should think the post to Bohemia will soon be re-established.

Vienna, August 5, 1866.—I have not much to tell you, for my life is a very monotonous and solitary one, as you may imagine, and I am getting very weary of it, and only wish the peace negotiations were progressing satisfactorily. Those with Prussia will not begin before Wednesday. Then I do not see much chance of an armistice with Italy, because the Italians want to keep what they have taken in the Tyrol, and Austria will not agree to this, so that if Italy does not choose to *render* what she has taken we may have more fighting. Four corps d'armée are moving south again, which does not look like giving way, at all events.

I found Mensdorff very low and ill yesterday, and he told me he required repose on account of his health, so I suppose he will not remain long after peace is made. Who is to succeed him I cannot guess, and I only hope the Emperor will find as honest a man as he is to put in his place. He at all events is not to blame for the war and its disastrous consequences, for he was always opposed to it, but I suppose it was fate, and not to be avoided, and the great question now arises, what is to be the future of Austria ?

Note.—Count Alexander Mensdorff was first cousin to the Queen and Prince Albert, and a most charming, amiable, and distinguished man. He died at Prague on the 14th of February, 1871, aged 58. He was born at Coburg, and married Princess Dietrichstein.

Yesterday I was sitting quietly in my room about six o'clock when the Princess Mary sent to invite me to her box at the Opera. I went there at eight, for I never dine till seven when I am alone, and I often eat my meals in solitude when you are away. After the Opera I went to the Casino, and met Szeczen, who has just come from Nachod in Bohemia, where he had been about his poor brother-in-law, Wimpffen, who was wounded and has since died. He says he found the country less devastated than he had expected, barring the total absence of all four-footed animals. The destruction to the harvest was partial, but no animals were to be seen. The peasantry were in the highest state of exasperation, and he was told by Prussian officers to whom he had applied for information as to his journey that they advised him not to go without an escort. It seems that the Prussians dare not move from their military stations, and that a guerilla warfare is being carried on. What a state of misery has been brought on that unfortunate country. There is nothing to eat, and a spirit of revenge is lurking which it will not be easy to pacify.

Vienna, August 7, 1866.—The news is sad, for I see no chance of preventing fresh hostilities in Italy. The Italians will not content themselves with Venetia, and are determined to fight for that part of the Tyrol which they have taken possession of, and Austria is equally determined not to give it up to them. The Archduke Albert goes to the army to-morrow to direct the future operations, and much blood will probably be shed by another needless war.

Vienna, August 17, 1866.—I was at Ebergrassing [1] yesterday, and never saw the garden look so nice as it did, or the flowers so abundant. There has been such a quantity of rain, and the grass was really green and beautiful. A lot of soldiers arrived there about 4 P.M., to remain some weeks : 400 men and the usual amount of officers. The greater part of the latter are quartered at the house. It was a Hungarian regiment, and I never saw nicer-looking fellows, or a more quiet,

---

[1] Baron Schloissing's place near Vienna, where Lord Bloomfield often went to shoot.

respectable, well-conducted lot. A number of poor wounded men are about the place, for every proprietor has provided for the care of these unfortunates, and it must be a great comfort to them to be able to move about in good fresh air away from the over-crowded hospitals, and the fevers and illnesses that are now spreading in all directions. By-the-bye, the Prussians have lost a fearful quantity of people latterly in Bohemia and Moravia, and of course will leave a pestilence behind them in addition to the devastation of every village and residence they have occupied.

Vienna, August 19, 1866.—How very sad about the poor Hanoverian country! Prussia appears to have annexed it simply, and the money sent by the King to England is in Hanoverian notes, so the payment will be stopped, and I know not what the unfortunate King and Royal Family will have to live upon. He and the Crown Prince, notwithstanding all, are wonderfully plucky. The King seems to hope against hope, and place his trust in God. Poor man! I pity him more than the others who have been simply annexed, for he was loved in his country, and governed it well and justly.

Vienna, August 23, 1866.—We made a bag

of 120 head at Ebergrassing yesterday, amongst them a bustard which had evidently strayed away. Such a magnificent bird, and such grand plumage, and I was reported to have been the fortunate gun that shot him. Schloissing fired, but he was so excited at this unexpected visitor that he missed the creature, strange to say, for it was nearly as big as an Irish cabin.

There have been some serious hitches in the treaty negotiations, but I hope that next week a compromise as to the charges to be borne by Venetia will be settled. Last night I heard that Vienna is likely to be the seat of the negotiations with the Italian Government. I wish they could take place anywhere else as far as I am personally concerned, and Paris or Geneva would be better for me. I suppose, however, the first thing will be to settle preliminaries of peace, and then the general negotiations will begin. General Menabrea, the Italian Plenipotentiary, is already at Paris waiting for orders and a hint to come here, so that if even the preliminary negotiations take place here I can hardly think they would be very long ones.

I see the 'Times' is now writing articles about the defenceless state of England. I am glad of this, and I hope our people will be roused in time ;

but there is such a strong free-trade element of peace in the Government and country, I dare say these articles will not be responded to as they deserve to be. However, with the example of Austria's late inefficiency before us, we might take a hint and put our walls in order, and prepare for a showery day, or we shall be at the mercy of the first invader, which God forbid !

Vienna, August 24, 1866.—The night is lovely—a full moon, brilliant beyond anything, and really an appearance of fine weather. I have been at the Volksgarten, where there was a grand illumination which had been prepared for the Emperor's birthday on the 15th, and postponed on account of the weather.

I sat a long time with Henri Zichy, who was just come up from Pesth. He seems in great force, and hopes there will be a fine vintage, and that something good will come out of the late disasters for Hungary, but at present all is in the dark. I am happy to say the Convention ceding Venetia to France was signed to-day, so that is another thing out of hand ; but it is important, as the negotiations with Italy could not commence until this was done.

So Julian Fane is engaged to Lady Aline Cowper. Do you know her ?

Vienna, September 23, 1866.—I am still more in hopes than I was yesterday that I shall be able to start on the 29th, so pray send any letters to Paris.

After dinner Aldenburg and I started for Liesing; of course we arrived too punctually, for the King of Hanover did not come for an hour, and then the actors delayed for some time because the cord of the curtain got out of order and had to be put to rights, but the performance was really very good indeed. Princess Mary acted admirably, and was very dignified. The society was extremely select. The King and Crown Prince of Hanover, and Princess Frederica who has just arrived, and is such a fine-looking, handsome creature ; she and her lady dressed in mourning, as is the fashion now with all the Hanoverians ; the Crown Prince of Saxony and some Saxon officers, and a few ladies. After the play there was some tea and cold meat, and I got home a little before twelve. To-day the Princess Mary and Prince Teck came to church and to luncheon.

Vienna, September 17, 1866.—The news is better for Saxony. The army will be allowed to remain in the kingdom and not be embodied at once in that of Prussia. The King will therefore return to Dresden. The Elector of Hesse and the Duke of Nassau have made peace with Prussia and saved their private property. The poor King of Hanover is now the only one who won't give in, though I fear it is useless to attempt to resist the force which is brought against him. I saw His Majesty last night at Princess Mary's. He is looking much better, and enjoys the villa at Hietzing as he is able to be much out in the open air.

Vienna, September 24, 1866.—The affairs of Saxony are settled, but things have gone back again; however, I hope the Diplomatic Body will continue yet at Dresden. The King of Hanover protests against the annexation of his country, but what is a protest against overwhelming force and the determination of a great Power in 1866, when treaties cease to avail anything, or to be considered any protection for the weak?

[Lord Bloomfield left Vienna on leave soon after this and joined me in Ireland, to my intense relief and joy.]

CHAPTER XVIII.

Dinner at the Swedish Minister's—Anecdotes—I go to Kissingen—
    Coronation of the Emperor at Pesth—Letters from Lord Bloom-
    field—Death of the Emperor Maximilian in Mexico—The
    Emperor is invested with the Garter—The Sultan visits Vienna
    —We go to Italy—Curious conversation with Count Chrepto-
    wich—Lord Bloomfield has an audience with the Pope, Pius IX.
    —Mr. Story—Miss Hosmer.

Vienna, April 25, 1867.—We dined with
the Swedish Minister, Mr. Due, and I had an
interesting conversation with Heyder Effendi,
the Turkish Ambassador. He said he wished
to ask me a question—whether I believed in the
eternity of Paradise? I answered, certainly.
' But,' he observed, ' you believe, do you not, that
God is omnipotent and immortal, and that he
has created all things in heaven and in earth,
therefore he created Paradise, and what he
creates he is likewise able to destroy. Is it not
so?' I answered in the affirmative, but added,
'I know not what the Mahometan idea of
Paradise is, but the Christian notion is that the
presence of God will constitute Paradise hereafter,

therefore, where God is, there is Paradise, and consequently it must be eternal like Himself.' The Turk agreed, and said that was the right view to take of the question, but he had not found it was one generally adopted by Christians.

He then told me the following legend, which I think pretty. A poor shepherd was one day feeding his flock in the wilderness, when he met Moses. They entered into conversation, and spoke about God. The poor shepherd said he loved him, and wished he would come and dwell with him ; that he wished to serve him, and would wash for him, cook for him, and dress his hair! But Moses indignantly reproved the poor man for his ignorance, and told him that God was in heaven, omnipotent, that he gives us all things, but needs not our poor services in return ; and the poor man was so disheartened and discouraged that he went away weeping. Then God had pity on him, and looked down in mercy upon him, and sent the archangel Gabriel to Moses to tell him he had done wrong ; that if *he* had spoken like the shepherd it would have been profane in him because he knew better, but that God wished to draw others to himself, not to drive them away from him, and therefore our business is to make religion attractive to our fellow creatures, and teach them to love and serve God to the very best of their ability and knowledge, never to discourage and dishearten those who are earnestly seeking the way of salvation.

Vienna.—Last night I was talking about ghost stories at Princess Schönburg's, when Baron Stockhausen, our Hanoverian colleague, laughed me to scorn, upon which the Princess rebuked him and said he was aware that her mother, Princess Schwarzenberg, perished at Paris in the great fire which took-place at the Austrian Embassy. She had left her youngest children here at Vienna. The Cardinal being then a baby of six months old was in his cradle one night, when suddenly his nurse, an old and very respectable, but by no means either a clever or imaginative woman, fell down on her knees and exclaimed, ' Jesu, Maria, Joseph ! there is the figure of the Princess standing over the baby's cradle.' Several nurserymaids who were in the room heard the exclamation, though they saw nothing, but to her dying day the nurse affirmed the truth of the vision, and there being then no telegraphs, it was not for many days after that the news of the Princess Schwarzenberg's untimely fate reached Vienna.

1867.—The Emperor of Austria's coronation as King of Hungary took place at Pesth in the month of June, but I did not attend it as, owing to a curious old precedent, the ladies of the Corps Diplomatique were not officially invited with their husbands, and I felt I could not well appear at Pesth as a private individual whilst Lord Bloomfield was present as the Queen's representative.

I had been ordered to Kissingen, and accordingly went there in the beginning of June, but as, owing to a severe cold, I was forced to interrupt my cure, I took the opportunity of paying a long promised visit to an old friend of mine in the Grand Duchy of Hesse. My friend came to meet me, and then we drove some distance along a good chaussée, but suddenly turned into a field, and then to my extreme astonishment, not to say alarm, we drove into a river which had been considerably swollen by some heavy rains. The water was so deep it came into the carriage, and the horses began to swim, but my friend only laughed and assured me there was no danger, so I complacently tucked my legs up and sat still. In course of time we got safe to the opposite bank, and then drove up a very rough road to the house, which was perched at the top of a conical hill, and looked like the house a child draws when it first attempts to delineate an object, viz., a door in the middle with a window on each side, and three windows above, surmounted by a high roof and a stack of chimneys. There was no attempt at ornament of any sort or kind, and no flower garden, but at the back of the house there was an avenue of fine old lime trees, which being in flower were deliciously sweet. The house looked as if it had not been inhabited for at least a hundred years. The walls of my room were painted in the Pompeian style, and furnished with Japanese wicker chairs.

There were no books or resources of any kind, for the Germans have a notion that when they go to the country comforts are superfluous, and certainly their mode of living is simple, unostentatious, and primitive to the last degree. But my hostess was very amiable, and I met a friend of hers who was divorced from her husband because she was extravagant, but they continued good friends, and I was assured that though each was at perfect liberty to marry whom they pleased, if the lady would only amend her ways and spend less, her spouse was quite willing to re-marry her. They had eight children, and I believe there was really nothing against the lady except that she had a madness for spending more money than she had, and could not keep out of debt.

I amused myself with trying to teach a clever grey parrot to talk, but never succeeded. Six weeks after my departure my friend was suddenly surprised at hearing me call her! This was the parrot, who suddenly imitated my voice exactly, to my friend's great surprise. Her husband had introduced a quantity of snakes from Schlangenbad, which considerably disturbed my equanimity during my long solitary walks.

Extracts of Letters from Lord Bloomfield.

Vienna, June 1, 1867.—The Emperor went to Pesth last night. The weather is warm, but not uncomfortably so, yet I think we shall have it hot enough at Pesth.

Beust is full of hope that the addresses will be satisfactory to the Government, and that the great question of the 'Ausgleich' with Hungary will meet with no serious difficulty. Mensdorff has done much to soften down the asperities which the party in opposition (reactionaries) wished to introduce into the address of the Lords.

I went to see Beust yesterday, and, poor man, he seemed completely done! He has had a hard job in hand, but he has at all events the satisfaction of feeling for the present that all is going on smoothly enough.

The accounts of the Archduchess Mathilde[1] are as good as could be expected under the sad circumstances. There seems no immediate cause for anxiety, but all say that after such severe burning, people rarely recover. She has been moved to Hetzendorff (a small Imperial palace, not far from Schönbrunn) to-day, and got there in an hour and a half, having been carried in a chaise à porteur.

I shall send my horses, carriages, and servants to Pesth by the Danube on Tuesday morning, and go there myself on Wednesday. The public entry takes place on Thursday, which will be a fine sight, and no function for us diplomatists, which will be so much the more agreeable. On Friday the reception will not be fatiguing, but on Saturday the work will be severe.

I am told that I shall want two hundred visiting cards.

---

[1] The young Archduchess Mathilde was the beautiful daughter of the Archduke Albert, and a most charming young Princess. Her dress caught fire from, it was supposed, a lucifer match, and she was so badly burnt she died the day before the coronation, to the inexpressible grief of the Imperial family.

What a sad thing for the Emperor to have his brother (Maximilian, Emperor of Mexico) in captivity—perhaps worse—and his cousin lying dangerously ill at this moment. Nothing, however, is to put off the coronation, but it takes place under sad auspices.

Vienna, June 2, 1867.—I tried to see the Duchess de Gramont yesterday, but I was not admitted. She and I will probably go to Pesth together to-morrow, but I mean to take the precaution of ordering a compartment, for fear of accidents, as the train will probably be tremendously crowded. Dr. Russell is coming to Pesth, accredited by the 'Times' for the occasion, so you will have a brilliant account of the whole proceedings there. It is said there may yet be some postponement of the coronation, as the formal abdication of Kaiser Ferdinand (the Emperor's predecessor) and the renunciation of the claims of his father, the Archduke Franz Carl, to the throne of Hungary have yet to be obtained. It appears these formalities have only just been thought of, but I should not think the necessary documents require much time to prepare. A dispensation from the Pope has been got to allow the ceremony to be performed on the great fast of the eve of Whit-Sunday.

I believe it is nearly settled that the Emperor will go to Paris in July, and I hear that the Queen gives up Buckingham Palace to the Sultan. I only hope that this travelling to and fro of all these Sovereigns will end in peaceful dispositions towards each other. That is the only right view to take of the present state of things.

It appears that unhappy Maximilian is really a prisoner, and only capitulated because resistance was no longer possible. No details are known, nor anything as to his chances, but it is said Juarez has treated two hundred other prisoners taken at Puebla well, so we must hope.

There are to be no Court balls at Pesth, nor anything but great dinners, and the necessary formalities of the coronation, and not much in private society, so I hope to be there only a week, and a hot and fatiguing one it will probably be.

Vienna, June 5, 1867.—I dined yesterday with Rothschild. The heat was tremendous, as he chose to light candles at half-past five. I met the Motleys and Ayllons. After dinner we retired to the north side of the house, which was cool and pleasant, where Wodehouse and the young ladies sang.

I hear a bad account of the poor Archduchess

Mathilde this morning; her appetite is failing, and she is very ill. Beust is said to have made an admirable speech yesterday in the House of Commons; to-day he is at work in the Lords, and altogether I apprehend he is sure of a good majority in both Houses. He is a powerful orator, and that tells.

Pesth, June 6, 1867.—We made a good and prosperous journey yesterday. The day was cool, the train not overcrowded, but there was an awful crowd at the station here; it was almost impossible to get through it. And you would certainly not have liked the discomfort and crush, for the Hungarians ignore the existence of police, and therefore I suppose do not understand the value of that establishment on these occasions.

My carriages were at the station, and we drove to the Hotel, the ' Königin von England,' where I found a nice apartment prepared for me, but the whole town is so crowded it is impossible to lodge my servants and the Secretaries', who have come each supplied with a valet. The night was excessively hot, the rooms clean and comfortable enough, but at daylight there was hammering going on at the tribunes erecting in front of this hotel. The town does present a most festive appearance, but I have not yet been out, as I have had an invasion of visitors, and English are pouring in expecting to see the sights and get places in the Churches.

To-night there is an evening party at George Karolyi's. We shall dine early, and take a drive in the Prater afterwards. In the meantime I have started Bonar and Sartoris in uniform to pay visits to Prince Hohenlohe, and compliment Count Andrassy as the Prime Minister.

Conceive that the ceremony of the coronation will commence so early! We shall have to be dressed in full uniform before six A.M. How long we shall be out and moving that day I cannot guess, but it will be a tiring business, and alas! the report to-day is that the poor Archduchess is dying, and received extreme unction yesterday.

Lord Lorne and Mr. Leeson are here. I have sent all the applicants for places to see the sights to Bela Széchenyi.

The poor Archduchess died at six this morning. How sad!

Pesth, June 7, 1867.—The party at Count George Karolyi's was very handsome: the house lovely, but so hot. The garden was prettily illuminated, but not intended for walking in. It was curious to see all the men in their long braided coats (the national costume), just as funny as *we* must perhaps have looked among them. A niece of the Count's did the honours—a very handsome, amiable person, who has been a great deal at Paris.

His daughter, Countess Clarisse, is also a very pretty girl. The Countesses all collected in what they could have wished the ball-room, only unfortunately there was no music there. How we shall get through to-morrow I know not. The carriage at six A.M., and no chance of getting home before two P.M. I think you have had a great escape, for really the heat and noise are insufferable.

I hope we shall have a little rest, by way of an *entr'acte*, on board a steamer which is to bring us across from Buda to Pesth. The Emperor has to go through two Church functions on the other side of the river, and I believe one here. The life of this town is wonderful, and the smart Hungarian liveries and equipages very striking. Such splendid fellows as there were last night at Karolyi's, such hussars in scarlet pantaloons!

I am glad you have discovered some roses and flowers at Kissingen, and I have no doubt your room is very different from mine, where there is an air of *graillon* which is not particularly odoriferous, and I am obliged to keep the windows closed on account of the sun and the dust.

I must conclude in haste, as I have been over to Buda to see the procession of the crown jewels, and only returned in time to dress for dinner.

Pesth, June 8, 1867, 3 P.M.—Well, everything has gone off admirably from beginning to end. The morning was clear, still, and cool. About nine o'clock it became clouded and threatening, but the advantage we derived from this was that we were not scorched alive. At six we left the hotel, and at seven the *cortège* of the King and Queen left the Burg for the Cathedral. The costumes were wonderful, strange, and altogether surpassed my expectations. We were nearly two hours in the Church, and had plenty of room. The ladies were opposite to us, and were splendidly attired. The Countess Nako looked very handsome. Lady Ashburton is with her, and I only hope saw everything pretty well.

The Primate Archbishop of Gran presided at the dinner at the Palace, and Andrassy, as representative of the Palatine, dined before the public, served by the great dignitaries of the Court. I hear it was a most curious sight, and I am grieved you have not seen it all, but it was very tiring indeed, and you would have been completely knocked up. How happy their Majesties must be that all has gone off so well. They return to Vienna on Thursday. To-morrow I have an audience to deliver the Queen's letters of congratulation.

I send you the bill of fare of yesterday. A magnificent meagre dinner, which does not suit me, so *I* fasted, as others ought to have done. The banquet was perfectly magnificent. The Empress made very tender inquiries about you, and spoke very much about the poor Archduchess Mathilde.

Vienna, June 8, 1867.—I hear that the Queen of the Belgians and the Comte de Flandres are to pass through Vienna to-day on their way to Miramar. They think it right the poor Empress Charlotte should know what has happened to her husband, but I am told it would not be safe to tell her, but remove her to Belgium, which is now her natural home.

Pesth, June 9, 1867.—It was fortunate the coronation finished at the time it did, for it came on to blow so desperately later in the day that all out-door amusements would have been simply impossible. At night there was heavy rain, and it has been clouded over all the morning, but the air feels deliciously fresh, and one can enjoy leaving the windows open without having a burning sun and clouds of dust to overwhelm one. I have just had my audience of the Emperor King, and was most pleased to see him so well. He told me he had no headache yesterday, which he expected to have, and altogether he seemed as well as could be expected under the circumstances.

To-night there are illuminations, and at three o'clock we are invited to see the great banquet of the town of Pesth. I am glad I am not to take part in it, for it will last many hours, and I believe the Emperor proposes a toast, and no doubt plenty of wine will be consumed on the occasion. 5 P.M.—This moment come back from the grand banquet, one thousand and eight guests in full dress. Their Majesties marched round and between the tables, and then came opposite the Primate, who made a speech in, to me, an unknown tongue. Such vociferations in and out of the hall! The Emperor and Empress spoke to us as they passed. The 'Eljens' were deafening, and are still ringing in my ears.

The afternoon is very fine again. I told the Empress, who seems wonderfully fresh and well, that she had 'Queen's weather for the coronation.'

Pesth, June 10, 1867, 2 P.M.—I have been since ten o'clock A.M. at the Burg *en frac*, to see the arrival of the deputations from the two Houses of Parliament, and other representatives of the kingdom, and the offerings of the cities of Pesth and Buda ; also the two magnificent silver cans containing the one hundred thousand ducats, voted as a present to their Majesties by the Counties. The gold coins looked very pretty indeed, fresh from the Mint, and produced from the mines of this country. Then I went to see the crown and jewels at the Church of Buda, and am just returned pretty well tired out. I have a great dinner at Andrassy's, and am asked to an evening party, but shall excuse myself, as I must try and write some despatches, which will go by the messenger to-morrow.

Pesth, June 11, 1867.—I had a hard day and a hard night of it, for the dinner at Count Andrassy's, though a small party only, lasted some time, and then I had to work for the messenger, and felt I must go to a great party where all the world assembled. The house was handsome and well arranged, but the crowd was considerable and the heat excessive. I came home before twelve, and then had to write till past two.

I was glad to have an opportunity last night of speaking to Count Andrassy. He and his wife are a very handsome couple, and they have a charming official residence at Buda close to the Palace, with a splendid view of Pesth and the river up and down. I made the acquaintance of your old friend Count Alexander Erdödy, who presented himself to me in the Church at the coronation, and, as you may imagine, I was well pleased to meet him.

Pesth, June 12, 1867.—To-morrow morning I hope to leave for Vienna. I have had an interesting morning, and assisted at the sittings of the two Houses, Magnates and Deputies. There was nothing of importance going on, but the forms of the House are worth seeing, and these are certainly a parliamentary people. I made the acquaintance of Déak (the great Hungarian patriot) in the lobby, and we exchanged a hearty shake of the hand. These are proud doings of his, and one sees what can be obtained by the steady and loyal resistance of a whole nation. The Hungarians are a strange mixture of constitutionalism and absolutism, but there is much good in the people, and we soon found this out in the awful crowds during the illuminations on Sunday night, when all passed with the greatest good humour. A policeman was hardly to be seen, and none was required, but we had hard work to keep our legs, and were nearly carried off them several times.

Last evening we had a magnificent party at Count George Festetics'. He has a beautiful house, handsomer much than the one at Vienna, built somewhat on the same model with improvements. It is hardly completed, but must be a charming habitation, and is almost out of town. To-day I dine there, and am very glad to think that to-morrow I shall return to the quiet of the Schenken Strasse, and have a little solitude after the tremendous fuss of these last days. I saw Count Nako at the House of Magnates.

The telegraph reports that the Emperors of Austria, Russia, and the Sultan are to receive the Garter. If so we shall have a special mission to Vienna, and all the paraphernalia of the Order to accompany it.

I have made Lady Ashburton's acquaintance, who seems clever and amiable. You know the people here are very English, and to-day when I arrived and was going upstairs to the palace the people found out who I was, and gave a tremendous 'Eljen.' I thought, in the innocence of my heart, it was some national celebrity, and turned round to see who was coming, when there came another, and I found I was the object of their vociferations. So then I made a grateful bow, and there was another cheer. They are funny people, and I wish you could have been here, but I am sure you would have knocked up after the first day, particularly as all the functions begin at such a very early hour. The weather on the whole has been most propitious ; rain would have done a deal of harm.

[As my husband, having written very hurriedly during his visit to Pesth, omitted to record one important scene in the coronation function, I venture to add this note, with the account published at the time from 'Our Special Correspondent.']

From the Special Correspondent of the 'Times.'

Pesth, June 10, 1867.—As I said yesterday the Diplomatic Corps mustered strongly, and some of their uniforms shone out conspicuous amidst the gay throng. On landing on the Pesth side of the Danube, we had to walk about 150 yards to reach the entrance by which we could gain admission to the grand tribune erected in the large square for the Queen of Hungary, her Court, and the Diplomatic Corps. No sooner does the Queen arrive than it is a signal for a long and protracted burst of cheering, which causes the hills on each side of the majestic river to re-echo with the sound. When she has taken her seat the procession is seen crossing the bridge, headed by a detachment of the Lichtenstein Hussars, a Hungarian regiment, and the only one which takes part in the proceedings. Then follow a large body of Hungarian peasants, all mounted and dressed alike in brown tunics, with pelisses slung over their shoulders, and wearing the inevitable Hungarian boots. These are succeeded by the standard-bearers of the different Counties, all on horseback, and wearing the gayest dresses that the world has probably ever seen. Then came the magnates of the land, each on a steed caparisoned as in the times of Louis Quinze, and attended by a couple of running footmen ; to these succeed the bishops, all mounted also. Then come a stream of general officers and the Ministers, and succeeding them is a careworn, handsome face, with hair prematurely grey, which, whenever it appears, is greeted with wild and enthusiastic ‘Eljens.’

This is the man whom Hungary delights to honour, for it is to the good counsels of this man that this happy day in the annals of Austria and of Hungary is attributable; this is the man who has had the far-sightedness to see that Austria and Hungary, at variance and disunited, are on the verge of ruin, but that, when they shake hands and join in a common bond of friendship and brotherhood, they secure to each and both a permanent and a happy future, which foreign nations will do well to leave alone; this is the great Minister De Beust himself; but hardly has he passed when the cheering is again taken up, and its heartiness and continuance show that the King is approaching. Preceded by the great officers of state, with Count Edmond Zichy in front who holds the sword of state in front of his Sovereign, comes Francis Joseph, with the crown of Hungary on his head, and the ancient coronation robe falling over his shoulders, and seated on a magnificent white charger, caparisoned in cloth of gold, which he manages with a grace and dexterity worthy of so distinguished a horseman. The King rides into the square amidst an ovation which he cannot but feel he has a right to expect, and as he passes the tribune where his lovely consort is watching the scene, like a preux chevalier he bows his head and salutes her. The procession is closed by another detachment of the Lichtenstein Hussars, and so well are matters arranged that, as the tail of the procession disappears on one side of the square, its head appears winding itself in again on the other side. As they pass along the different nobles are recognised, and the hearty cheers which greet the Sczecheynis, the Erdödys, and the Karolyis show the veneration which their fellow-countrymen entertain for them. Then comes the most interesting part of the day. As the procession emerges from the side streets and files into the square, in the centre of which stands the coronation mound, all are drawn up in line, with the horses' heads facing inwards, and when the square is thus completely filled, a more magnificent *coup d'œil* could not be effected, for just then the sun shone out in all its glory, and lighting up the variegated dresses and plumes, the armour and jewels of the hundreds there assembled, it produced a dazzling effect upon the eyes, and an impression which cannot easily be effaced. Then there was a slight pause, and then a reverberation as of thunder. It is the roll of cheering that greets Francis Joseph as, emerging from the procession and leaving all his attendants behind, he puts spurs to his horse and gallops on to the coronation-hill.   Here he pauses for a moment while he reins in his steed.   And now we have the spectacle before us which we have all come so far to see.   The King of Hungary himself, in all his majesty, is in the centre of his subjects.   He pauses for a moment, and then draws his sword—that ancient sword which the venerable Archbishop had placed in his hands in the great Cathedral—and with a clear, distinct motion, he cuts towards the east, then wheeling his horse sharply round, he cuts towards the west, then towards the south, then, again wheeling, he cuts towards the north.   There is another pause, the sound of the cannon's roar announces that the ancient kingdom of Hungary has now a free constitution, and an acknowledged lawful king, and Francis Joseph again wheels round and gallops down the hill, and as soon as he reaches his attendants he sheaths the sword, which we may trust he will never be called upon to draw again, and the coronation scene is over.

Vienna, June 13, 1867.—Here I am again, and I have no wish to see any more coronations; they are curious sights, but very fatiguing, and the idea of a little quiet after all the bustle of the last week is very pleasant.   We had a handsome dinner yesterday at Count George Festetics', and a fine party at Count Andrassy's. The town was again illuminated, notwithstanding the Emperor's desire to be allowed to depart quietly on account of the mourning in the Imperial family, but crowds rushed to see their crowned King again. We met His Majesty and the Empress Queen driving down the hill from the palace at 10 P.M. as we were driving up to Count Andrassy's. Their Majesties started at 10.30 for Vienna, and had a pleasanter journey than I had to-day in the hot sun and dust.

The terrible news of the death of the poor Emperor Maximilian will have reached you before this letter arrives. Some people try to think it may not be true, but alas! one can hardly believe a telegram would have been sent across the Atlantic by an Austrian Minister if there was any doubt as to the fate of this unfortunate Prince. The news arrived here yesterday from New York and Washington that he had been shot on the morning of the 19th ult. at Mexico, and that the other foreigners would be at liberty to return home. The reason which may have impelled the Republican Government to order this execution may be explained by their desire to prevent Maximilian coming to Europe and establishing himself as a Pretender, and thus becoming a centre of intrigue against the *de facto* Government in Mexico. The Emperor and Empress will have learnt the dreadful news at Munich, where they were yesterday afternoon on their way from attending the funeral of the Prince of Taxis. Trauttmannsdorff was telegraphed to from here to communicate on the subject with the Emperor. What a sad *dénouement!*

Last evening I went to the Motleys, as the last chance of seeing them before their departure. Mr. and Mrs. Motley seem to deplore leaving Vienna. They both grieve at it, and are dreaming of nothing but coming back.

Vienna, June 26, 1867.—After dinner yesterday we adjourned to the Volksgarten, and enjoyed Strauss and the cool of the evening very much. It is the regular rendezvous of all the men in town now, for ladies there are none, and the only place where one sees a human being to speak to. Beust never fails, and I really do not comprehend how he finds time for everything. He is a most remarkable character, and I suppose his light-heartedness and confidence in himself is what carries him through all his troubles and difficulties. I have been discussing with Prince Constantin Hohenlohe the great question of the Emperor's dress when he will be invested with the Garter ; and Beust and I were arguing the subject last night, when he said that he had been telling the Emperor that after all there is no costume so neat as knee-breeches, and that he does not despair of bringing him round to the idea. I suppose His Majesty is practising civil clothes, for he would have to wear them at Paris, so the question of breeches will not be so outrageous a one to press on his consideration.

Vienna, June 29, 1867.—I hear that Lord Bath is appointed to be the Queen's Commissioner with the Garter. The Emperor and Empress are just gone from Ischl to Ratisbon to attend the funeral of poor Prince Taxis, who died the day before yesterday.

The messenger brought me a letter of adieu from Lord Cowley, who had received his letters of recall and was to deliver them the end of next week. I should think he must be delighted to have brought his embassy to a close, for really the last months of his residence at Paris must have been anything but suited to his taste, and certainly not advantageous to his pocket. I know nothing of Lord Lyons' departure from Constantinople, but should think he must be on his way to Paris.

Vienna, July 1, 1867.—Though you are in

such a secluded spot (I was then paying a visit in Ober Hesse), I dare say the sad intelligence of the Emperor Maximilian's terrible death will have reached you.

Vienna, July 6, 1867.—I received a telegram from the Queen yesterday, to convey her sympathy to the Emperor and the parents of Maximilian. It is a sad, sad business, and I see it has created an immense sensation in Paris.

Vienna, July 10, 1867.—Mallet (Sir Louis) paid me a long visit to-day, and brought two iron-masters and experts from England, who have come to assist in the Commissioners' inquiries. They have just returned from Gratz, where they have been doing some works under the management of Mr. Hall, which are admirable, and to judge from their reports, rails are being now manufactured in Styria at lower rates than we can ever deliver them at Hull.

Vienna, July 12, 1867.—I have received a letter from Lord Stanley, dated from Windsor Castle, where he was, I believe, with the Viceroy of Egypt. He was in a peck of troubles on the questions to be put to him about the poor Emperor Maximilian ; and well he may be, for between the feeling of horror at the murder, and the necessity which will exist in a short time to hold communication with whoever governs in Mexico, or abandon the British interests which will be at stake in that country, besides departing from our principle of acknowledging *de facto* Governments, he is in a mess altogether. I wish him well through it.

Vienna, July 13, 1867.—The Garter Mission leaves London on the 20th, and will be due here about the 23rd. The Sultan will arrive, I believe, about the same time. I am glad to see that he had fine weather for his entrance into London, and I hope that matters will please him in England.

[The Sultan was Abdul Aziz, who was afterwards cruelly murdered at Constantinople].

Vienna, July 24, 1867.—I saw Lord Bath yesterday evening, who is pleasant and intelligent, and he is now with the Emperor, who came to town from Ischl this morning. Lord Brownlow is a fine, tall, handsome fellow, Lord St. Asaph somewhat diminutive, Sir Henry Storks a good-looking English soldier, Colonel Fielding also. Corry, of the Foreign Office, acts as Secretary. We are to dine with Beust on Friday, and Saturday there is to be a great affair at Schönbrunn for the Austrians. On Sunday, I understand, the Corps Diplomatique are to be invited. and I suppose presented to the Grand Turk.

The Emperor is going to send the Order of St. Stephen to the Prince of Wales.

Vienna, July 26, 1867.—The Garter ceremonies went off well and in all due form. The Embassy were only admitted as spectators, and had no part to perform except that Garter-King-at-Arms proposed that Bonar should carry something in the procession.

The ceremony did not last too long; the Court carriages were very handsome, and the Marquis of Bath did his work well, and was rewarded with the Order of Leopold, in which he appeared yesterday at dinner. No decorations are given to the others, as they would not be allowed to wear them. The dinner at Schönbrunn was very handsome, the gardens lovely in freshness. I sat on the Emperor's right, Lord Bath on his left, and I suppose there must have been forty people present. Afterwards we were shown the Palace, and the Sultan's rooms, and then we drove round the Gardens escorted by Hohenlohe, went through the Menagerie, and finished at the Neue Welt, where I introduced Lord Bath to Princess Schwarzenberg, and came home.

Vienna. July 28, 1867.—The presentation to the Sultan, Abdul Aziz, went off very well. He spoke to me for some time ; our old friend Fuad interpreted. He spoke of the kindness of the Queen, the Royal Family, and the English nation, and seems to have come away deeply impressed by everything he saw. I observed that he shook hands with the Ambassadors, not with the Ministers (considering the former no doubt as what they are, the personal represent-atives of their Sovereign, whilst the Ministers only represent the Government). The Sultan looked very tired, and seemed as if he would prefer rest to anything else. Fuad Pasha looked well, and as cunning as ever.

Extracts of Journal in Italy.

1867.—Lord Bloomfield and I left Vienna on the 17th of December, and in spite of a heavy fall of snow, we reached Venice without being delayed. We stopped an hour at Udine, a lonely little town on the Adriatic, where there is a miniature Palazzo Vecchio, and some very pic-turesque old buildings. The weather was rainy and not warm, though the change from the harsh air of Vienna was very pleasant.

We visited the Belle Arti, where there is Titian's magnificent picture of the Assumption of the Virgin, and also his first work, the Visitation, painted when he was sixteen, and the Deposition from the Cross, the last work he painted, when he was ninety years of age.

We were much interested with Salviati's glass works, where we saw the manufacture of mosaics, and also that of the Venetian glass beads, and at the church of San Giovanni we saw the blackened remains of Titian's famous picture of the Martyrdom of St. Peter, which, with a fine Giovanni Bellini, was burnt in the autumn of last year. The origin of the fire was never discovered, but it is supposed that it was caused by the tapers which had been used during a service not having been properly extinguished !

We left Venice on the 23rd, and arrived at Florence.

We visited Mr. Power's studio, and were delighted with his Greek Slave. His allegorical statue of an Indian woman, intended to represent the extinction of the Indian tribes, was full of expression and dignity. Mr. Power himself had a remarkably fine head, and most expressive eyes.

We went to the Chambers in the Palazzo Vecchio, but there was no debate going on. We saw Count Menabrea and Madame Ratazzi, who was still very handsome. We went in the evening to a small party at the Minghettis'. Madame Minghetti sang delightfully, and her salon was one of the pleasantest in Florence.

On Wednesday, the 11th, we went on to Rome, where we settled ourselves very comfortably at the Hotel Costanzi. I found on revisiting Rome, after an absence of fifteen years, that my impressions of the place were as unchanged as the town itself.

The Coliseum I consider by far the most interesting building I ever saw! Its colossal size, the interest which is attached to its history, and the wonderful beauty of its colours, shape, and vegetation, exceeds all powers of description. St. Peter's is gorgeous and splendid, but never impressed me one half as much as many of the old Gothic cathedrals I have seen in England and elsewhere, and the music and theatrical character of the ceremonies conveyed no religious impressions to my mind, but rather the contrary.

I had an interesting visit from Count Harry Arnim, then Prussian Ambassador at Rome. He told me that the Pope (Pius IX.) often spoke with him on religious questions, and was convinced that all Protestant countries would in time return to the bosom of the Romish Church, and that he looked upon us all as his subjects, albeit rebellious ones! Count Chreptowich came to see us, and recounted the following interesting episode of the year 1848, when he was Russian Minister at Naples, and the Pope had taken refuge at Gaeta. Prince Felix Schwarzenberg had just been appointed Minister for Foreign Affairs at Vienna, and sent a special messenger off to Naples to ask Count Chreptowich's opinion on the position of affairs at Gaeta, and the possibility of re-establishing Pius IX. at Rome, which was then in the hands of Garibaldi and Mazzini. Cavaignac was at the head of the Republican Government at Paris, and nearly all Europe was in a state of revolution. Count Chreptowich determined at once to take a bold step, and go in person to Gaeta, and endeavour to persuade the Pope to apply for the protection of the great Roman Catholic Powers, who were disputing among themselves which should offer His Holiness an asylum, but had not thought of uniting in his defence.

Being anxious to avoid publicity, Count Chreptowich determined to go to Gaeta in the night, and he applied to Count Filangieri, then Governor of Naples, for a steamer, and asked the Count to accompany him to Gaeta on a mission of great importance, telling him he would give him all particulars during the passage. Accordingly at 10 P.M. a steamer was in readiness, with Count Filangieri on board, and they started for Gaeta, and arriving there at midnight found that the Pope and the King of Naples had already retired to rest, so the first step was to awaken the King, who, much surprised, received Count Chreptowich, and was told that he, the Count, must have an audience of the Pope and Cardinal Antonelli at once. There was some demur, but at last, at 1 A.M., Count Chreptowich was admitted to the Pope's bedroom—a very small room, with a simple camp bed, a sofa, a chair and a table. The Pope had just risen, and after hearing the Count's proposition, declared he could give no answer till he had sought guidance from God and heard mass. Count Chreptowich agreed to this, but said he must be back in Naples early in the morning, as it was of the utmost importance his mission should be kept secret, so the Pope heard mass at 5, and gave his answer at 6 A.M., and in accordance with the Count's advice, the appeal to the Roman Catholic Powers was drawn up by Count Chreptowich, Count Filangieri, and Cardinal Antonelli ; and at 9 A.M. the two former were back in Naples, and a messenger was despatched to Prince Schwarzenberg to inform him of the steps which had been taken, which resulted in the occupation of Rome by the French, and the reinstatement of the Pope in the Vatican.

I met Count A. Apponyi at a dinner party, who told me a curious fact, showing the independence of the Primate of Hungary, when he came to Rome to attend a canonisation. When he went with his suite to St. Peter's he found his proper place had not been assigned to him, so he remonstrated, and on being told that no change could then be made, he and his suite left the Church.

Rome, February 10, 1868.—Lord Bloomfield having heard from Lord Clarendon that the Pope (Pius IX.) expected all travellers of distinction to ask to be presented, and that, moreover, his Holiness had spoken of our presence at Rome, my husband considered it right to ask for an audience, which was granted to him two days after his application.

The Pope received him most graciously, rose to receive him, and Lord Bloomfield kissed his hand. He was seated on a sort of low throne in a small room, with a table before him, and desired Lord Bloomfield to sit down opposite to him. After welcoming him to Rome, the Pope first expressed his regret that the winter had been so unpropitious, and said a few civil words as to his hope that we should have time to enjoy our visit to Rome. My husband replied that the newspapers had busied themselves with our movements, and had tried to make out that he (Lord Bloomfield) had been charged with a mission from his Government at home, but that he begged to say this was not the case, that we had come as private individuals on account of my health, and to avoid the severe cold of a Vienna winter.

The Pope then spoke of the generally perturbed state of the public mind in Europe, expressing regret that the excitement had extended to England, and alluded to the Fenian movement in Ireland. My husband replied that as an Irishman that question particularly interested him, but that serious as it was, he hoped the strong arm of the law would be sufficient to restore order, especially since the Roman Catholic clergy had shown a disposition to support the executive, but that lately things had been less satisfactory, and the reports of a mutiny at Limerick caused him anxiety. He hoped the Pope would take notice of them, as that would prove very useful to the cause of order. The

Pope then spoke of the changes going on in Austria, and Lord Bloomfield ventured to tell him that Baron Beust had found matters in a very hopeless condition, and that nothing but fundamental changes in the administration of the Empire could avail—the remedies applied were severe, but were apparently doing good.

The Pope then referred to Victor Emanuel, without any expressions of ill-will; he spoke of Prince Humbert's projected marriage, and wished him all happiness ; and on Lord Bloomfield observing that Count Menabrea was exerting his best energies to arrest the movement of the democratic party, his Holiness said he willingly believed all this, and had no doubt Victor Emanuel had spoken in that sense, but he could not trust him.

The audience lasted nearly half an hour, and Lord Bloomfield was much struck by the Pope's fascinating manner, and thought his Holiness appeared in good health and spirits.

On leaving the Pope he called on Cardinal Antonelli, with whom he had an interesting conversation on the state of Austria and Fenianism. The Cardinal seemed to think there was little prospect of arriving at an understanding with Austria on the question of the Concordat, and that with regard to Ireland he believed the conduct of the Roman Catholic clergy had satisfied the Government. Lord Bloomfield then begged to draw his attention to events which had recently occurred, as it was possible they had not yet come to his knowledge, and there the conversation ended. Cardinal Antonelli is a tall, handsome man, with a remarkably intelligent eye, but he had a bad countenance, and I never made his acquaintance. I was too delicate to frequent the society at Rome much, and studiously abstained from mixing myself up with politics there and elsewhere, in accordance with my husband's wishes, who had a great horror of women meddling in matters which do not concern them. Political feeling ran very high at Rome then as it does now, and it interfered very much with the pleasure of society.

Rome, February, 1868.—I had the pleasure of making the acquaintance of Miss Hosmer, the American sculptress, to whom Mrs. Sartoris had given me a letter of introduction.

As she was at that moment occupied with a model, she regretted that she was unable to admit me into her working studio, but I was delighted with the beautiful fountain she had made for Lady Marion Alford—a siren arresting the attention of children, seated upon dolphins. The figures were most graceful, and the whole conception charming. Her statues of Puck and a sleeping faun also delighted me; and during my stay in Rome I frequently visited her studio, and enjoyed the witty conversation of this gifted artist. I also often met the Abbé Liszt, both at his own home and elsewhere. He is quite a man of the world, and his conversation is as brilliant as his pianoforte playing.

My husband dined at Monsieur de Sartiges', the French Ambassador, and had a curious conversation with his wife, an American, who told him she was a Protestant, and that since she came to Rome great efforts had been made to induce her to change her religion, but she had no wish or intention of doing so. Among other things she had been assured that she could be received into the Roman Catholic Church without any public ceremony, and that she need not be re-baptised, to which she answered she hoped not, as perhaps in that case she should also have to be re-married.

One day we had a long visit from Monsignor Talbot, and my husband presented a petition from the landlord of our hotel, who had received orders to close all the south windows of the hotel because they looked upon a nunnery, which, however, was some way off. The nuns had complained of their privacy being disturbed by the curiosity of travellers visiting the hotel, and the hotel-keeper averred that his house would be ruined were he obliged to shut up all the south side. Monsignor Talbot promised to inquire into the knotty points, and endeavour to arrange matters.

A friend of mine at Rome was occupied attending the Garibaldian sick and wounded. Nearly a quarter of them died from their wounds, and had it not been for private charity the prisoners would have fared badly; as it was they were well looked after and clothed before leaving prison, and the lady visitors met with great civility from the officials, Sisters of Charity, and the surgeons at the hospital; but Rome is considered an unhealthy place for wounded men, and a large proportion in hospital die. We visited several studios and ateliers, and were much pleased with old Mr. Coleman's pictures, some of which we purchased. He is a charming artist, and his sketches of the Campagna are first rate. He told me he had been thirty-four years at Rome, having gone there with the intention of only staying a few months, but he could never tear himself away from it, and remained there till he died, a few years after I saw him. Miss Hosmer gave me an interesting account of Gibson, with whom she studied for some years. He made a curious discovery, by which he could accurately ascertain the proportions of the human figure by subdividing a triangle, so that if any one part of a statue be determined on, according to this measurement all the other parts can be easily ascertained, and the scale has been verified over and over again on the best Greek models, and Miss Hosmer assured me it is invariable, and a most valuable discovery for artists. Miss Hosmer is the only person I ever met who believes they have actually seen a spectre ; she told me she had a maid named Rosa who lived with her a long time, but left her service because she was in a consumption. Miss Hosmer took a great interest in her, and used to visit her frequently. One day she called, but did not find her worse than usual, and thought she might still live for some weeks ; she promised to return the next day and bring something the poor woman wanted. The following morning Miss Hosmer was in bed, but woke at dawn with the conviction that some one was in her room. She heard the clock strike five, and at that moment the figure of Rosa appeared at her bed-side and outtered the words, ' Adesso sono contenta, son felice' (now I am content and happy), and then disappeared. Miss Hosmer said the whole thing seemed so natural that she was not alarmed, but she got up, found her door locked as usual, and the room empty. At breakfast she told the lady with whom she resided what had occurred, adding she was so convinced that Rosa was dead she should not go to her as she had intended, but would send to inquire after her. The answer came back that Rosa had departed this life exactly at five o'clock that morning.

We paid the Abbé Liszt a visit, and his playing of the Erl König was one of the finest things I ever heard—a *chef d'œuvre* of poetry, feeling, and execution really marvellous. One might have imagined he had six hands instead of two; his touch was delicate and beautiful, and at the same time so powerful.

We afterwards drove to see some interesting excavations which are being made under the Gran Commendatore Visconti at the Emporium on the Tiber, where fine blocks of marble are dug out after having been buried for probably upwards of 1,500 years. The view of Rome, lighted up with the glowing evening tints, was quite lovely, and the colouring exquisite.

We had what might have proved rather a disagreeable adventure the day we drove to Frascati to visit Tusculum. We had intended returning by Grotia Ferrata to see some very famous Domenichinos there, and my husband ordered the carriage to be ready to meet us on our return from a donkey-ride to Tusculum. The day was very hot, and we were surprised to find no signs of the carriage at the appointed hour. My husband went off to look for the coachman, and at last found him at a small pot-house leisurely smoking his pipe, and on being asked why he had not harnessed the horses he replied, in the coolest and most impertinent manner, that he had not the smallest intention of doing so for two hours, and should certainly not drive us to Grotia Ferrata, but return quietly straight back to Rome. We were very indignant, but as we were completely in the man's power, and had no other means of returning to Rome, we were obliged to submit and dawdle about till he saw fit to start, when he drove us back safely, and seemed much surprised when my husband informed his employer that we utterly declined his services in future. He actually had the impudence to bring the carriage the following day, but we positively refused to drive, and at last succeeded in dismissing him.

We visited M. D'Epinay's studio to see a fine statue he was making of the young Hannibal. The boy, the determined enemy of Rome, is struggling with, and endeavouring to strangle, a large eagle. The expression of his countenance is fierce and powerful; and the hair, dressed according to the Nubian fashion, stuck out in two straight plaits from the head, as it is represented on the Nubian coins, and still worn by young lads in that country; but in a statue the effect was strange and inartistic. We also saw a fine bust of a brigand's wife, done from nature. The woman was imprisoned at Rome, and was afterwards sent to Cayenne, having committed atrocious crimes. She was sent to M. d'Epinay's studio attended by gendarmes, and he told us her expression was so diabolical, that although her features were remarkably fine and classical, he sometimes felt alarmed at being left alone with her.

We had a pleasant dinner at Mr. Story's, the American sculptor, who lived then in the Palace Barberini. We met Lord Clarendon, Lady Emily Villiers, and her *fiancée*, Mr. Odo Russell, then acting as Chargé d'Affaires at Rome, Mrs. Bruce, and various other guests. Mr. Story told me

some curious details of his experiences of spiritualism, which he is firmly convinced is not humbug.
He also told me he had begun life as a lawyer,
but had always been fond of modelling, and the
first thing which induced him to give up the law
and become a sculptor was his getting an order
to make a statue of his father, which he undertook
with all the energy, and, he added, the audacity
of a young inexperienced man. Once when he
was called upon to defend a woman accused of
murdering her husband, he adduced as one of the
proofs of her innocence the fact of her having
attended him on his deathbed, and said to him,
when he was dying, 'Good-bye, George.' The
counsel for the plaintiff declared this ought rather
to be taken as a proof of her guilt, and that the
words she had used were 'Good, by George!'
Mr. Story also mentioned some curious facts which
are mentioned in Tchoeke's autobiography as to
his powers of knowing people's characters and
antecedents by intuition. Among other instances
he once found himself in the society of a young
man, a perfect stranger to him, who doubted these
powers, upon which Tchoeke said he would
prove them to him, as he knew perfectly what
he was doing on the night of the 13th of April,
1766. That he had entered his employer's room

with a false key, and opened his bureau with the intention of robbing it, when his courage failed, and he left the room without committing the crime. The young man turned deadly pale, and acknowledged the truth of the accusation, adding that he believed no one on earth knew the facts, as he had never revealed them. With regard to spiritualism Mr. Story declared his own experiences had been so very awful he could not repeat them, but he was firmly convinced they resulted from causes which are as unnatural as they are inexplicable and extraordinary.

Mr. Story's father was an eminent judge, and to please him William Story studied law, and was in good practice when his father died. He then determined to follow the bent of his own inclinations, and came to Rome to study sculpture, for which he always had a passion. One day an American called upon him and sat for some time in his studio, looking at him without speaking. At last he said, 'Story, I wish to ask you a question ; in Heaven's name tell me what induced you to give up the glorious profession of the bar to come to Rome and pinch up mud ? ' Mr. Story said he could only answer by a fit of laughter. Mr. Motley, the eminent historian, broke his chair at dinner, upon which Miss

Hosmer immediately inquired what was the difference between a Roman chair and a cow? the answer being that while one gives milk the other gives way (whey). Miss Hosmer was busy for many months finishing a pendant to her sleeping faun for the Paris Exhibition, but was dissatisfied with her work. She was, however, most anxious to complete it. It was actually finished in marble, and packed to go to Paris, when driving one day to the meet of the hounds, Miss Hosmer had an inspiration of another statue, which she thought would so far exceed in beauty the one she had executed that she determined, *coute que coute*, to suppress her work, which she accordingly did, and assured me that no mortal eye would ever see it again. I have often watched her at work with the deepest interest, and been much struck by the conscientious manner in which she works, first modelling the muscles and veins, and then, as it were, clothing them, and this gives wonderful life and finish to her statues. One day one of her best workmen in chiselling out a marble statue had the misfortune to chip off a finger. When Miss Hosmer entered her studio she found the poor man pale and speechless, and he led her up to the statue to show her his misfortune. She said nothing, but turned upon her heel. I asked

John Arthur Douglas.
Lord Bloomfield. G.C.B.

whether the mischief was irremediable, and she answered, 'Oh no. It is so well mended scarcely anyone could perceive it, nevertheless it would never do for me to allow a maimed statue to leave my studio ; if I once did that I should never have a whole one again, so I told Cesare we must go shares in a new block of marble, and begin all over again.' The cost of a large block of marble is 100*l.* before a chisel touches it.

We visited the Vatican with Sir Charles Locock, and saw the picture painted by the Pope's order in commemoration of the dogma lately promulgated of the Immaculate Conception of the Virgin Mary. It is certainly fine as a work of art, but particularly offensive to the eyes of Protestants, as the Virgin is represented in heaven between the Father and the Son, the Holy Spirit in the shape of a dove being above her, thus making, as Sir Charles Locock aptly observed, a quartette instead of the Trinity !

We left Rome with great regret, and returned to Vienna by Florence, Bologna, and Venice.

CHAPTER XIX.

Letters from my Husband during a Cruise with the British Fleet on the Adriatic.

Caledonia, off Trieste, August 18, 1868.—Our journey was prosperous. The night was clear, and though there was no moon, Venus shone forth more lovely than ever. There was much mist and clouds about Gratz, but about eight o'clock the sun shone forth brilliantly, and I never saw anything more fresh and lovely than the country from Gratz. Quantities of grass and green crops, not a yellow leaf, and the river charming. I found the Consul (C. Lever) and Lord Clarence Paget's Flag Lieutenant waiting at the station at Trieste, and the Admiral's barge at the quay. Lord Clarence Paget received me most kindly and cordially, and seems well pleased to have me on board. He has given me a large cabin with a very comfortable bed, and all the accommodation which a ship can afford. It is the cabin which Lady Clarence occupies when on board, so I am not to be pitied ; but the heat was tremendous last night, notwithstanding a thorough draught and my cabin door being open to the stern gallery all night. There was thunder and lightning and heavy rain from time to time, and at day-light, it being the Emperor's *fête* day, an Imperial salute was fired from some castle, which effectually roused me. The Admiral came to ask me if I would come to prayers.

The chaplain, a tall, devout-looking man, read a few prayers and a psalm, and the officers and crew attended. Lord Clarence told me this takes place every morning on board each ship in his squadron. He seems a most kind, just man, and so fond of his people, taking such great interest in the well-being of all around him.

The view of Trieste and the adjoining country is very pretty from our anchorage : Miramar is very near, and if there had been more time and less rain, I should have gone there this morning. At twelve all the men-of-war will fire a salute in honour of the day, and at half-past one we are to lift anchor, and be off for Lossini, south of Pola. There the squa ron will anchor, and the Admiral then proposes going in the *Psyche* to Fiume, and afterwards to coast to Zara, and so back to Lossini, where we shall rejoin the squadron, which will afterwards go on to Ragusa, the Bocche di Cattaro, &c.

I am sitting in the main cabin, with two large doors open to the stern gallery, with sight of a British man-of-war from each. Captain Gardiner commands this ship, and seems such a good, nice fellow.

Poor Lever (our Consul at Trieste) is in great trouble, his wife lying so dangerously ill she is not expected to recover.

Caledonia, at Sea, August 19, 1868.—We are having 'Queen's weather;' there is so little wind that this heavy ship—which has been under sail since yesterday afternoon—can hardly be kept in her course. The air is much cooler than it was yesterday, at least it feels so from being distant from the land, and it is very enjoyable both on deck and in the cabin. In my sleeping cabin the thermometer holds to 20°, but the heat is not so oppressive as it was at Vienna, and I wish you were here to try this ' Dolce far niente ' life. Yesterday we got under way in two lines. The three ironclads in one line, the three wooden ships in the other. The two frigates—*Endymion* and *Arethusa*—the former especially, are lovely ships, and seem always wanting to separate from us and go their own pace. They are rigged like ships of the olden time, and can go equally well under steam or sail. Now that I have got used to the *Lord Warden*, who keeps about half a mile in our wake, and always in view from the stern gallery, I consider her a fine handsome ship of war. We have had all sorts of little amusements by way of manœuvring, forming, and changing line, and knocking about like people in a quadrille! The crew and officers are magnificent, and look a deal better than they did yesterday, having had a quiet night at sea, instead of broiling in the anchorage at Trieste. The views of the coast of Istria, and especially the town of Pirano, famous for its fights in former days with the Venetians, were pretty, but not very striking. We dine at half-past six at sea, so we have a longer evening than I expected, but whist is the order of the night. At half-past ten it was over, the others retired to the stern gallery, I to bed. The Admiral is most kind and amiable; it would be impossible for any one to be more so.

We have a band that plays in the morning,

and again at dinner—but otherwise the quiet of this great ship is wonderful. There is not a sound to be heard in the great cabin, which I am occupying all by myself, and one would think everybody had followed the Admiral's example, and were taking a siesta after luncheon.

Captain Wood, a son of Lord Halifax, commands one of the small ironclads, the *Enterprise*. He came on board yesterday, and seems a very nice fellow. All the captains came off to be presented to me before we sailed from Trieste. Captain Gardiner commands the *Caledonia*, and there is a most admirable tone amongst all the officers I have seen of this ship, and such order and cleanliness it is pleasing to behold.

Thursday, 2 P.M., *off Pola.*—Yesterday was cool and pleasant, and as the Admiral is in no hurry, and there was no wind, he decided that the squadron had better anchor, which we did in twenty-three fathoms. After dinner we played at whist, and I won four rubbers, but am no richer in consequence, for the points are only threepence, and nobody pays, though a book is kept and the scores of each player are noted. About half-past ten I was thinking of going to bed, when the Admiral asked if it would be disagreeable to me if we beat to quarters, as he has orders to do at night and without giving notice to anybody, once in every quarter, at sea, so he turned out all hands clear for action, and fired three rounds from each gun of the ships in the squadron. I thought it would be good fun, so away goes up the night signal. The ships soon answered, and up came all the poor fellows with their hammocks on deck, and in due course of time bang bang from the squadron. After it was over, and it lasted about three-quarters of an hour, I went all along the main and lower decks, which were well lighted, and it was a curious sight to see the grim looking tars all ready for battle, not over and above encumbered with clothes. By-the-bye, there was an amusing sight after anchoring yesterday. Permission was given to the men to bathe, one of the quarter boats was lowered in case of a man getting the cramp, or any accident occurring, and in about ten minutes there were a hundred fellows swimming about the ship, making themselves clean and comfortable for the night.

We are now running for Lossini, an island which was taken possession of by the French in 1859, and from which they intended to prepare for the attack on Venice. It is said to possess but one interest, that of having a fine harbour, where we shall anchor, and in the morning proceed to Fiume in the *Psyche*, which will be due from Trieste with letters. The weather is cool and pleasant, but it feels very relaxing, and I do not think, though I am most comfortable, as far as food and accommodation are concerned, that I should care to pass the remainder of my days on board a ship, particularly as where I am sitting I feel every stroke of the screw ; but the 'deep and dark blue ocean' is very lovely. The coast as far as Pola seems green and nicely cultivated, but all beyond it to the southern point of land looks bare and barren.

Psyche, *August* 21, 11 A.M.—Here we are steaming away for Fiume, where we expect to arrive this afternoon. We made Lossini in good time yesterday, and as the harbour was completely unknown to every one on board, we moved gently, and found ourselves safely anchored in the most sheltered harbour imaginable, with plenty of water and conveniences of every kind. The village, or town of 'Augusta,' as I see it called in the log book, seems well to do, and to be a great place for ship-building : one or two largish vessels were lying on the stocks, and others being rigged. As soon as the ship anchored and all was in order, we were told to dress for dinner, and sat down about half-past seven. The evening heavenly, not too hot, a pleasant air, and the stars shining brilliantly. I was looking at the Great Bear, and afterwards at Venus, and thought perhaps you might be out and doing the same thing. I slept soundly for the first time since I came on board, and, strange to say, heard nothing of a tremendous storm of rain, wind, thunder, and lightning!

We must have been a great source of interest to the inhabitants, for all the bands on the ships played during the dinner, and until nearly nine o'clock, and boats came off to see the sight, and the lights of all the ships produced an extremely pretty effect. There is a battery facing the entrance of the harbour, which would effectually stop any ship trying to enter as an enemy. There were a few soldiers in the battery of some Hungarian regiment, who doubtless were amused at the novelty of our appearance.

Edward Adeane is commander of the *Arethusa*, and he and Captain Coote, who is, I think, the senior officer of the squadron, and left in charge till we return to Lossini, came to breakfast with the Admiral, who signalled to Adeane to come on board. The tone Lord Clarence Paget has established on board is wonderful. He is considerate, strict but not a martinet.   As yet I see nothing remarkable about the coast and islands, but the mountains are increasing in height, and I dare say Fiume will open out grandly by-and-bye.   This vessel is beautifully easy, and I am writing my letters in the stern cabin, where the Admiral takes up his quarters.   There is no more motion than there would be on the Danube ; we are running about ten and a half knots an hour, and could go sixteen if necessary, but the Admiralty never care to press their engines, and shake their vessels unnecessarily. These wild islands produce lots of wine according to our pilot of Lloyd's establishment, and are well to do ; but he gives such an account of the Bora in the passage we are going up that one would certainly not care to be exposed to it.   He says the gales usually commence after the equinox, so our Admiral, who has no desire to be out in one with his squadron, has made up his mind to move south in proper time.

Psyche, August 22, 1868.—Steaming for Zara Fiume is prettily situated at the base of a high hill, and the run up the bay was very fine.   The old Vice-Consul, Mr. Hill, and the authorities came off as soon as we had moored, and we afterwards went on shore.   We were taken to see the Casino, a good club, with assembly rooms attached to it.

The Consul got us a smart four-inside carriage, belonging to an English paper manufacturer, a Mr. Smith, in which we drove up the hill to poor old Field-Marshal Nugent's former residence, where he and his wife are now buried. There is an attempt at a castellated building, and the effect from the sea and at a distance is very striking, and the view magnificent. The dwelling itself is wretched, but the mausoleum, built partly out of an old ruin, is rather nice, but so neglected. It never was finished, and I have no idea what plan he had in his head for the construction, but there was a collection of old marbles and statues which he had brought from Italy, some of which, columns taken in war, were by way of trophies. It is such a queer-looking place, reminding me of what one might see in Ireland! We went afterwards to see a handsome building just finished in the town—a Naval Academy—which is excellent in its internal arrangements. No expense has been spared, and it has excellent professors. The cadets, eighty in number, are now on a cruise for the holidays, and were last at Naples, where they were admirably received. Mr. Hill dined with us, and after dinner we went off to hear the military band of a Hungarian regiment play. The music was good, and we sat down at a table in front of the café to listen to the music, the colonel of the regiment at our side, and a naval officer called Henriquez.   At ten o'clock we returned on board, and went to bed.   As we breakfast at eight, one must be up at half-past six.   The air is deliciously cool to-day, and the vessel went comfortably and easily.   The sea quite smooth, and everything goes on as prosperously as possible.   We steamed away at eight, and went into a charming harbour—Porto Ré, about twelve miles off.   The situation is pleasant, but there is no cultivation ; and, in fact, no soil to cultivate, for the islands seem to produce nothing but vines, and only here and there does one see a good vineyard.   Shipbuilding and fishing seem the only occupations of the few inhabitants of these wild districts.   Here and there the hills are covered with stunted trees or bushes ; but they are generally wild and rocky, and some islands are perfectly bare, and the pilot says they mark the line of the Bora, which appears to ravage whole districts, and to be a fearful destroyer.   We have just passed at the back of the Lossini island, where we saw the masts of the three big ships we left there, about fourteen miles off. I find my field glasses excellent, as good as any in the ship, but the single telescope is still in vogue, because it is said to be better for night work than the binocular one. To-morrow we are to steam off at 4 A.M. from Zara to Sabenico, and thence to a famous harbour' and waterfall, which is one of the wonders of the Dalmatian coast. We hope to get through the expedition, about eighty miles, in good time, and return late at night to the squadron in Lossini harbour.

We have a nice party on board. The Captain, Sir Francis Blackwood, is a charming fellow; then we have Captain Gordon, of the *Caledonia*; Lieutenant Stewart, the Flag Lieutenant, the Secretary, and a Dr. Forbes, the staff surgeon. The weather perfect, so if I do not thoroughly enjoy my trip it is my own fault. Lord Clarence is the most amiable of hosts, and does everything to make life agreeable on board without boring one in any way.

Steaming between Zara and Lossini, August 24, 1868.—My last letter was posted at Zara; we got there about 6 P.M. Saturday. It is a curious fortified old town, once Roman, then Turkish, afterwards Venetian, then taken by the French, and finally ceded to Austria in 1815. It was situated on a peninsula, but now it is an island. The streets are very narrow, scarcely room for carriages. There seem to be plenty of shops and food, and no end of fruits for sale. A nice-looking Hungarian regiment, and some artillerymen and engineers were all about the place. There are pretty walks on the bastions; the air of the place is quite southern and eastern, and some of the costumes pretty, but there was nothing pretty to be bought there. Maraschino is the great business of the place. There seem to be good public offices, and the people orderly and well to do. We had intended starting off for Sabenico very early, but stopped for letters, which was a mistake, as it threw us back and out of our calculations. We steamed off on Sunday. At 11 Divine Service was performed by Sir Francis Blackwood, our captain. We passed between some wild rocky islands, but there is great sameness in the Archipelago. It is charming for sailing about in this weather, and the Admiral wonders our yachting people have not yet discovered its merits. The passage up Sabenico is very narrow and pretty. We anchored about 3 o'clock in front of the town, which is a curious looking place, and said to have a fine cathedral, but we did not go ashore, as we were in a hurry to get off to the ' Kerka ' falls, ten miles off. The boats were manned, and we had a fair wind. The water immensely deep, and perfectly adapted for steam navigation, though at times the passages are very narrow ; great black masses of rock of all shapes, few houses, and fewer villages. We opened an immense lough, a couple of miles wide and six long, and then got to the Kerka river, passed the village of Scardona, and then about one and a half miles further we found the falls. The whole river comes tumbling down in several streams, but there is one great fall, more, however, like a torrent than a waterfall. It is, however, fine, and worth coming to see, but unfortunately our time was very short, and so we could only go behind the mill, which is established there, and appears to do the grinding work of the whole country. The miller seems to have lots of work, and to be well off; several boats were waiting for cargoes. Above the fall there is a monastery, and a lake from whence the cataract is supplied. The labourers at the mill are very picturesque—dark, brawny-looking fellows, with strange countenances, and each would have made a picture and a study for your pencil. The excursion would have pleased you much, but it was rather a fatigue sitting in a boat without moving for five or six hours. At the village of Scardona on our return we halted to give the boat's crew some bread and wine ; and the poor fellows certainly deserved it, for they pulled right well, and did not seem a bit the worse for the day's work, though they have not much practice in rowing, and the captain says it is capital exercise for them.　It was a lovely night, the young moon shone brightly, and at half-past eight we got back to the *Psyche*, and there found Mr. Paton, the Consul, awaiting to pay his respects, who had arrived on the Lloyd's boat from Fiume on his way to Ragusa.　After compliments he departed, and we got to dinner about nine o'clock.

We left our anchorage at Sabenico at 4 this morning, and hope to reach Lossini at 1 o'clock P.M. There will be plenty of signalling to the squadron as soon as it is in sight, for the Admiral talks of getting to sea as soon as possible.

Trieste, Tuesday, August 25, 1868.—Here I am on shore again.　We had a charming sail to Lossini, and found the squadron ready for sea, so after luncheon I had a long talk with the Admiral, who did his best to persuade me, in the kindest possible manner, to go on with him ; but after examining the chart and talking over the time required I made out that it would be useless for me to think of getting back to Vienna before the middle of next week, as his project was to cruise about and take the squadron into the fine harbour of Gravosa, Bocche di Cattaro, and Ragusa, all of

which I should have been delighted to see, but
. . . I felt I could not stay from you so long. If
we had been taking a turn in the *Psyche*, it would
have been another affair, then one could make
accurate calculations, so I told the Admiral I must
get back to Vienna and my wife. This he
admitted was an unanswerable argument, into
which he could enter perfectly, so then it was
settled I should land, but first I said I should like
to return the visits of the captains, and after
doing this I would come on board the *Caledonia*,
and bid him (the Admiral) good-bye. So he
ordered his barge for me, and then signalled to
the ships that I was coming on board them all.
The officers and men were prepared to receive
me in full dress, bands playing 'God save the
Queen,' rigging manned, and all the usual sailors'
demonstrations. It was a severe climb up and
down the two small vessels, as they were ready
for sea, and it was straight up and down. The
Arethusa's main deck is magnificent, one of the
finest I ever saw, and in fact all the ships were
really beautiful. After I left the *Caledonia* and
got by her bows, up went the Jack to the main-top,
and I had to listen to the salute of nineteen guns ;
but happily the sensible Admiral has pop-guns, as
he calls them, for this sort of work, so my ears

were not damaged. On returning on board the *Psyche*, after all honours shown me, I saw the signal for sailing, and I got the captain's gig, and had a stroll about the town, which is a flourishing little place—good ships, and no appearance of poverty. The captain of the port walked about the place with me, and told me that last year they had built fifteen large vessels. When the squadron was off and out of the harbour we started after them, and passed close by each ship, taking another good look and farewell ; and when we got alongside the *Caledonia* the Admiral told me he proposed to make a pretty manœuvre, and the *Lord Warden*, which had been out cruising for three days, was ordered to take up his position—the squadron to form in two lines and make sail. This was done with beautiful precision, and it was then 6 o'clock, so I took leave and steamed for Trieste. The night lovely, a little air to cool us, dinner at 7, bed at 10, and up at 6.30, and here I am waiting for letters. I shall, please God, be with you Thursday, sooner probably than you expected. My idea is to leave by the 6.45 train this afternoon, sleep at Adelsberg, see the caves, and proceed to Gratz and Vienna.

I have been to Miramar, which is like an enchanted palace. I wish you could have seen it, but it was blazing hot, and you would have been roasted. The Bishop of Gibraltar is in this hotel. I have called on him, but did not find him at home.

Gratz, August 26, 1868.—Such a change in the temperature; we seem to have got into regular autumn. We.were up at five this morning, and the grotto at Adelsberg is certainly one of the most wonderful things I ever saw. Its extent and variety marvellous ; we walked hard for an hour and forty minutes, seeing everything perfectly.

Lady Ely once told me the following curious anecdote of Sir Charles Locock. He was convinced he had disease of the heart, so he wrote a note to the great authority in London, who did not happen to know him personally, and said he sent him a patient he was anxious about, and requested him, after a careful investigation, to tell him, Sir Charles, his opinion honestly. He took the note himself, waited on the doctor, and was examined with the stethoscope. The doctor said he was happy to inform him he had no disease of the heart, so Sir Charles said very well, will you kindly write a diagnosis of my case to Sir Charles Locock. The doctor said he would send it, but Sir Charles said he was in no hurry, and would rather wait for it ; accordingly the doctor sat down and wrote, ' Dear Sir Charles, I am happy to inform you that your patient's heart is as sound as yours or mine.' The letter was brought to Sir Charles, who immediately opened it, and, much relieved, went back to the doctor, and told him what he had done.   The doctor was extremely angry, and asked how he could play him such a trick, so Sir Charles said for the simple reason that he wished to know the truth about his own case, and was convinced in case of mischief the doctor would not tell it.   ' Set a thief to catch a thief.'

London, November 15, 1869.—I read this remarkable passage in Sir Henry Bulwer's ' Life of Lord Palmerston,' in which, writing to his brother Sir William Temple, he says, ' Metternich must be an idiot if he does not see that Russia is the windward quarter of the heavens, and that his dirty weather must come from thence, and therefore that he should look for shelter westward.' This was written October 19, 1827.   Alas ! the shelter westward has a good deal changed since then.

I had the honour of knowing H.I.H. the Archduchess Marie at Vienna, and she was very amiable, clever, and agreeable, the daughter of the great general, the Archduke Charles. She told me she once travelled incognita in Scotland, and was anxious not to be known. On board one of the Caledonian steamers a gentleman entered into conversation with her, and finding from her accent that she was a German he inquired whether she knew the South of Germany. She answered she did. He then asked her whether she had been at Vienna, and whether she knew the Archduke Charles. The Archduchess then made sure that the gentleman knew who she was. She was sorely puzzled, not liking to deny her own father, and she blushed up to the roots of her hair. The gentleman, much astonished, repeated his question, and added, to the Archduchess's great relief, ' Oh, you know what I mean by the Archduke Charles, the great hotel at Vienna.'

I left Vienna on Monday, May 9, 1870, on a visit to my dear friend Countess Clam Martinĕ, *née* Altgräfinn Salm, one of the most distinguished women at Vienna. I found her carriage at Amstetten station, which took me to the Castle of Klam in about three hours by Grein, which is a picturesque old town on the Danube, one of the stopping places between Linz and Vienna. The castle there, which is very large, belongs to the

Duke of Coburg, who possesses several large châteaux in that neighbourhood. Klam is a most picturesque old place perched upon the top of a high rock, with a deep wooded ravine below, and commands a magnificent view of the whole range of the Upper Austrian Alps, which were still covered with snow. The castle is an irregular building, and part of it is very ancient. A two-storied stone cloister surrounds the inner court, and the round tower, with its painted roof, may be seen for many miles, and is quite a landmark in that country. The staircase is open to the outer air, and leads across one of the cloisters to a large room, from which there is a very fine view of the mountains. The morning after I arrived, as my friend was busy, I thought I would poke about the old Castle by myself, and I descended to the courtyard and terrace. Coming back I missed my way ; the staircases at the different angles of the court being all similar, I could not find the one which led to my apartment, and wandered hopelessly about for a considerable time, till at last my friend discovered me, to her infinite surprise and amusement, on the second floor. We drove to Wallsee, another castle on the Danube, which had lately been purchased by the Duke of Coburg; coming home we visited a convent belonging to the order of the ' Good Shepherd,' at Baumgartenberg. The superior, a middle-aged, cheerful looking woman, showed us all over the establishment, which is a school and penitentiary, as well as a nunnery. The sisters, who are very poor, make everything they require : linen, shoes, white and black serge, artificial flowers for decorating the church ; and one of the lay sisters does all the carpentering. The building is very large and airy, but must be dreadfully cold in winter, as there is no means of warming the cells. It is surrounded by a large garden full of fruit trees. The order is not a very strict one, and I thought the nuns all looked cheerful and happy. They rise at 5, have service till 7.30, when they breakfast on weak coffee and bread. They dine at 11, have meat three times a week except during the fasts ; sup at 6, after which they attend vespers, and go to bed at 10. Each nun has a separate cell, except those who superintend the children and penitents. They work hard, and I could not see that their life is more conducive to their spiritual welfare than that of other industrious members of the community, though perhaps they may be rather less exposed to temptation. After spending a few happy days at Klam, which looked like one vast orchard in full blossom, the fields carpeted with the most lovely wild flowers, I accompanied my friend to Ottensheim, a château near Linz belonging to Count Coudenhove. The drive along the banks of the Danube was pretty and picturesque. We had the pleasure of meeting Baron Hübner there, who was formerly Austrian Ambassador at Paris and Rome, and is a remarkably clever agreeable man, who has seen much of life, having been a great traveller, and knows perfectly how to adapt his conversation to his audience.

I left Vienna on the 13th of September ; met Countess Clam at Skaliez station, and we proceeded together to her father's château of Raitz in Moravia. It was dark when we arrived, but we were shown through the entrance hall into a large vestibule which led to a handsome drawing-room hung with family portraits, where I was very kindly received by Prince and Princess Salm and their family. The château is like an old French one, red brick with a high roof. It is well situated above the village of Raitz. The pleasure grounds are well laid out, and extensive, with fine timber. I was particularly struck by a very pretty fountain surrounded with ferns. The sun shone brilliantly, lighting up a birch tree round which hung a scarlet Virginian creeper ; the whole scene was like fairy-land, and quite unique. The 15th of September was the Prince's birthday. We mustered a large party at breakfast, and after dinner the Prince's band attended, which was composed of miners and the men who work at the large iron foundries on the estate. They played wonderfully well, and a taste for music seems innate in the inhabitants of Moravia and Bohemia. The music set the whole establishment, young and old, dancing, and wherever I looked I was amused at seeing groups of people waltzing. It was a festive scene, every one appeared to enjoy it, and it was characteristic of the country.

April 17.—I visited the exhibition of Schwindt's drawings and pictures. He died a short time previously, and had a great reputation in Germany, though his works are little known in England. He was employed in the decoration of the new Opera House at Vienna, and I met him once at a party at Dessauer's. He was then an oldish man, stout, with a very jovial countenance, and certainly did not give me the impression of being the poetical and sentimental man his drawings would lead one to imagine he was. His illustrations of Melusine were charming, especially the details of the plants and flowers, which he introduced with the utmost taste and refinement, and there was a power of imagination and humour in many of his works which almost amounted to caricature. I did not admire his colouring, and his oil pictures were hard and vulgar. I thought there was an absence of truth in them, and that the colouring was very heavy without being rich.

Markhardt's painting, on the contrary, was the very reverse of Schwindt's in this respect. It is marvellously rich and powerful, whilst his drawing was exceedingly faulty. As a decorative painter I consider he is one of the great geniuses of the present day. There is wonderful variety in his pictures, which remind me in the richness of their colouring of Paul Veronese and Rubens; the draperies are splendid, and his groups are well composed, but his pictures are often disgustingly coarse, and he earned such a great reputation whilst still very young that he was spoilt and got careless.

I asked Dessauer one day whether he admired Wagner's music, then much in vogue at Vienna. I shall never forget the pitiful expression of his face when he answered me by saying, ' Mais, my lady, après tout la musique ce n'est pas le chinois.' Wagner dined with us once, and after dinner read us the libretto of his Minnesänger. He had a cracked voice, and could neither sing nor play, but had, in spite of these impediments, the most wonderful power of rendering the effect he wished to produce upon his audience, and I was excessively interested and amused with his performance, but did not otherwise consider him the attractive individual he had the reputation of being.

On the 1st of May I left Vienna with Countess Clam Martiniez for Prague, where I took up my quarters at the Hôtel d'Angleterre. Prague is certainly one of the most picturesque towns in Europe, infinitely more so than Vienna, and the situation of the Hradgin or royal palace, which rises up above the Moldau, is extremely fine. The old bridge, the palaces and streets are very striking, but I was told that the society is decidedly dull, and remarkable from the absence of the male sex, who all prefer a club life. One lady told me she always felt it was quite ridiculous to make a 'grande toilette' to receive her most intimate female friends, whom she would much rather receive *en robe de chambre.* I had a very pleasant visit from the Abbé Liszt. We discussed the state of affairs at Paris, where at that moment communism and revolution were rampant, and no one could foresee what was likely to happen. I was amused to observe how careful the wary Abbe was not to implicate himself in any way, and how he avoided pronouncing any decided opinion. He evidently was not sure of the ground under his feet as he sang the praises alternately of the Orleans faction, the Comte de Chambord (Henri V.), the Republicans and the Imperialists; and then kept watching me to see what impression he had made. It was very droll! I visited the exhibition of modern pictures, where I was much struck by a fine Achenbach of the Villa d'Este at Rome, which was remarkably well painted and very good in colour; a Gude, of a storm on the coast of Norway, which was very spirited; a pretty *tableau de genre* by Hayn, of Munich, of an alchemist; and some landscapes by Franken and Bertha von Grab. A quatuor by Saitz was very highly finished, and worthy of the old Dutch school, but the price, 2,600 thalers, I thought exorbitant, and in general the prices were very high.

On May 5 we left Prague for Count Clam's château at Smečna. The weather was terribly cold, with occasional snow showers, and vegetation was at least three weeks later than it was at Vienna; for there I had left the fruit trees in blossom and the lilacs coming out, whereas in Bohemia all was mid-winter.

The rooms were warm and comfortable, and

there was a look of occupation in them which was pleasant and rather unusual in foreign houses, where in general rooms look as if no one ever entered them except to have a cup of chocolate. I admired a fine picture by Saitz, which is rich in colour and good in composition, the centre being a figure of our Lord, with the Virgin and St. John. Below there is a fine figure of St. John the Evangelist, sitting on the sea-shore with an eagle beside him. To the right there are the figures of St. Theresa and St. Dominic; to the left St. Augustine and the Magdalene. The whole is a striking work of art, and there is a feeling about it I seldom find in sacred subjects by modern painters, which generally strike me as being either bad imitations or else wholly devoid of religious sentiment. Whether this is owing to the rationalistic tendencies of the present age or to a want of genius in modern painters I know not, but the fact that sacred subjects generally displease me is undeniable.

I had some very interesting conversation with Count Clam Martinič, who is a clever, agreeable man, who has taken a prominent part in politics, and was considered the leader of the aristocratic Czech party in Bohemia. At that time the Czechs refused to attend the Reichsrath at Vienna,

the consequence of which was that their party
was unrepresented in Parliament, and, though a
large and important element in the empire, had
no influence. I could not help contrasting the
position of the opposition in Austria with that of
the party out of office in England, and wondering
what would happen in my country if the chiefs of
the opposition retired to their estates, and refused
to take any part in public affairs ? Count Clam
gave me an interesting account of an adventure
he had in 1848, when he was serving under the
minister Count Stadion, who had been condemned
to death by the revolutionary party at Vienna,
and been forced to make his escape with the intention of joining the imperial family at Olmütz.
Count Clam Martinič spent one day in great
anxiety at Vienna, not knowing what had become
of his friend, and then he learnt that Count
Stadion had gone to Moravia, where Count Clam
Martinič joined him, and they stopped at a small
inn at Zoraim. There Count Clam went to speak
with some officials, who warned him that the innkeeper had a very bad reputation, and was extremely violent in his political opinions, and that
therefore the sooner they left his house the better.
When Count Clam returned to the inn to join
Count Stadion he observed that a pair of pistols

he had left with the luggage had been put into
water to prevent their going off. The innkeeper
came into the room, and Count Clam told him he
wished to have some refreshments and to start
immediately. The innkeeper, who was also the
postmaster, made some trifling excuse, and said
he had no horses at that moment. The key of
the room where they were was inside the door,
and Count Clam observed that whilst they were
talking the innkeeper stood at the door and put
the key into the lock outside. This put Count
Clam doubly on his guard, and he went to the
door and stood upon the threshold while Count
Stadion had his breakfast. The innkeeper kept
pressing him to sit down, but he said he was not
hungry, and preferred standing; so at last, seeing
the Count was not going to be hoodwinked, the
innkeeper asked where they were going? Count
Clam said to Nicholsburg; so after some further
delay the horses were harnessed and they started;
but as soon as the travellers were well out of the
town Count Clam desired the postillion to turn
the horses' heads and drive in exactly the opposite
direction. The postillion looked very much embarrassed, and remonstrated, saying he had been
ordered to drive to Nicholsburg and could not go
elsewhere; but Count Clam told him they had

changed their minds, and had a perfect right to go where they pleased; and so they got off safely, but were firmly convinced that they had had a narrow escape, and that at one moment they were in imminent danger.

I left Vienna in October to spend the winter in England, and paid Mr. and Mrs. Morier a visit at Darmstadt. Mr. Morier had just returned from Metz, where he went in the interests of the sick and wounded, and the accounts he brought back were dreadfully harassing. The wounded were as well taken care of as circumstances allowed, but the sick were packed off anyhow without a doctor, and left to find their way to their homes, or die, as best they could. They frequently died at the railway stations, where typhus and dysentery raged. Whilst at Metz Mr. Morier lived in a charming villa occupied by Prince Louis of Hesse Darmstadt, but his description of some of the places he visited made me shudder. He says the wells smelt of disinfectants, so it was no wonder cholera, dysentery and typhus were prevalent. Mrs. Morier was very active attending the sick in the hospital at Darmstadt, and seemed quite accustomed to the work, talking of deaths and amputations like any surgeon.

The first sign I saw of the war was at Munich, where I saw some French guns ; five cannon and a mitrailleuse were in front of the Residency. I had never seen a mitrailleuse before ; it looked like any other gun, except that the mouth was full of little holes, and it was worked by a handle. I saw a good many French prisoners at Ingold-stadt, and we were somewhat delayed waiting for a train conveying a number of sick soldiers.

The Government only allowed 50 kreutzers a day for the sick. The French were accustomed to better food than the Germans, and complained bitterly of hunger. Mrs. Morier told me they seemed much more grateful than the Germans, and were pleasanter to deal with.

Princess Alice spent many hours every day in the hospital, and devoted herself to the sick and wounded. Her Royal Highness kindly sent for me, and the first remark she made when I arrived was, 'I hope, dear Lady Bloomfield, I have not got the small-pox.' I asked why Her Royal Highness imagined such a horrid thing, and she said the fact was she had been helping to lift a wounded man, when it was discovered that the disease was full out upon him ! The Princess had the most winning, charming manners. Her husband was at Metz, but she was so brave, and never seemed to imagine anything could go wrong!

Reichenhall, August 21, 1871.—I met an interesting young Prussian officer, who was badly wounded at Gravelotte. He was shot through the knee and the right lung, and is quite lame. The Prussians had a glorious victory, but they paid dearly for it, and their losses at Gravelotte were fearful. Out of thirty-six officers in one regiment only four remained, and young S—— told me the major, nearly distracted, rushed about crying, 'Wo ist mein bataillon, wo ist mein bataillon!' Alas! they were nearly all killed.

Who should I see at Freylassing, the station between this and Salzburg, but the great Prince Bismarck! He was sitting on a sort of balcony outside his state carriage with his wife and another lady. A large crowd had assembled, and he was much cheered as the train moved off.

Lord Bloomfield and I went to Gmünden, where we lodged one night at Countess Schmiedegg's pretty villa. The following day we dined with the King and Queen of Hanover, and were much touched by their Majesties' kindness when we took leave of them. The King was an old friend of mine, and remembered running races with me at a breakfast my parents gave William IV.

and Queen Adelaide when I was a child. He
was then Prince George of Cumberland, such a
handsome youth, and at that time he had not
lost his sight. He had a wonderful memory,
like all the Royal family, who seem to have a
peculiar gift of recollecting events and people.
His Majesty mentioned by name several of our
contemporaries : Lady Fanny Cowper, afterwards
Lady Jocelyn ; Lady Sarah Villiers, afterwards
Princess Esterhazy, and her beautiful sister Clementina, who died unmarried ; the present Lord
Denbigh, then Lord Fielding ; Lord Seaham,
now Marquis of Londonderry, James Stanhope.
and others. When we took leave their Majesties
expressed great regret at our approaching departure from Vienna, and gave me a handsome
locket with a turquoise and diamond ' forget-me-
not,' containing photographic portraits of the
King and Queen, both excellent likenesses. We
made a very charming little tour from Gmünden to
Ischl, where I had an audience of the Empress of
Austria, and then we went to Aussee and Lietzen,
returning to Vienna *viâ* Leoben and Bruck. The
scenery was most beautiful, the views very striking
and the weather most enjoyable.

On Monday, October 2, my dear husband went
in state to present his letters of recall to the Em-

peror of Austria. Although for many years past it had been my wish to retire into private life and live among my relations in England, I could not see my husband depart on his errand without deep emotion. He had been fifty-three years in active service, having begun life as an attaché at Vienna in 1818, when he served under Lord Charles Stewart, afterwards Marquis of Londonderry. He afterwards served at Stuttgart, Lisbon, and Stockholm, where he was Secretary of Legation for eleven years before he was appointed Secretary of Embassy in 1843. On Lord Stuart de Rothesay's retirement he was made Envoy and Minister Plenipotentiary in Russia, remained there till 1851, when he was moved to Berlin, and appointed Ambassador at Vienna in 1860. Lord Bloomfield received his promotions in the diplomatic service from alternate Whig and Tory Governments, and during his long career was never censured ; so naturally we both felt his leaving the occupation and interest of his whole life, though God knows I did not regret his retirement. For several months previously rumours of his intended resignation had been afloat, and when I was in England in the winter of 1870 I tried to ascertain whether Lord Granville had any intention of recalling my husband, but was distinctly assured he had not ; but in the month of June following my husband received a private letter from Lord Granville, saying he had been frequently told that Lord Bloomfield intended to retire, and that, having some very important diplomatic appointments to make, he wished to be informed whether there were any grounds for those reports. Lord Bloomfield answered in the negative, and said that had he intended resigning he should certainly have thought it his first duty to inform the Minister for Foreign Affairs of that intention ; but, on the other hand, he had no wish to make any block to promotion, and therefore if the Government wanted his post to dispose of, he was quite ready to place his resignation in their hands. It was at once accepted, and thus terminated my dear husband's long and useful public life. Diplomatists cannot live abroad as travellers ; they necessarily take root in the place to which they are accredited if they remain there long enough, and are treated with the kindness, sympathy, and affection we always met with. It is sad to part, ' it may be for years, or it may be for ever,' from those who lightened one's sorrows, doubled one's joys, and who have been the chief objects of daily intercourse and friendship.

Monday evening we were invited, with all the members of the Embassy, to dine at Schönbrünn, and were accompanied by the Hon. Robert Lytton, Mr. St. John, Mr. Smythe, the Hon. Frederick Henley, and Colonel Goodenough. I sat next the Emperor, and nothing could be kinder or more flattering than his and the Empress' expressions of regret at our departure. After dinner the Empress talked to me for some time, and said we had been so long at Vienna she could not understand any one coming there to replace us; that she looked upon us both as personal friends, and hoped we should one day return to see her and the Emperor.

Thursday, October 5, we left Vienna, and never can I forget the sadness of leaving what had been such a happy home for ten years. Our servants crowded round to kiss our hands, all sobbing bitterly. We were both so overcome we could not speak, and when we entered the carriage my dear husband threw himself back and said, ' Oh, this is really dreadful : it is like assisting at one's own funeral.'

Thus ended our diplomatic life, and with that I conclude these Reminiscences.

THE END.

Spottiswoode & Co., Printers, New-street Square, London.